MERMAID WATERS

MERMAID WATERS

CALL OF THE OCEAN, BOOK ONE

by

GINNA MORAN

SUNNY PALMS PRESS

ISBN 978-1-942073-72-7 (soft cover)

This is a work of fiction. All of the characters, organizations, and events portrayed in this novel are either products of the author's imagination or are used fictitiously.

Cover design by Silver Starlight Designs
Cover images copyright Depositphotos

For Inquiries Contact:
Sunny Palms Press
9663 Santa Monica Blvd Suite 1158
Beverly Hills, CA 90210, USA
www.sunnypalmspress.com
www.GinnaMoran.com

For all the mermaids in the oceans and those who dream of being one.

LIFE ON LAND

OH, OCEAN. NOT AGAIN.

Tears blur my eyes as a cartoon rainbow cuts across the TV of the best movie I've ever seen before the credits roll. I'm embarrassed to admit this is the thirtieth time I turned it on this week while my roommate Giselle chases the swells on the beach right outside our back patio.

But I can't help myself. A movie about a princess mermaid grabs hold of the spark in my chest, sending the warmth of my mermaid essence through me. I confess, I'm addicted to the idea of love, of finding the perfect mate to share my existence with, but the ocean has declared it's not my time yet.

The backdoor slides open, lighting the dark room with early afternoon sunshine, and Giselle steps inside our cool condo, dripping sand and ocean water across the tiles. She jerks her attention from the blaring TV to me sitting on the couch, cocooned in a knitted blanket in the shape of a mermaid tail she bought me as a late Winter Solstice gift a few months ago.

Narrowing her copper eyes, she points from me to the TV. "You're seriously not crying over this damn movie again, Luna."

I sniffle, laughing through my tears. "It's so perfect. I need it to be my life."

Giselle carries in her surfboard and sets it on the rack against the wall. Pulling a towel from the chest beside it, she soaks up the water trickling from her bronzy hair. "You need to get out more is what you need. You haven't left the condo in a few days. I'm starting to worry about you. You didn't leave Pearlestria for land to beach yourself on our couch."

Her remark stirs a drop of sadness in me at the mention of my home in the ocean—the home my dad ruined for me because he failed his job as the ocean's king. And now, it no longer feels like home. But being on land with my ocean-chosen human best friend? She feels like home. But the human world is strange and scary, harder than I imagined.

"But our couch is comfortable," I say with a pout.

"Luna."

I sigh.

Picking up the remote, I turn off the TV and lean back on

the couch to stare at the ceiling. Giselle's worry is unwarranted. She's human and doesn't understand what it was like for me to transition from living in the water full time to suddenly coming onto land. She wouldn't get that I've always lived a simple life within the palace walls of Pearlestria only ever leaving when I wanted to collect pretty stones and shells.

It wasn't long ago that I merely gazed at the surface from afar. A mermaid come to land wasn't supposed to be my future, but the ocean made it possible. And now, I want to sit here on this comfy couch and breathe air, hear the sound of music, smell the sweet sugar of the doughnuts Giselle bought last night, and do nothing for another day.

Giselle claps her hands when I don't respond to her, still staring off into my memories. "Come on, Luna. Get changed into your bikini. We're spending the day out."

I frown.

She laughs. "Jeez, don't look at me like hanging out is pure torture."

"It's not that. I just—" I groan and snap my mouth shut. She's right. If I don't leave the condo, how else am I to adjust to my life on land? If only humans weren't so intimidating. I've gotten better at controlling my mermaid nature, but for those who haven't been deemed worthy by the ocean to know my mermaid secret, it's hard to socialize. They make it clear that I'm strange. Silly humans. They're the strange ones.

So I like to hide away.

"Just nothing," Giselle says. "You can't find your future

mate if you don't look for him."

I roll my eyes. "You said it wasn't important." She's trying to use my dreams and desires of finding my perfect mate against me.

Giselle shrugs. "It's not."

On the first day I moved into the condo, I had my mind set on thrusting the front door open, charging into town, and finding my eternal mate, but it didn't happen. Everyone looked like strangers and was frightening, and no one even smiled at me in the food store. The only human who offered me anything to eat was a man in an apron. He was handsome enough, and smiled a lot at me, but then he fed the man next to me and then a whole pod. He was feeding everyone in the entire store like it was his job—and it was! Giselle couldn't stop laughing.

So, I turned around and decided human dating wasn't for me. I'll wait for the ocean to wash someone ashore instead. But it still hasn't happened. It takes Giselle reminding me that the most important thing for me to do on land is to discover who I am as a human, that courting—dating—could wait. And she's right.

The fact that I'm two hundred and nineteen full moons doesn't mean anything on land. But I'm not human. I'm an eighteen-year-old mermaid in disguise no matter how much fun Giselle says I should be having.

But that's just it. As a mermaid, this is my time to think about my future mate. A mermaid's bond is the most important thing in the ocean. It's how I was raised. Because love makes the world a better place, at least, that's what my mom said to me as a merbabe, and I want to do right by the world and bring it everything I have to offer.

"And the whole dating humans process is the worst, but I think it'll be good for your little mermaid heart if you at least get out. No more moping. There is a great, big world out there," she adds, poking each of her index fingers on the sides of my mouth to pull my frown into a smile.

Laughing, I nod and let out a breath without arguing. I stroll to my bedroom and swap my sweatpants for a bikini and sundress. Sliding into my flip flops, I glance once at my reflection in the mirror over my dresser before meeting Giselle on the back patio. Warm sun caresses my tan skin, and my midnight hair catches on the salty breeze.

I inhale a deep breath of sea air into my lungs. "Where to now?"

"Reefaria?" she asks, smirking.

"You have class tomorrow," I remind her, though I think she's joking about swimming to the Tasman Sea, where the merpeople colony we visited over Winter Solstice is located. I'm pretty sure she couldn't make it that far on my back, though, not with having to surface all the time.

She sighs. "Why is my boyfriend so far away?"

I pout my bottom lip at her. "You could ask Sun to come ashore. I could figure out my own living arrangements." Because that's what happens when you find your mate, and Giselle found hers, though she hasn't accepted the idea of an eternal commitment.

Her eyebrows shoot up on her head. "No way. It's been four months."

"Time doesn't matter when—"

"Don't even say it, Luna," she says, cutting me off.

So I don't.

I couldn't imagine living in separate parts of the world from my intended mate. But I know mermen, and the one who adores Giselle is probably not even in Reefaria. He'd be nearby. I don't tell her that, though. She'll never understand how deeply the merman bond runs until she commits to him completely and couples under the light of the full moon that anchors all merpeople to the sea.

Giselle doesn't realize it yet, but Sun fully believes she's his intended mate. My heart swells thinking about it. I can't wait until the day he asks her to officially couple because I love, love, love planning ceremonies. I've already designed her a special mermaid top and everything. She'd push me back into the sea if she knew. It's a good thing he's waiting for her to finish school with good reason. She clearly doesn't feel the same as me when it comes to finding the person who completes me. She follows her humanity while my heart drifts in the sea.

Pushing the thoughts of her future away, I twist my lips to the side and stare at the ocean stretching out to merge with the clear sky in a gradient of blues. Giselle shades her eyes from the sun and motions a ways down the shore at the crowded sand of the public beach. I never imagined humans could claim the shores of the ocean, but having a private beach outside the condo makes for coming and going through the surf much easier. I'm still learning human norms and understanding how living on land works, and I'm lucky to have Giselle, who's basically my personal human guide. If it weren't for our mutual best friend Ava, the human-born, ocean-chosen queen who replaced my dad, I'd have never met someone worthy of the mermaid secret. I'd never get to constantly breathe air, either. Because according to my ocean-shunned father, a princess's place is behind the glittering walls of Pearlestria's castle.

"Let's go to the pier," I finally say, yearning to be immersed on the crowded beach on this perfect spring day. People watching, studying how humans interact with each other, is one of my favorite things to do.

Giselle hooks her arm through mine. "Only if we swim."

She doesn't have to ask me twice. Tugging my dress over my head, I leave it on the back patio and jog with her to the waves. It's been days since I've transformed into a mermaid, and the sea filling my lungs sends a wave of relief through me. I love the land, but my heart really does belong to the ocean.

Giselle treads the surface above me, and I pop up next to her, spitting water over her head. She laughs and splashes me before hooking her arms around my neck. She could probably swim on her own if she tried, but I'm faster. I wait for her to take a deep breath and then dive into the waves, taking her farther from shore with me.

I swim as fast as I can, jetting through the water and past a menagerie of fish that inhabit the kelp forest not far from shore. A seal darts around us, swimming circles, trying to get me to play, but Giselle squeezes my shoulder, reminding me she needs a breath of air. She's gotten loads better at holding her breath since the first time we swam together. If only I could risk swimming the surface. Thankfully, my mermaid essence protects me from being seen in the water. I try to be as careful as possible, because the ocean would rise to swallow anyone who could threaten my existence. I'd rather it didn't.

Giselle releases me to swim up for air, and I give her a moment before I tug her back under. We make our way down the shore, and I avoid a few small boats floating along the California coast. It wouldn't fare well if someone spotted Giselle getting tugged under by some mysterious force. The last thing I ever want is for someone to fear the sea.

The shallows sneak up on us, and I let go of Giselle once more to transform back into my human form. My muscles tighten and relax as my pectoral fins smooth into my arms, and my golden tail splits into my tan legs. The temperature of the water shifts to feel cooler after my transformation, but it doesn't bother me. Sliding my bikini bottoms back on, I peer around the now blurry water once more before kicking to the surface.

I expel the sea from my lungs and suck in a deep breath. Trailing my eyes over the beach in front of us, I peer around for a place for us to emerge without drawing too much attention. But it's not like people will automatically assume I'm a mermaid.

Giselle grabs my hand and swims me forward. "Come on. No one will even notice we came from the sea. People aren't that observant." She points at a crowd gathered around a small pop-up tent. "Plus, they're all too busy looking at the sand."

I let a wave carry me to shore and drop to the beach. It takes me a minute to adjust from sea to land, and I lie in the waves, feeling the sand tug out from under me and back into the ocean.

Giselle rolls onto her stomach and rests her head on her arms. "We couldn't have picked a better spot to wash ashore."

Tilting my head back, I glance at the beach behind me upside down and read the sign staked into the ground outside the pop-up tent. *La Tortuga Point Beach Cleanup.*

My heart flutters at the sight of the group of people, who care about the ocean as much as I do. But watching a woman in a tank top and shorts as she passes out reusable bags to carry trash left behind by beachgoers isn't the only thing making me smile.

"He's cute," Giselle says, flicking my arm.

She's right. A guy, who I think is my age, with the most incredible green eyes, sparkly and vibrant like my favorite color sea glass, tugs his dark blue T-shirt over his head before setting it on the table. He combs his dark hair from his face with his fingers and smiles at the woman passing out supplies.

"He's perfect," I whisper, my heart racing the longer I look at him.

Giselle laughs and nudges my arm. "Does he have mate potential?"

I don't respond. I can't take my eyes from him. And I think he feels my stare. Turning away from the woman, the guy glances in my direction, still smiling at something she said. And then his smile widens.

"Since you're too busy checking him out to respond to me, I'm going to say he definitely has mate potential," Giselle whispers.

"I—" I don't even know. There's not a mermaid's handbook to finding the perfect mate. It's something my pod should've told me about, but Mom wasn't there and Dad swore I'd find a merman in the sea—but no one ever smiled at me like this guy does now. And I have the sudden urge to close the distance.

He breaks my stare, turning toward the group of people, and the woman sends everyone off. My heart still races, though now disappointment washes over me watching him stroll down the beach and away from me.

"I don't think so," I say. "Mermen usually approach the mermaid they're interested in."

Giselle groans. "He's not a merman."

She's right about that. If the guy could possibly be a potential mate, he wouldn't even know. He doesn't have the same spark in his chest like mine, which gives me my mermaid essence, though the glittering, magical sea stone ring on my finger gives me my legs all but on the full moon. "So what do I do?"

Pushing up, Giselle gets to her feet and offers me her hand.

"Go say hi to him."

I peer in the guy's direction. He strolls the sands alone, stopping every few feet to pick up something he finds on the ground. This goes against my very nature, making the first move, and I'm scared. "You make it sound easy."

"It is." Giselle gently kicks my calf. "At least you have a voice."

Giselle laughs at her own joke, teasing me about my latest TV obsession. She beams me a smile and motions for me to hurry. Taking another breath of the ocean air, I channel Giselle's confidence. I straighten my back and toss my long tresses over my shoulder, something I've seen her do a dozen times around Sun.

"You got this. I'll be at the pop-up. Might as well join since we're here." Giselle meanders away from me, kicking up sand, and motions toward the guy once more.

I keep my eyes on the sand and trudge along the rolling surf.

I can do this. I know I can do this. I say hello to strangers all the time at the food store and any time we go out to dinner. It's one little word. But I'm so nervous. Maybe it's a sign. I should be feeling all sorts of pleasant emotions and not like I want to dive into the surf and swim away.

"Hey," a masculine voice says, surprising me.

I stumble back, my legs acting like they did the first time I emerged from the sea, and I fall into the lapping waves. Embarrassment rises from the spark blinking in my heart and to my cheeks. "Oh, Ocean! You scared me."

A weird expression crosses the guy's face, and I realize I said something that would be strange to him. But I couldn't stop the words from escaping my lips. I was too focused on summoning the nerve to approach him that I had no idea he approached me. *He approached me!*

He steps forward, his hand outstretched, and says, "Here, let me help you."

Oh, Ocean. He's so handsome and wants to take care of me. I almost don't believe it.

His hand encircles mine, and warmth blossoms between our fingers. He smirks at me, a hint of curiosity in his sparkling eyes. I can't resist smiling back. Being close enough to notice the shadow of facial hair on his cheeks ignites something unfamiliar in me, but it sweeps my nerves out to sea.

"Thank you. I was trying to figure out how to approach you without being weird. When I came ashore and saw you at the..." Okay, this is me being strange. I can't believe I said I came ashore. I take a deep breath. "It's nice to see someone who cares about my home as much as I do."

He laughs, his handsome smile lighting up his entire face and crinkling the corners of his eyes. "I appreciate that. Want to help me?"

Bobbing my head, I grin. "Sure, I'd like that." It takes everything in me not to squeal, because not only did he help me to my feet, he asked if I'd help him make our world a better place.

"I'm Ryan," he says.

"Ryan is the most interesting name I've ever heard," I say. *Ryan.* I repeat his name in my mind, liking how it sounds. *Ryan.* It's cute and fits him perfectly. "I'm Luna."

"I think you have me beat. Luna is pretty."

I giggle and release a breath at his compliment.

Ryan smiles and holds out his bag to me, and I take it, strolling next to him along the water. The sun bounces off his dark hair, shining like streaks of chocolate against lava rock. In my peripheral vision, I trail my gaze down his muscular chest to his toned stomach. He's athletic, but not in the sculpted muscular way mermen are from swimming all the time. But that doesn't matter to me. Because I really like how his legs look as he walks next to me.

"You have nice legs, you know. They look strong," I say to fill the silence falling between us. Mermen love a compliment about the strength of their tails.

He chuckles. "Thanks, I guess."

My smile falters though his doesn't. "I mean, I'm sorry. I don't know why I said that."

I peer over my shoulder at Giselle still talking to the woman under the pop-up tent. She waves to me, and I beg her to rescue me with my eyes. If only we were both mermaids and in our true forms, then I could tell her I'm failing miserably to sound normal, and I need her to save me.

Ryan picks up a plastic water bottle and shoves it in the bag, split into two sections to separate the garbage from the recyclables.

"It's probably the best compliment I've heard," he says a little late, just as the looming silence starts to feel awkward.

It's my turn to laugh. "Really?"

"Definitely." His green eyes hold mine for a moment, staring at me in a way that makes me step a little closer to him. I doubt my awkward compliment was the best one he's ever heard, but it's nice he tried to make me feel better.

The roar of the ocean hums in my ears, washing my nerves out to sea the longer we stroll along the beach, collecting every piece of trash that made its way to shore before there's no more space left in the bag.

Something sparkles from the sand, and Ryan bends down and scoops it into his hand. He dusts the sand off a silver chain bracelet. He dangles it out to me. "Who knew a beach cleanup could be fun? You never know what you're going to find."

"I love finding stuff," I say, staring at the bracelet in the light. "There are some cliffs nearby not accessible from shore where I've found some of the prettiest sea glass."

"So you're a treasure hunter," he says, grinning. "Maybe you could show me sometime?"

"Yeah, I'd like that," I say, before I realize how hard it would be to show him without swimming him to the spot myself as a mermaid. The cliffs are technically jumpable if you go during high tide, but there's no way back up without a long swim through potentially rough water. "But we need a boat. My friend took me last time."

"I think I can manage that. Are you busy tomorrow?" he

asks.

I shake my head. "Not really." My only plans consisted of watching TV on the couch.

"Cool. Should I pick you up or do you want to meet at the marina?" He pulls out his cell phone to hand to me.

I enter my number even though I rarely ever carry the phone Giselle bought for me. "If you don't mind picking me up," I say, smiling. I point at my complex in the distance. "I live in the condos down the beach."

He takes his phone back. "We can grab breakfast, too."

I bounce on the balls of my feet because he wants to feed me. This is going better than I expected. "I love to eat," I say, and then cringe.

He laughs. "Great, me too. It's a date."

"It's a date," I repeat.

Oh, Ocean. I hope I don't mess things up.

POTENTIAL MATE

"YOU DIDN'T," GISELLE PRACTICALLY squeals, covering her mouth with her hand.

I scrunch my face, nodding. "It was bad. I was certain he would run away from me at any second."

Her eyes glass over with laughter. "At least you'd have gotten to see those strong legs of his in action."

A low knock on the back slider draws our attention away from each other. The door whooshes open a second later, and Ava smiles and reaches into the chest by the back door for two towels. I've been anxious for my self-proclaimed pod to come over to help me work through what's going on inside me. It takes everything in me not to hop to my feet and shake every piece of information I can from Ava. She would take this life-changing day more seriously than Giselle, who doesn't get how huge Ryan asking me out is.

"What's so funny?" Ava asks, moving out of the way to let Carter, her merman mate, inside. They visit every day at the same time to eat dinner with us like they would in the sea since their home is just a swim down the beach. "I could hear you laughing from the swells."

Giselle tips her head back and laughs again before she can even spit the words out. "Luna hooked herself a potential mate." She fakes reeling a fishing rod while bouncing. "At a freaking beach cleanup. How perfect is that?"

Ava's face brightens even more, her cerulean eyes sparkling in the light from our open kitchen. She rushes forward and hugs me, her wet blond hair dripping to soak into the fabric of my shirt. "That's amazing, Luna. I told you it was only a matter of time."

"That's not the best part," Giselle says, her voice rising in a pitch I'm sure only dolphins, whales, and merpeople can hear.

I groan, blush sweeping across my cheeks. "Talking to humans is hard, but especially cute ones."

"She told him he had nice legs." Giselle's laughter echoes through the room again.

Carter chuckles from the door. "But it worked, right?"

I nod. "We're supposed to have breakfast, and then I'm

taking him to the cliffs."

Ava's eyes widen. "The cliffs? But—"

"By boat," I say, cutting her off before she can remind me of the dangers humans face without proper thought and care in the ocean, especially around a mermaid like me. Things happen. The ocean likes to test people's worth. But I fully believe it wouldn't do that to me.

Ava and Carter share a silent conversation with their eyes. I can almost feel Ava's worry, because she knows how dangerous the ocean can be if our mermaid secret is revealed to someone who isn't trustworthy, and as for Ryan, I don't even know him. But I want to get the chance. He's already done everything right in gaining my attention without even realizing it.

Carter pulls his gaze from Ava to look at me and slowly nods his head. "I'll drop off some gear later tonight. It'll look strange if you free dive without at least a snorkel and fins."

I didn't even think about that. The water will be shallow, and there is a section of beach that appears with the low tide, but I wouldn't be able to explain that I can see pretty clearly underwater even without transforming into a mermaid.

"Thanks. I appreciate it. I just—I suck at this whole communicating thing," I say. "I was sure I ruined it, and he wouldn't want to see me again, but then he asked me out. With food, even. You know how that costs money here." Mermen hunt for fish to give to mermaids, and Ryan, while not a merman, is using his own money to bring me food. That stuff is not as easy as I thought to get, and I'd be eating in the sea if it weren't for my pod taking care of me.

"If he's your intended mate, I doubt anything could ruin it," Carter says, grinning. "Don't worry so much. It won't change anything. I should know. Ava was afraid of the ocean when I met her."

Ava slides her arms around him. "The ocean sure tested him for me."

"It was all worth it, Aves," Carter says. "And you'll see too, Luna."

"How do I even know if he is?" I ask. "My dad picked my mom based on her power. Their relationship was a lie." My parents didn't exactly have the love story I imagine living, so I try not to think about it. I don't want to fall in their footsteps to just coincide with someone. I want to be all in.

"I didn't know for certain until I almost lost Ava." Carter turns to peer at Ava again. His turquoise eyes light from within, glowing with his merman spark. The way he looks at Ava with such love and devotion makes the world feel like a better place because they're together. I get the same feeling when I see Giselle with Sun. There is something about finding that perfect person that runs deep in a mermaid's nature. I sometimes wish I could shut it off and stop thinking about it. It's driving me crazy.

I hum under my breath and run my fingers through my hair. "That's a terrible way to find out."

He shrugs. "Definitely."

"I know it's hard, but try not to over-think it," Ava says,

crossing the room to sit next to me again. She places her hand on top of mine and squeezes my fingers. "I'm sure it'll work out how it's supposed to. Don't fight against the call of the ocean like me. There's no right way to go about things."

She's right. If Ryan has any chance at being my mate, the ocean will let it be known. But for now, I need to enjoy that I have this chance. That these new feelings coursing through me are there to begin with. They make me anxious and excited and a little restless, but they remind me of Ryan and all the possibilities.

"Yeah, start with tomorrow and work from there," Giselle adds, speaking up. She's been quietly listening, surely trying to absorb the advice from the two people who have been through what Giselle and I are going through now. Except Giselle's the human and knows the merpeople secret. I wish I could already tell Ryan. "You need a lot of patience when it comes to guys, and basically all humans."

"Sun could probably give you some pointers about how to handle it," Carter quips, raising his eyebrow to Giselle.

She rolls her eyes at him. "Can we not talk about my love life?"

I giggle. "But it's so much better than talking about the lack of mine."

"Or how about we go out to dinner?" Ava says. "Because we have something to celebrate."

Giselle squeals and claps her hands. "Did you two set a wedding date? Please tell me it's going to be a summer wedding.

Maybe sailing on the *Ocean Jewel*."

Ava laughs, shaking her head, pelting us with the sea water clinging to her hair. She reaches into the waterproof bag that never leaves Carter's side in the sea and pulls out a small envelope. "Not yet, but we got this in the mail from Carter's parents this morning. It's for you, Luna."

"Me?" I wasn't expecting to receive anything from the mermates who check on me every few days to make sure I'm doing okay.

She hands me the envelope. "You're officially one step closer to establishing a real human identity on land."

I blink a few times. "Huh?"

"Luna, your great-grandfather was human. He never coupled with your great-grandmother. He kept his life on land," she says, resting her hand on my shoulder.

I knew this. I hold the memory of my mom playing in the water with her grandfather, who was human because my grandmother also chose someone on land. I come from a long line of mermaids that have yearned for the land. And now I see the reason more clearly. I have the land in my blood even with the sea in my heart. "But what does that have to do with me?"

Ava's eyes glitter in the light. "You have family apart from your dad."

I blink. My grandparents might've decided to live out their lives on land and never return to sea, but all they had was my mom, who returned to the water as a teen.

"On land," Carter adds, confirming that what I know

about my lineage isn't as telling as I had thought.

My mouth drops open, and I rip my finger through the envelope seal, nearly tearing it apart to pull out the papers inside. There are a few pictures of my mom as a merbabe in human form. Across the back, the name Grandpa Charles and Celestiana appears in blocky scrawl.

"My mom figured you'd want these, but you can also take them with you when you meet your cousin."

My eyes widen. "My cousin?"

"Well, distant cousin. Crazy, right?" Ava asks.

Giselle bounces on the couch next to me, shaking the three of us. Her dark hair falls loose from her messy bun, and she pushes it off her face. "Where? We have to go."

Carter clears his throat. "San Francisco."

"I didn't know Luna's mom was from where your parents came from, Carter," Giselle says, scrunching her brows. "Whatever, it doesn't matter. Spring break is next week. We can all go together."

Carter and Ava glance at each other having another silent conversation. They're so in tune with each other that they don't even need their ocean telepathy to know what the other is thinking. "We're supposed to make a trip to Coralista over break. I promised my grandparents."

I smile at the thought. I know how much Ava enjoys visiting the colonies, and I know she hasn't had the chance to visit the Caribbean one much.

"Ugh," Giselle says. "Fine. Road trip for me and Luna

then, and we're going to have all the fun."

Ava releases a breathless laugh. "Good. You both deserve it. I promise we'll plan something together this summer."

"Just not a coupling ceremony," Giselle says. "Unless it's Luna's."

My heart flutters at the thought, but I push it away. If Ryan is truly my intended, which I'm not even sure about, then I have to prepare myself for a long courting process, especially if he's anything like Giselle.

"I—"

"Enough about relationships," Giselle adds. "Let's talk about this human relative. No wonder you love the land. It's in your blood."

My head whirls with the information, my mind wandering from Ryan and to my cousin. I never thought about having human family members, but now that I know, I can't help wondering what they're like. If they have any idea who my great-grandfather loved. This is so much to take in.

Ava touches my hand. "You okay?"

I nod. "I'm just—whoa."

"Whoa is right. A potential mate and a human family." Giselle takes my hands and pulls me off the couch. "Ava was right. This is something to celebrate."

"Luna! My mom loved, and I mean *loved*, the necklace you made her. She wants to know if she can commission you to complete the set with earrings and a bracelet," Chloe says from outside Sushi Days. She skips up to me and rocks me back and forth in a hug.

"Commission?" I ask.

I stare at the girl, who like me, hasn't found someone to spend her life with. But unlike me, she doesn't care. She takes Giselle's side because she's human and thinks like one. Chloe pulls back and grins, her wavy hair smelling like the salt of the sea. She spends more time in the water than I do, but floating on top, catching waves instead of diving in the deep.

"Like, pay you," Chloe answers.

"Oh."

The second hardest thing about living on the land besides fitting in with humans is money. I had no idea I needed it for everything—clothes, a home, TV, to enter certain places, and even talking to people on the phone. And food. The fact that Giselle loves taking me out for dinner, which is definitely different from how I eat in the sea, it's not the same as a warm meal. It's overwhelming. Money is one of the biggest things that prevents most merpeople from venturing onto land.

"That's okay. I'm happy to make her something for free. I'd like to," I add. Because I love giving people things.

"No, you wouldn't," Giselle says. "Money is good."

Chloe laughs. "She's right, Luna. My mom wouldn't take anything for free from you, anyway. She knows how much time you put into everything you make. Not to mention where you get your materials. Everyone in Azure Waters will soon want a coveted Princess Luna piece."

I've always created things made from stuff I found in the sea for fun. I had no idea humans would actually love it. It's one of my ocean-gifted talents apart from navigating the seas and creating things to help the colonies thrive.

I smile. "That would be amazing. Makes this all feel more permanent until I return to sea."

Everyone frowns except for Carter, and I'm not so sure why. I've dreamed of living on the land all my life, but I couldn't possibly stay ashore forever. Most merpeople return to the sea, because we live much longer lives than humans. It's where we go to extend our pods until our merbabes are old enough to remain on shore.

"Well, you better give me some warning. It was seriously the worst weeks of my life when Ava couldn't come to shore. I just—I need to be prepared if you choose not to," Giselle says.

I smirk. "Oh, I'm sure you'll visit me in Pearlestria after your coupling ceremony."

Giselle groans. "Okay, you grossly romantic mermaid, I know you love to dive head first into this whole mermaid marriage stuff at eighteen, but you need to take a step back and inhale a breath of fresh air to clear your head. Who says I want to even transform into a mermaid?"

I blink a few times, flicking my gaze to Carter. He understands what it's like for a merman to find his mate, and once Giselle realizes how amazing a life with Sun will be, she'll change her mind. It's unusual for a human to deny such an experience born from love and the ocean, so rare, that I only know the mermaids before me to do it—but I don't even know why. And Giselle? She's made for the water. She'll make Sun incredibly happy and live in the happiness she deserves. Once the ocean chooses you, there's not much you can do. It's fated by the light of the moon.

Ava laughs. "You do whatever you want, Gi. Don't let these two pressure you."

Giselle relaxes her shoulders. "Thank you, Aves."

"Poor Sun," Carter says, fake pouting. "You're going to put out his merman spark."

I press my lips together to keep from laughing. Because Sun wouldn't be fazed by her purposely stubborn resistance. He'll continue to court her and sweep her off her feet. She'll be lost to the deep but found at the same time.

Giselle points at me. "I would never!"

I smile. She's right. That was enough to prove my point, though I don't mention it. Humans aren't as adaptable as mermaids. We welcome change and thrive because of it.

"I know," I say.

We all enter the restaurant, and after ordering enough sushi to feed an entire colony of merpeople, I sit back in my chair and listen to my friends talk about their plans for their spring break from their first year of college. If I had all the necessary documents, I'd consider enrolling at one of the local colleges to help me adjust and socialize, but my heart isn't into it much. I don't even know what I want to do with my life. I always assumed I'd couple and create my own pod, and that would be that, but listening to my friends, I'm starting to think there's so much more.

"So, tell us about Mr. Nice Legs," Chloe asks, leaning across the table. "What's his name?"

Heat warms my cheeks as Ryan's name crosses my mind. Just as I think it, a phone beeps from Giselle's bag, and she rushes to pull it out. She sets it on the table in front of me, and I realize she must've unplugged it from the charger, knowing I wouldn't have because I'm with the only people who'd call me.

"You have to remember to keep this on you from now on. It's how humans communicate," Giselle says. She swipes her finger across the screen. "And Ryan just wanted to say hi and asked what you were doing."

"Oh, I bet he can't stop thinking about you," Ava says.

"Ryan?" Chloe asks, repeating his name. "What's his last name?"

I open and close my mouth. I always forget people on land have those. I've always been Princess Luna, or just Luna to my friends. "I don't know. I didn't ask."

"That was probably a good thing," Giselle says. "He might've asked for yours."

I press my lips together, now adding another thing to my list of reasons to freak out about this dating humans situation. "But I don't have one."

"You're a Stevens right now," Carter reminds me. "My sister, remember?"

"Or you could be a Nash," Giselle says. "I can pay someone

to make you an ID. You might need one if you're going to start abandoning me for Ryan No-Last-Name."

The phone beeps again, and I stare at the same text message blinking across the screen. When I don't move to reply, Giselle steals the phone back and taps her finger across it. She raises it up and snaps a picture of me and Chloe before sending it to him.

Giselle taps her flip flops on the tile, nearly trembling with excitement in her seat, taking way too much pleasure in pretending to be me. I let her because I'm the slowest texter ever, at least compared to her. Not to mention she'll make sure I don't sound like a mermaid.

She holds the phone out, beaming her most brilliant smile. "Guys, isn't he hot?"

My heart flutters at the sight of the picture he sent, drenched in the light of a beach fire pit. His dark hair hangs just out of his face, and he's still shirtless. I can almost picture him as a merman now.

I shake the thought away. I'm getting ahead of myself.

"I know him!" Chloe says, smacking her hands on the table. "Well, sort of. That's Ryan Reyes. He's a sometimes surfer. Travels a lot."

I scrunch my face. "He doesn't live here?"

She shrugs. "Sometimes, I guess. I don't know much."

"That's what tomorrow is for," Giselle says. "You can find out everything you want to know. All you have to do is ask."

Why does that sound so terrifying? I'm using my voice

right now. I can respond to whatever people ask me. But small talk? Asking questions that might make me out to seem strange? Oh, Ocean. Please help me.

Another text message pops on the screen. *Low tide at 6. Still up 2 goin?*

I consider begging Giselle to change our plans to something around people with an easy escape if I can't do this whole dating a human thing. I'll be alone with him. *In the sea where you're most comfortable,* I remind myself.

Giselle taps on my screen, letting me watch her type. *See you before sunrise.*

Can't wait, he replies.

I hold the phone, stopping Giselle from responding and reply myself. *Neither can I.*

Now, I can't stop smiling, because he's looking forward to seeing me as much as I am to seeing him despite my nerves. Tomorrow can't come soon enough.

SEA PRINCESS

GISELLE PINS A FEW strands of my black hair back into my braid and out of my face. She woke me up over an hour ago, playing one of my favorite songs about being madly in love through the surround sound in our condo.

I glance at my checklist of human hygiene daily tasks like I'm afraid I missed something like brushing my teeth with the mint toothpaste or putting on deodorant I don't even need but like the flowery scent of. Giselle laughed when she saw it and reminded me I've been doing these things for months. I don't need a list. But hanging up my list makes me feel better. Doing the things the ocean has done for me makes me feel human.

Giselle spritzes her citrusy perfume into my hair like it won't wash away with the waves. "You look amazing. He's not going to know what to do with himself or what to say. It's perfect. You'll both be awkward messes and connect over it."

I smile at her in the mirror. "Luckily, we'll be in the water most of the time."

"Just don't accidentally transform," she says, teasingly.

Ice rushes down my face, stealing away the color from my cheeks. I hadn't thought about the possibility. Sure, it's never happened to me because I'm ocean-born and deeply connected to the sea and don't constantly long for it, but now she put the thought into my head.

"I'm kidding," she adds, squeezing my shoulders. "And if that happened, your dad would be thrilled to meet Ryan."

I glare at her. "Not funny." Because Dad would summon the sea to swallow Ryan whole if he had any ocean magic left in him. Now, he's taken to island living in Celestiana Cove a few hours from Pearlestria—a place named after my mom. Taking Ryan there would never, ever be an option unless we were coupled, and I was introducing him as my chosen, not because I messed up and revealed my secret, and he turned out not to be deemed worthy by the sea.

The doorbell rings, stopping me from saying anything to Giselle, and she spins and runs away from me before I even have a chance to get to my feet. The door clicks open and voices mumble through the condo as I swipe the bag of diving gear Carter left outside my door while I was sleeping and saunter to the living room.

I hover in the hall for a second and listen.

"Luna will be out in a minute," Giselle says. "It's nice to officially meet you, Ryan. I'm Giselle."

"Nice place," he says. "You surf?"

Two shadows stretch out across the floor, and Giselle comes into view. She glances at me in the hallway. "Yeah and thanks. The condo is ours for a few more years until college graduation."

"Where do you two go?" he asks. His deep voice stirs something inside me, and I inch forward, drawn to him like the call of the ocean on a full moon.

Giselle talks to him so effortlessly. I want to remain in my spot and let her find out all the information she can before I come in and fumble over my words, my nerves even worse than last night.

"Just me. UCSD. Luna's still figuring her life out."

"So am I," he says.

I release a tiny breath. We have something in common.

Ryan steps into view, and I force my legs to work to close the distance. His gaze trails from my bare feet and up my legs to the short sundress I borrowed from Giselle's closet. He then turns his sea glass green eyes to mine and smiles, showing his straight teeth. He hasn't shaved, his cheeks peppered with a shadow of a beard, longer than yesterday, making him look older in the still dark of early morning. But he's still so handsome. My whole body buzzes at the sight of him smiling at me in a way that feels completely for me.

"Wow, you look incredible. I should've done more than roll out of bed," he says, chuckling. He steps closer to me and surprises me with a hug I hadn't anticipated, making me giggle.

"Luna wakes up like this." Giselle grins. "Makes me totally jealous."

I blush, feeling the intensity as they both stare at me. "Thank you," I say to Ryan, flicking a glare Giselle's way. "You look great, too. Perfect for the water."

Ryan holds out his hand to me. "Ready?"

I nod and slide my fingers through his. Something as little as holding hands shows his desire to be near me—at least that's how it is with mermen. "I think so."

I hope so. Oh, I'm so nervous, I'm afraid he'll notice my hands shaking. If he does, he doesn't make it obvious, and he's quick to let go of my hand to hook his arm around my waist to guide me out the front door, leaving Giselle nearly bouncing in the living room. Heat blossoms on my side through my sundress, and I glance at Ryan in my peripheral vision, catching him looking at me.

He smiles again. "I could barely sleep last night."

"Oh, no. I'm sorry. We can go some other time if you're tired."

He chuckles. "I'm not complaining. I—" His cheeks tint red. "I'm looking forward to this is all."

"The sea glass beach is amazing."

"I meant hanging out with you."

I beam a smile. "Oh, me too." My spark blinks so furiously, I'm almost afraid he'll see it, but he keeps his eyes trained on mine.

Ryan leads me into the parking lot of my complex and to a lifted black truck, giant compared to Giselle's Mustang. He helps me climb in, and from here, I can see a view of the ocean from over the short block wall with a gate to the beach for those not beachfront.

Music hums from the speakers when he starts the engine, and the scent of something sweet and savory wafts through the air. He reverses and exits the complex to drive toward the small marina only a few minutes away.

"I hope you don't mind I stopped to pick up breakfast on the way. I figured we could eat it and watch the sunrise over the cliffs," he says, motioning toward a paper bag on the backseat. "It's a little of everything."

I smile at his thoughtfulness. He really planned things out. "I love everything." Oh, Ocean. I need to think before I open my mouth. "I mean, I'll eat anything, really, and it smells delicious."

He chuckles. "Good to know."

Ryan parks in the lot nearest to the entrance of the docks and jumps out to open the door for me. He helps me from his truck, shoulders the bag I brought and grabs his stuff, before leading me to the locked gate. Only slip owners have access, and Ryan hits in a combination to open the gate.

"You own a boat?" I ask.

"My dad does. He's not around much, so I take it out whenever." Ryan guides me to a surprisingly big motorboat in charcoal gray. It looks as long as an orca, but it's hard to tell from the surface. I spend more time glancing at the bottom of boats than anything.

"I don't see my dad much either," I say. "But I guess it's a good thing. He doesn't approve of my life choices."

"Because of college? I can relate in a way. My dad wants me to join the family business, but I like doing my own thing." Ryan steps aboard the vessel with the name *Sea Princess* declared on the side. I can't help feeling like the ocean led me right to this moment, and now it's showing me glaring signs I can't and don't want to ignore.

He motions for me to board, taking my hand to help me in, a smile lighting his face in the pre-dawn light. He sweeps a flashlight around, doing a visual check of the vessel before storing our bags in a compartment under a bench seat at the stern of the boat. I pull out the folded piece of paper Carter wrote the coordinates on to give to Ryan, since I navigate the ocean by instincts and currents. Visually, too. From above water, it all looks the same to me. I'd get us lost and would have to dive in to make sure we were going where we were supposed to, something I'm sure Ryan would find weird.

"Here, enter these in," I say, motioning to the navigation system in the cockpit.

He raises his eyebrows. "You do this all the time?"

I shrug, wishing I could tell him that of course I do because

I'm a mermaid. Instead, I say, "You look surprised."

"Intrigued, too. I wasn't sure what I was getting myself into, only that I knew it would be an adventure for sure." He grins again, brushes his dark hair from his face, and meets my gaze. "Which I definitely like."

I giggle under the weight of his stare, heat overflowing from my spark. It glows so brightly from my chest that I'm nervous it might light up the ocean around us for him to see, especially since I keep thinking about the moment I can tell him my secret. "Good. I hope it is."

Ryan touches my cheek with the backs of his fingers. "It already is to me."

I sit in the cockpit with him, and he navigates from the dock and toward the open sea. Ocean spray mists the air, sending goosebumps over my skin. Ryan shrugs from his jacket to give me. I nestle my face in the fresh fabric, catching a hint of sunscreen.

The boat jumps across the water, cutting the calm surface, and I close my eyes, letting the wind whip my braid behind me. I soak in the world around me—how close to home I feel leaving shore, how each breath of salty air reminds me of millions of breaths I've taken surfacing after being under, how my heart races, trying to escape me only to dive toward Ryan in hopes he'll catch it.

"I think we're here," Ryan says.

I open my eyes as he turns the wheel to face the cliffs on shore and stare at the quiet world around us. With the low tide,

I spot the stretch of beach along the rocks, which is where sea glass gathers. The sky lightens from navy to lavender with the rising sun in the east.

"Yup, this is the place. With the way the cliffs are, things gather along the rocks. You can see some tide pools, too." Pulling my necklace out from under my dress, I hold up my pendant to him. "This is one of my favorites."

"You made this?" He shifts the smooth, heart-shaped glass I strung on a braided piece of fishing line between his fingers.

I nod. "Even the line is from the sea."

He stares at it, running his finger over the four pearls I've strung on both sides of the heart. "It's awesome. You're talented, Luna."

I smile and tuck my necklace away. "Thanks. Collecting things from the sea and creating stuff is one of my favorite things to do besides swimming and free diving."

Ryan bobs his head while turning away to drop the anchor. He grabs the breakfast he picked up for us and offers me the bag to pick what I want first just like a merman would do. I was expecting him to be so different with his human nature, but he's more similar to me than I realized.

Silence falls between us while we eat, but it's not awkward or uncomfortable. It's just the silence of us being together, watching the sun peek over the cliffs, lighting the sky aglow in pale yellow. Everything feels so perfect—calm yet exciting, new but somehow still familiar. I'd be okay sitting here with him all morning, but I suddenly want so badly to swim and see him underwater, to let him see me in the place that brings out everything good in me even in my human form.

"So, you ready for this? The water's probably freezing," I say, balling up the trash from the French toast sticks. "But it'll be worth it, I promise."

He grins, hopping up from the seat we share and tugs my bag from the cargo space before getting his. I unzip my bag and see Carter also packed me a wetsuit along with the snorkel and fins hooked to the outside. I pull it out and set it on the railing.

I tug my sundress over my head and drop it on the seat. Ryan does the same with his shirt, and we both glance at each other for a second before smiling. I like how I feel under his gaze. No one's ever looked at me the way he does. It's hard to even process every emotion pulsing through us.

I smirk again, turning my gaze toward the sea and reach for the ties on my bikini top to undress completely for my wetsuit. His mouth opens as he takes in my body, and then his eyes widen. He spins to look the other direction, his whole face reddening with the rising sun.

I cringe, holding up my wetsuit to cover myself, realizing the mistake I made. "I'm so sorry. I didn't know this was the first time you've seen a female body before. I wasn't thinking."

Carter warned me a dozen times about how uncomfortable many humans are about naked bodies, but in this moment, under Ryan's gaze, I forgot. He was peering at me in surprise and wonder like I was all he wanted to look at, but then something shifted in his demeanor. I inspect myself to make sure I didn't start transforming into a mermaid, but I'm just me.

"It's okay to look at me if you're curious," I add. "I don't mind." Because I want him to continue to stare at me like he first did. I don't care if he sees me in my human form.

"I—" He chuckles, craning his neck to peer over his shoulder while keeping his gaze trained on my face. "You don't need to apologize. It's just—it was unexpected. You keep surprising me. And you're right. It's not a big deal." He smiles again, turns to face the water, and undresses completely to change into his own wetsuit in front of me. "I prefer to wear a wetsuit this way, too."

He drags his hands up his face and into his hair, and I watch his chest expand and push against the suit as he gulps in a deep breath. I can't stop smiling. He's so cute, more boyish than man, being flustered and slightly embarrassed, though he goes with everything like doing something out of his comfort zone excites him.

I turn away, still smiling, and grab my snorkel and fins. "I should've warned you. I'm not from around here, and I'm still getting used to what's normal—nudity is one of those things. Changing in and out of clothes to dive is just life." A lot of mermaids don't wear tops at all in the sea.

"Where are you from?" he asks.

I shouldn't have tried to explain myself, because I'm not familiar enough with the land to tell him one place in specific. "I—a little bit of everywhere."

His footsteps thump on the deck, and I feel him come up

behind me, but I don't turn to meet his gaze. A few fish swim around the boat through the clear water, helping me keep my racing heart under control.

"It's amazing how much we have in common." He rests his hand on my shoulder and touches his other hand to my lower back, his warm fingers grazing against my bare skin under my still open wetsuit. "Here, let me help you with that."

I shift my hair so he can pull the zipper up. His breath tickles my ear, and I lean my back to his chest when he's through, remaining utterly still against him to watch the calm water lapping along the shore. He brushes my braid from over my shoulder, letting it fall down my back, and I finally turn to face him.

"Thanks," I say, my voice lowering to a whisper.

He bobs his head and grasps my hand, pulling me to the small platform. We sit together on the step, so close that I feel myself leaning into him. Cold water splashes my cool legs, making me laugh, and I puff a breath of air through my lips.

"So, we'll head to the beach first?" he asks.

I nod, holding his gaze. His vibrant green eyes sparkle with flecks of caramel in the rising sun, and they trail from mine to look at my mouth. Neither of us says anything again for a long moment. It takes the boat bobbing, the ocean begging me to return even in my human form, to get me to break our stare.

I adjust my mask over my head and slide on my free diving fins. Ryan tips himself backward into the water first and treads the surface, opening his arms out for me to jump into. Saltwater splashes between us, and Ryan hugs me against him, pressing his body to mine, staring at me through the water droplets speckling across my mask.

He points with his thumb downward, and I nod, following him under. Without letting go of my hand, he swims with me toward the shore. It takes me a minute to get used to the fins, pushing me faster than my feet but not nearly as fast as if I had my tail.

A few small fish jet around the shallows, and Ryan points out an opaleye darting along the bottom. It swims right up to me, its yellow body and blue eyes vibrant in the morning sun. I reach out, and it pokes its nose to my outstretched fingertip.

Ryan reaches his own hand out, and the fish whizzes away.

I offer him a close-lipped smile. Even without my tail, animals know I'm a mermaid. The smaller fish tend to congregate to us because we have no natural predators in the sea and usually stick to eating much larger species when it comes to food. But I can go weeks without eating in my mermaid form.

We close in on the shore and thousands of pieces of sea glass glitter below us, the larger pieces weighted in the sand while smooth fragments move with the waves dragging toward shore.

I peek at Ryan, watching his eyes light up. The sun streaks beams of light so perfectly it looks like we're hovering over thousands of jewels. With the way the ocean floor dips below the cliffs, it all gathers here, waiting to be collected.

I let go of his hand and dive down, scooping up a handful

of smooth glass pieces without sorting through them. Ryan waits on the surface, watching me run my fingers along the bottom. I pick out a few larger pieces of sea glass the same color as Ryan's eyes and stow them in my net pouch before following him to the beach.

"I had no idea a place like this existed, and I've seen the shores of nearly every continent," Ryan says when we make it to the tiny stretch of glass beach nestled between rocks.

"You're worldly," I say. I can imagine showing Ryan all the oceans, taking him places he could never see as he is now. I try not to get ahead of myself because he's human. But even after just talking to him this morning, it's like the ocean knew what it was doing when it assured we crossed paths.

"Grew up on the sea," he says. "It's in my blood. My dad's a fisherman."

I smile. I can't help it. Because it's in my very essence. "But you don't want to join the family business?"

"Nope, which is a good thing, because then I'd never have had the chance to meet you." Ryan leans back on his hands, tilting his head to the sky.

"So, what do you do to survive on land? Everything's so expensive. I wouldn't be able to be here if it weren't for Giselle." After the words come out, I realize how strange I must sound. "I mean, living in a beachfront condo."

"Inheritance," he says without looking at me.

"Your dad must be great at what he does." Which means he doesn't fish anywhere near any of the colonies. Because merpeople will mess with lines, empty nets, and release traps. It used to not always be this way, but I've worked hard with Ava to find a balance to unite the sea and land to help the oceans flourish. It's just a start, but now that more merpeople are surfacing, things will change.

"Inheritance is from my mom. She passed away when I was a kid," he says, glancing at me in his peripheral vision.

I reach out and touch his hand. "Oh, I'm so sorry. I've lost my mom, too. I was only a merb—I was a toddler at the time."

A strange look flickers across his eyes as he scrunches his brows. Sliding his fingers between mine, he shifts and tugs me to my feet, grabbing my fins from the sand. He strolls us toward the edge of the rocks to peer into the tide pools teeming with life. A few crabs scurry across the rocks to hide as Ryan reaches over to brush his fingers across a sea star.

"What's wrong?" I ask, his sudden silence feeling heavy instead of comfortable. "Did I say something weird?"

He shakes his head without looking at me. "No, it's just— we have so much in common it's almost freaky."

"Oh." I blink a few times, disappointed by the way he says it. The ocean wouldn't have fated us to be mates if we didn't have similarities.

He turns to me. "Hey, no, I didn't mean it as a bad thing. I'm just a little scared of messing this up, because I like you, Luna."

My heart warms at his admission—at how he might sense the same thing I do, that we're destined to be mates. I can feel it within me. But it's hard to explain why or how. My mermaid essence draws me to him, but he's human. He might sense something between us, but he'll never know until the moment he agrees to transform and couple with me. Now, I just have to take it a day at a time.

"I like you, too," I say, barely a whisper. "A lot."

Leaning closer, Ryan cups my face and brushes his lips to mine. I stand frozen in surprise, my heart pounding so hard it's all I can hear. I run my fingers up his arms and to his neck, and kiss him deep enough to taste the sweetness of syrup through the salt of the sea.

Feeling the softness of our lips together, his strong hands wandering down to my sides to hook onto my hips, his warm tongue caressing over mine—everything about this moment ignites something inside me. I think about the first time our eyes met and he smiled, and how I never imagined he'd be the first one to ever kiss me like this.

He gasps against my lips, and I suck in a breath at the same time. Because I opened my mind to him. I accidentally showed him what he looks like to me in this moment, and I'm sure such a thing was enough to startle him. I didn't even know it was possible with a human, because no one told me. No one had a reason to. Kisses between merpeople are a way to quickly share information, but they're never kisses like the one Ryan gives me full of so much more.

And the kiss ends too soon, but not by either of our doings. I grab Ryan's hands, dragging him back from a rising swell, but with the cliff behind us, there's nowhere to go. Fear rushes through me, and instead of trying to hold onto the rocks and risk getting pummeled into the cliff, I drag Ryan with me. At the same time the wave crests to crash into us, I dive us forward.

But the current's too strong.

I scream out as the roaring surf drags me over the slippery rocks toward the shallows and away from Ryan. I try to stop myself, but there's nothing I can do. The call of the sea doesn't give me a choice, and panic cascades through me.

This can't be happening.

Why would the ocean do this? Ryan's my potential mate.

Unless he isn't.

The last thing I hear is Ryan yell out my name from the sand where we were standing.

Then the sea swallows me.

JEALOUS OCEAN

THE ROUGH CURRENT ROCKS me back and forth through the water, clouding the sea. Without my fins and mask, it's harder to break the surface. But I need air. Because I can't risk transforming. If I do, there will be no returning to my condo. Ryan knows where I live, and I could never explain how I disappeared into the sea to resurface. He'll get the human authorities involved.

Oh, Ocean. Why allow me to get as far as sharing my first romantic kiss with Ryan only to pull me under? He's so perfect. I don't understand. I know deep within me that he could be my one, and it's unfair the sea tries to change that.

I sway with the waves, kicking my feet, wishing my legs didn't suck so much at swimming. A current pulls me toward the bottom of the shallows instead of allowing me to ascend, and I close my eyes, suppressing my panic the best I can.

I'm going to have to transform. There's no other way. If I don't, I'm sure the ocean will trigger my transformation before I can drown.

Arms lace around me as I close my eyes to will my body to transform into the form fitting for the sea, stopping me. Ryan hugs me from behind and propels me toward the surface. The current dissipates, freeing me from its rocking hold, allowing Ryan to tread the surface with me. I gasp a heaving breath, the edges of my vision shadowing. Ryan spins me in his arms, combing the strands of my hair now free from my braid out of my face. His wide eyes search mine, worry puckering his brows.

He hugs me and releases a groan. "You're okay. God, you're okay. Just catch your breath."

I don't say anything as he pulls me with him, swimming back toward the boat. My mind races, everything playing over and over again. I'm so confused. I can't decode the ocean's signs. It allowed Ryan to rescue me, but dragging me under was its doing. Maybe it's warning me that it was wrong, and Ryan isn't my potential future.

Ryan pushes me up onto the step to get back in the boat and then pulls himself up. I stare at the seawater dripping from my disheveled braid and onto the deck. My fingers shake in my lap, and Ryan wraps a towel around my shoulders.

"Say something, please," he asks, kneeling in front of me.

I open and close my mouth for a second, gathering my thoughts. "The ocean's mad we kissed."

He releases a breathless laugh, shaking his head. "I'd be jealous, too."

Cupping my cold hands in his, he brings them to his lips and blows out a warm breath. Even under the morning sun, the chill from the spring night still hangs in the air. Ryan grabs his own towel and moves from in front of me to sit beside me, wrapping his arm around my back.

"I don't think I've ever been that scared, Luna. You were underwater forever. Longer than I can hold my breath." His voice quakes as the adrenaline washes away from him. A mixture of emotions collides inside me at his admission. How can I still like him so much when it's obvious I shouldn't draw anything out between us? The ocean could have very well taken me back to sea, stopped my human life here on land because of Ryan, but it was only warning me. And I can't take such a thing lightly. I can't risk Ryan's life and world like that.

I lean into him, resting my head on his shoulder. I can't stop myself. This is the last time I'll get to. Once we return to shore, I'll have to tell him I can't see him anymore. "I was seconds away from breathing in water." And not as a human.

"There must've been an earthquake or something." He points at the now flooded shore, the sea glass beach hidden beneath the waves crashing against the side of the cliff. "Look, the beach is gone. Just my luck a freak wave had to interrupt something I've been dying to do since you smiled at me yesterday on the beach."

I tilt my head to meet his green eyes. His gaze bores into mine, sending my heart racing all over again, but in a good way. Running his finger along my jaw, he tucks my still sopping hair behind my ear.

And then he kisses me again, leaving me as breathless as the ocean did minutes ago. The boat rocks, startling me, and I pull away and release a small yelp.

Ryan squeezes my hands, turning away to peer around the ocean. "I think that's a sign I need to get us back to land."

All I can do is nod.

So much for finding my perfect mate.

"It was a disaster," I say, leaning my elbows on my knees. "I'll swim back to the cliffs tonight to see if I can find your gear."

Carter tosses a marshmallow at me from over the fire pit. "No worries. I can go myself. You look like you can use a night away from the water."

I groan. "I don't understand. I was so sure, and I like him so much. But the ocean nearly forced me to change. That's a sign, right? The ocean was pretty clear."

Ava puffs out her bottom lip, turning her gaze toward the night ocean. The waxing moon hovers above us with tiny bursts of glittering stars sprinkled through the dark sky. The fire dances between us, casting shadows across her face, enhancing the worry crinkling her forehead.

She leans into Carter, using him as a backrest. He brings his hand to her chest, just holding it against her heart. "What's clear is that you like Ryan, and the thought of not seeing where things can lead upsets you. So, I think that's a greater sign than the ocean messing up your first kiss."

Her words fill me with the hope I had lost in the waves. "You think so?"

"Listen to my mate, Luna," Carter says, snuggling his chin into her shoulder. "I thought the same thing when Ava fell overboard when we first met. Now look at us."

Their relationship is exactly what I want, how I imagine love to be. A tear sneaks from my eye to splash on my cheek, and Ava shifts from Carter's lap to stroll around the fire to me. She hugs me, using her sleeve to wipe my face. "Take a breath and smile. I mean it. I see another sign."

I inhale the sea air into my lungs. "What do you mean?"

"Ryan looks exactly like his picture. He's cute." She smiles, releasing a quiet laugh. "He's also staring in this direction like he found the best thing he's ever seen on this beach."

I crane my neck to peer in the direction she's looking. Kicking up sand, Ryan strolls along the beach wearing board shorts and a T-shirt without shoes. He waves, a smile brightening his entire face. Ava whispers in my ear once more about being right about him showing up as being the sign I should follow. I push to my feet and stroll away from Ava and Carter to meet Ryan.

"Hey, I hope you don't mind I came by, but I found your

phone in my truck," he says, reaching into his pocket. "I think Giselle's annoyed you're not responding. It's been buzzing the whole walk here."

My phone buzzes in my hand right on cue with another text message from Giselle, asking if I decided to run away with Ryan to elope without inviting her.

"I swear I only read the first one. I thought you might've been texting to see if I had it," he says.

Blush warms my face as I scroll up to see exactly what he read. "I'm sorry you had to read that. I should warn you, my friends are—"

"The best," Ava calls from behind me.

Ryan chuckles and waves.

"You want to join us?" I ask. "We're waiting for Giselle to finish her last midterm and then going to dinner."

"Sure, I'd like that. Maybe it'll turn out better than this morning," he says.

"We heard you were Luna's hero," Carter says, trying to keep a straight face because Ryan doesn't know my mermaid secret. "Dinner's on me for that."

I never imagined I'd ever need rescuing from the water. But I'm glad he did. Ava was right. The ocean dragging me out to sea wasn't the sign of whether or not he could be my intended mate. Ryan pulling me to the surface and then showing up here is.

Ryan nods, smiling at me, though his eyes don't. "I wasn't going to let her get away from me that easily."

Sliding his arm around me, he hugs me against him. I can see the events from this morning replay in his green eyes, lit by the firelight, and it hardens his features as he clenches his jaw. I reach up and lace my fingers with his on my shoulder, and he squeezes my hand.

"Good. Don't let that big ocean mess with you," Ava says, trying to lighten the mood.

"You'd think after spending all day yesterday cleaning up the beach, it'd have been nicer." Ryan grins at me, and I can't stop the smile crossing my face. Because even though he's humoring Ava, he sounds like he could easily adapt to my life. He did say the ocean was in his blood.

"Well, we appreciate it," Carter says, wagging his eyebrows at me, because Ryan won't get that we, as a species, are grateful that he cares enough to make an effort in protecting our home away from shore.

The back door to my condo slides open, and Giselle peeks her head out at us on the beach. Everyone's attention shifts to her, and she trudges the few feet to our fire pit, her shoulders sagging, acting like the effort to reach us is exhausting.

"Long night?" Ava asks.

"Didn't think I'd survive my midterm. Then there was so much traffic. If only I could swim to school," she says, grabbing a marshmallow from the bag next to Carter before popping it into her mouth.

"Someday. It could happen sooner if you..." I close my eyes, letting my words trail off. I'm so comfortable in Ryan's arms, hanging with my friends, that it's hard not to say what's on my mind. I've always been honest. And I want to be with Ryan, but I can't yet. I'm not a hundred percent certain he's my mate—only my potential one. From the few merpeople who have chosen a human mate, I know it doesn't happen overnight. It can take months or years even. But things are changing. Merpeople emerge from the sea more and more. The risk isn't as great as it was. A human discovering our secret isn't a death sentence like it used to be under my dad's reign.

Giselle groans. "No more talking about me." She turns to Ryan. "I see Luna didn't scare you away." I'm thankful she manages to turn the conversation to Ryan to take the focus off me and my inability to keep my mouth shut.

"I thought I might've been the one to do so after this morning." Ryan tells his version of what happened on the glass beach. "And all I could think about was how I was not going to let the ocean have Luna before I even got a chance."

Carter stares at me from over the fire, a smirk playing on his lips. "Good thing Luna is part fish."

Ryan laughs, missing the truth to Carter's joke. "A real mermaid, huh? More beautiful, though."

Everyone falls silent for a moment. Ava and Giselle lock gazes before looking to me. Giselle laughs first, causing me to laugh. Carter rests his chin on Ava's shoulder, just smiling at Ryan. I feel his gaze on the side of my face, and I turn to him, sucking my bottom lip between my teeth, trying not the laugh. His eyebrows rise on his forehead, and I'm sure he thinks we're all strange for laughing so hard at his sweet compliment. If only he knew. *One day...*

"You got that right," Giselle says. "My best friends are mermaids."

Ryan laughs. "Not you?"

She shrugs, smiling. "Maybe one day. I hear ocean living is boring."

Ryan laughs. "I think the land's a little overrated."

I bump Ryan's shoulder, smiling at him. "You think so?"

"Well, maybe not entirely. You're here."

Leaning in, I brush my lips to his. I can't help myself. "You were wrong today, you know. The ocean wasn't jealous of you kissing me. It was jealous of me kissing you."

He laughs against my lips. "Let it be jealous."

I plan on doing just that.

MERMAID HEARTS

I SIT AT THE bar, watching Giselle drizzle pancake batter onto a skillet. The ocean breeze wafts through the air from our open backdoor, and I turn my gaze from her to the beach. It's only been a few hours since Giselle dropped Ryan off at his apartment, but I still can't stop thinking about him.

Dinner last night couldn't have been more perfect. I think my friends like him as much as I do. It helps assure me that my moment of doubt was unwarranted. Because I trust my friends' opinions as much as I do the ocean's.

And Ryan is exactly how I imagine my intended mate to be. He's friendly, easy-going, and loves the ocean. He likes adventure and exploring, and showed me dozens of pictures of shores he's visited that I've only seen from the water. I also enjoy how much attention he shows me, constantly holding my hand or putting his arm around me. Boys on land might not be so different from those in the sea after all. Or maybe because he was raised on the water.

"Luna?" Giselle asks, drawing my attention away from the waves and my thoughts of Ryan. "Did you hear me?"

"What? I'm sorry," I say.

She lifts an eyebrow. "I've lost you already, huh? You mermaids and your hearts. Think you can resist the call of love until after spring break? I thought we could make the trip up north after my aunt's gala this weekend."

"Up north?"

"To meet your cousin." She removes the pancakes from the skillet and sets them on a plate, sliding it in front of me. She hands me a glass of syrup she warmed up, knowing how much I love hot food. "You still want to go, right? I mean, you better want to go. I've already promised my mom that we'd help her plan the next three events if she paid for vacation."

I blink a few times. I haven't thought much about going to San Francisco since finding out I have family on land. I don't know how I feel about the information. My mom kept some huge secrets from my dad, which means they were kept from me. I wonder how he'll react if he knew. I wonder if he'd have handled me differently knowing I had a blood bond to the land. Or maybe he knew all along, and it was why he was so adamant about me remaining in the sea.

I exhale a breath through my nose. I'll ask him the next time I visit Celestiana Cove, but I doubt he'll tell me even now. He doesn't say more than two words to me, and can barely look at me with my legs. Yet, I still keep visiting him. I can't turn my back on my family. And the same goes for my mysterious cousin.

I nod way too late, cutting a piece of pancake with my fork. "Of course I haven't forgotten, and I'd help your mom with all her event planning anyway."

She points her fork at me. "I knew you would want to help, so might as well get a vacation out of it."

I stare at my dripping syrup. "I still can't believe all of this is happening so suddenly." The more I think about my land bond, the more excited I get.

"You sure you can handle being away from your potential mate for a bit?" Giselle smiles as she says it.

I don't even know the answer to her question. Can I? Would it be weird to invite Ryan along so soon? I mean, he loves to travel. And I don't think it would be that weird to do so with him if Giselle comes along. Ava was allowed to travel with Carter when they first met.

Instead of answering her with my millions of thoughts, something in the ocean draws my attention away from Giselle. I shift in my chair to turn to the beach through our open door. "Can you?" I ask her with a smile, spotting a tail cut through a wave.

Confusion puckers her brows, and she misses what I see. "Well, I have been, haven't I?"

I shake my head and point out the window, watching a head pop to the surface not far from shore. I was right about Sun waiting nearby in the water, because it's rare for a merman to leave his intended mate, and I had a feeling he'd pick today to come to shore since it's the start of Giselle's school vacation. He's probably been planning since the Spring Equinox.

"I don't think he's left since the last time he came ashore," I mention, smiling as Giselle's grimace morphs into surprise and then happiness so palpable I can feel it wash over me from across the kitchen.

She throws her spatula on the counter. "Why didn't you tell me he was here?"

"I didn't know for sure. He hasn't called out to me. But even if he did, he wouldn't have surfaced before now. He knows how important school is to you, and he's trying his best to control his merman nature, so he doesn't scare you away."

Giselle points at me. "You merpeople! I swear. That glorious man with his delicious abs and pouty mouth would never have me running away. Have you seen his arms? I'm going to jump into them now and listen to his sexy voice whisper into my ear how my soft hair blazes with streaks of gold in the bright sunshine like my damn smile."

I laugh, watching her race from the condo and to the waves. My heart swells at the sight of Giselle running into the ocean in her pajamas to greet Sun, who's already strolling through the shallow water, wearing only a pair of swim trunks.

Taking a couple more bites of the pancakes Giselle made me, I grab my waterproof bag and head out to the beach. I smile and wave at Sun. "I'm going for a walk," I call out. Because if I were them, I'd like to be alone to catch up. I don't know if my love-obsessed spark could handle listening to Sun sweep Giselle into the waves with promises of a magnificent life without crying from happiness like I do every time I watch my favorite princess mermaid movie.

Giselle blows me a kiss from Sun's arms and turns her attention back to her merman boyfriend, allowing him to carry her out of the waves. I head in the direction of the public beach near the pier to people watch. Instead of walking the surf, I wade into the waves, pulling my sundress over my head to tuck away with my towel in my waterproof bag. I'd rather swim than walk, especially with everything Ryan still stirs inside me. I feel like if I don't transform to swim, I'll get restless and end up at his apartment to knock on his door. It's too early for that. The sun barely rose.

The longer I think about Ryan, the more I need to take a breath of the sea so I can take a moment to think. The ocean calls to me, and I jog deeper, jumping over the cresting waves, letting them lift me off my feet until I can't touch the sea floor anymore. I spin once, peering at the shore for signs of anyone on the beach, but it's empty like usual and my condo is the only one with the blinds open.

I dive under, kicking my legs to swim myself a bit farther,

practicing what Ava calls a butterfly stroke in case Ryan ever asks me to swim instead of dive since I told him I liked doing both. Sand clouds the water, making it blurry, and I shoo away a few small fish who attempt to hide in my hair as one of the playful local seals passes me by.

Drinking the ocean into my lungs, I transform and dive deeper into the shallows. I swim along the bottom and trail my hands through the sand, clouding the ocean even more. Shadows of boats pepper the surface, and I automatically search for the Sea Princess, though I only recognize a few of the usual locals.

A few fishing lines stretch through the water in front of me, and I cut the hooks off with my sharp nails, dropping them into the small zipper pocket on the outside of my bag. I'll add them to the hundreds I have collected over the months here. Fewer and fewer fishing boats pick these shores, and Ava always messes with the currents using her ocean magic, keeping the visibility around our beach low to stop people from snorkeling and diving in our thriving kelp forests just in case. They'd never see us in our mermaid forms, but the last thing we need is to have thrill seekers or scientists searching for some mysterious creature newly arrived from the deep.

Swimming faster, I jet through a current and head toward the shore where I watch a dozen surfers float on their boards, waiting to catch the perfect wave. I hover in the sea, bobbing with the ocean, listening to the musical voices of a pod of dolphins in the distance. They sound nothing like I hear on TV, and it took me a minute to realize that as a mermaid, I hear things at a different frequency. The human transformation dulls everything, but I gain new sensations, too. I can't imagine being a human every day apart from the full moon, even if I spend days on the couch.

Out here, I feel most at home, but my heart draws me to the land even in this moment. Something pulls at my very essence, and I let it guide me toward the pier where barnacles decorate the huge wooden pillars. Bar-like shadows ripple across the surface, and I take a moment to transform into a human. My back arches with the tightening of my muscles and tingles rush through me. When my lungs start to burn from the sudden shift from breathing water to needing air, I tug on my bikini bottoms and kick to the surface, spitting out water.

I swim out from under the pier and stroke my arms to head toward the beach, using a wave to propel me forward. I don't bother standing up, even in the knee-deep water, and glide the rest of the way to the beach until I'm too weighted to drift back out to sea.

Flipping over, I rest on my elbows, and tilt my head toward the sun, soaking up the rays of warm morning sunshine. A shadow turns my closed eyelids from red to black, and I peek through my lashes at the silhouette standing above me.

"You really are a mermaid, aren't you?" Ryan's deep voice swirls to my ears, though he's hard to see from the starbursts dancing across my vision from the sun behind him. It wasn't the land calling to my heart. It was him, and he doesn't even know it.

I smile and nod, though he's only teasing. "I love swimming."

Instead of pulling me to my feet, Ryan plops down next to me in the surf. The sea washes over our legs and to our stomachs. Ryan laughs as sea spray mists our faces and glitters across his chest.

He takes my hand like it's the most natural thing to do, reminding me how much he likes me, and combs our fingers through the sea foam. "Wanna swim with me now?"

I like that he doesn't question that I randomly emerged from the surf, but instead gladly accepts I'm here and that our paths met again without even having to arrange anything. "You sure you can keep up with a mermaid?"

He bobs his head and tugs me to my feet with him and into the next wave. We go under together, sand blurring the sea, though I can see him staring at me underwater. He hooks his arms around my waist, picking me off my feet to stand us in the rising swells. Another wave curls toward us, and we both jump over it, letting it carry us a few feet toward the shore.

Another whitecap washes over us, and I drag Ryan back to the shore with it until the surf pulls back to leave us behind on the beach. He props up on his side, digging his elbow into the sand. His green eyes shine in the bright sun like the sea glass sparkling from my bracelet. I let strands of my wet hair fall into my face only to have him push them away.

"You know what's weird?" Ryan asks, holding me in his

gaze. "I was thinking about you, and I even texted you to see what you were doing, but then I look up and there you were in the waves like the ocean was apologizing for yesterday."

I release a small laugh, so caught up in the warmth pouring from my spark that I can't stop myself from closing the space between us to kiss him. He reacts to my lips, deepening our kiss, tasting of the salt from the ocean dripping from his hair.

I dig my hand into the sand, bracing for the ocean to rise up to wash me back into the water, but the waves remain the same. Maybe yesterday was a freak accident like Ryan assumes. Or maybe he proved himself by rescuing me.

I hate not knowing.

But the ocean has never been forthcoming with what it wants.

Slowly pulling away, I lean back and smile. "So, what are your plans for the rest of the day?"

"I was going to ask you," he says, playing with my long strands of hair.

There's no denying that I was meant to be here. Like Sun stayed offshore, keeping close to Giselle, I keep finding myself back with Ryan where my mermaid spark longs to be. "I was hoping you'd say that. I can't go home because Giselle's boy-friend just arrived and—"

He chuckles, cutting me off. "And you've been temporarily kicked out."

I crinkle my nose. "Actually, I ran away."

"Well, I'm glad you did because I have an idea," Ryan says.

"If you're not scared of the open sea after yesterday."

My eyes widen. "Me afraid of the ocean? I used to live there."

He smirks at my words, but I don't cringe or try to take back what I said despite it sounding weird. He's never once looked at me or treated me like I'm strange but takes it in stride. It's incredibly easy to be with him, how I imagined it'd be.

He grabs my hand again and pulls me to my feet. "Just checking. You were a little freaked out after diving yesterday, but since you were swimming..."

"You were scared, too," I say, smiling.

He tugs me closer, until our shoulders touch. "Not of the ocean."

"Of losing me?" I ask.

His face reddens with blush. "Have I told you I really like you?"

I smile and nod. "I'd like to hear it again."

Ryan kisses me once more and leads me from the beach and down a street away. A small gated apartment complex comes into view, and Ryan opens the gate for me. It looks different in the daytime, more alive with people, and I spot his truck parked in a resident space.

He points at an apartment on the second floor, which I didn't get to see from the car last night. "That's me."

I peer at it a moment, wondering what it looks like inside. But instead of showing me his place, he opens his truck and tosses a towel on the seat for me. Dropping my waterproof bag on the floor, I climb up and get in. He turns on the stereo and opens the windows, allowing the ocean air to gust inside the truck.

"I was thinking about the glass beach, and how you like to treasure hunt in the sea. So, I asked around for places I could surprise you with," he says, glancing at me in his peripheral vision.

"You told people about the glass beach?" I ask, a frown stealing my smile away. I wish I could control my expression. I should be excited Ryan told the people he's close to that he hung out with me. I should be bouncing in my seat that he thought about other ways to impress me to show me how much he likes me. But I can't help feeling sad that the spot I love to swim as a mermaid might start getting more attention.

He reaches out and touches my knee. "No way, Luna. I could tell that place was special to you."

Now I feel even worse. "Oh, I'm sorry. I didn't mean to assume you did. It's just—that place is incredible, and I wouldn't blame you if you wanted to share it with others."

Grasping my hand, he says, "You should probably know. I don't have a lot of close friends. Mostly acquaintances. No one like you do. Your friends are pretty awesome."

I purse my lips in thought, wondering how could he not have a ton of friends. He's the most fascinating human I've met. "They think you're pretty great for me, too."

"Glad they approve," he says, smiling.

"Oh, I—that doesn't matter to me."

He chuckles.

"Is it because you travel a lot? I mean, why you don't have many people you consider close to you? Because I get that. I had no one until I moved here."

"Something like that."

"Oh."

"I'm okay with it," he says. "It's better this way."

I don't say it, but he's right. The fact that he doesn't have a lot of close ties to the land makes him even more of an ideal mate. It's easier to disappear from land without having to worry about who you have to leave behind. It's why Ava and Carter remain on land most of the time. Ava's deeply connected to her family and her community.

"Well, I'm happy to share mine with you," I say.

He nods his head and releases a short laugh I enjoy hearing. It's not at me but like everything I say brings him joy, and his smile is so handsome...

"I'd like that," he says.

I know I should be a teensy bit sad he doesn't have many close friends of his own, because bonds of all kinds are important in the sea, but maybe it's because he was fated for this. It's why I left the water. There wasn't much left for me in the colonies—not with my friends on land.

I want to ask him more about his life, but he parks in the lot at the marina and shuts off the engine. Ryan grabs a bag from under the cover on the bed of his truck and surprise washes over me at the sight of two sets of free diving gear.

"You're so prepared," I say.

He scoops everything we need from the truck and slides his bag over his shoulder. "I told you I texted you."

"You should probably know I always forget my phone," I say. "I have a waterproof case and all, but I'm afraid of losing it, and would hate if Gi—I'd hate to have to buy another one." I'm glad I caught myself, because it would be weird to admit Giselle takes care of me like I know parents take care of their children on land.

Motioning me to walk with him, Ryan leads the way to the docks. "It gives me an excuse to stop by more if you're okay with it."

"Unless I swim ashore, huh?"

He grins at me. "Everything about you impresses me, you know. You're unlike anyone I've ever met."

I beam a smile. "I feel the same about you."

"I was hoping," he says, laughing. We stop in front of the *Sea Princess,* and Ryan holds up his bag. "I know you lost your fins yesterday, so I rented a pair from the Big Swell Surf Shop. I didn't know Carter owned the place."

I nod. "Yeah, he bought it a few months ago when the old owner decided to sell it."

"That's cool."

Ryan helps me board the boat, and I sit in the cockpit with him as he navigates from the marina and to the open sea. He waves to a fisherman we pass near the kelp paddies they favor fishing. The wind whips through my hair, and I quickly braid it with my fingers and tie the strands together to hold it in place.

After about an hour, Ryan drops anchor swimming distance from a cove nestled between two cliffs with caves. I've only seen them from a distance because humans love this area, and I never thought about exploring it in my human form.

"Have you been here before?" Ryan asks.

"Just passed by," I say.

"I should warn you. It's not as nice as hunting sea glass. There's a shipwreck that you can walk to during the low tide. But what's the fun in that?" he asks, tugging me to my feet.

"No fun at all."

"Who knows? Maybe we'll find some treasure."

I giggle, shaking my head. If there were ever treasure here, it'd be long gone. We both know it, but from what I know about Ryan, he's more interested in the adventure of it. And I am, too. Because I can't wait to see where the ocean takes us from here.

"Ready?" he asks, grabbing our free diving gear.

I nod. "Try to keep up."

Laughing, he says, "Lead the way."

6

MERMAID WATERS

"PRINCESS LUNA!" SUN'S VOICE echoes through the small living room of our condo. "Is this the potential mate my beautiful Giselle told me about?"

Sun's blond hair shines in the setting sun lighting the room aglow. He gets to his feet and crosses the room, his arms outstretched and ready to surprise Ryan with a hug I'm sure he's not expecting. It's customary for courting mermen to get together and give advice, guiding each other in presenting themselves as the best mates possible. It's not necessary since I've never in my lifetime seen a mermaid reject a merman once they begin the process, but it's more of a ritual.

And Sun's about to drag Ryan into customs that could scare him away from me. Mermen might like the challenge but a human? The pressure could be too much.

I step forward and fling my arms around Sun, intervening before he welcomes Ryan into the merman courting world. Ryan probably already thinks Sun is a little strange from the single sentence he's said, and I don't know how I can explain his word choices. Sun struggles with human norms more than I do, but only because Giselle finds him endearing and lovable. He doesn't have to be careful around her because she knows the merpeople secret.

"This is Ryan, Sun," I say, still hugging him to keep him back.

"It's awesome to meet you, Ryan," Sun says from over my shoulders. "Princess Luna is lucky to have found you."

Ryan chuckles, extending his hand out to shake Sun's, brushing off anything he finds bizarre. "I think I'm the lucky one."

Giselle comes rushing into the hallway from her bedroom, her hair half in curls. "Oh hey, Luna. I was wondering where you've been all day. I should've guessed."

"Exploring shipwrecks," Ryan says.

"Oh!" Sun's eyes light up. "Princess Luna, have you already told—"

"Free diving, like always," I say, interrupting him.

Giselle hooks her fingers around Sun's muscular arm, probably realizing she might need to catch him up to speed on how to handle the situation properly. Ryan's the first human Sun has been around in our circle of friends who doesn't know the mermaid secret. I can see how it's easy to assume I've already told him with him being my potential mate and all, especially with the growing union between land and sea.

"Come on, Sun. You still need to get dressed. Mom wants to see you in something other than swim trunks." She looks at me. "You need to as well or did you forget?"

I frown. "I did. I'm sorry."

Giselle notices the disappointment crossing my face. "Why don't you invite Ryan?"

"I'm sorry. You can say no. I don't mind. But I forgot I was supposed to have dinner with Giselle's aunt," I say. I hope he says yes because I'm looking forward to sharing another dinner with him, even if it won't be alone.

Ryan presses his lips together. "Oh."

"It's formal," Giselle adds.

I squeeze his hand, twisting my lips to the side. "You can say no."

He shrugs. "But I'm not."

Giselle claps her hands. "Well, hurry up and go get ready. We'll pick you up on the way."

Ryan smiles at me. "It's a date."

I can't take my eyes off Ryan. Dressed in a suit, clean-shaven, and with his hair styled back with product, he looks so different but perfect all the same. Ryan links his fingers with mine under the table, staring out at the panoramic view of the night darkened ocean and the moon lighting a silver path leading into the horizon. It glows blue for me like daytime water merging into a night sky, lit by the magic of my mermaid essence, but he wouldn't be able to see what I see.

I never realized that all humans can see is the darkness. I'd have never known if Giselle hadn't gone on a night swim with me and asked me to stay on the surface because the pitch blackness of diving freaked her out.

I can't wait for Ryan to see it as I do—all glowy and magical. The night livens all the oceans, drawing the most interesting creatures from the depths, but especially on the full moon.

Pushing the thought away, I turn from the view of the sparkling sea. There won't be any transformations any time soon, because I've only been with Ryan a few days. This is the land and not the sea. Humans shy away and can't grasp the idea that love bonds happen in an instant. They don't feel what merpeople feel. Things might be different if they could open up their entire beings completely.

"I feel like he does," Ryan whispers, nodding his head to Sun.

Sun messes with the collar of his jacket, shifting in his seat. Giselle loosens his tie some to help out with his comfort, but then he messes with the buttons on the sleeves of his dress shirt next. He's as fidgety as me in the too tight dress and heels I barely manage to walk in. If I hadn't held onto Ryan's arm from the car to my seat, I would've fallen.

"Sorry," I whisper. "I know the feeling. I'd rather be wearing nothing at all."

Ryan bows his head, grinning at his seared salmon. He shifts to look at me, amusement crinkling his eyes in the corners.

"What's so funny?" I whisper, bumping my shoulder to his.

"I like your honesty is all."

"So, Ryan, have you lived in the area long?" Ruby King asks from her place next to Anaya, Giselle's mom. She draws our attention away from each other, and I sit up straighter.

Ryan wipes his mouth with his napkin. "No, ma'am. I've only visited a few times a year until recently. I'm currently living with my aunt until I decide if I'm staying permanently."

I blink at his words. The thought never really crossed my mind that he wouldn't remain in La Tortuga Point. "Oh." My voice sounds a notch above a whisper, and I turn my gaze away. I didn't mean to voice my disappointment out loud.

He squeezes my hand. "It's looking pretty good, though."

Giselle gently kicks me under the table and winks at me. "It's a great place to live."

I bump my shoulder to Ryan's. "I like it."

"Were you interested in going to school here?" Anaya asks, keeping the conversation on Ryan.

Giselle clears her throat. "Hold off on the interrogation, you two."

Ryan smirks. "It's all right. I don't mind." He turns his gaze back to the two women. "And I don't know. I haven't thought much of it."

"Ryan's an adventure seeker," Sun says, like he's known Ryan more than the thirty minute car ride it took to get here. "He and Princess Luna will probably travel the world together. I'd like to take your daughter to sea eventually, too. The ocean is a beautiful place."

Giselle's face blooms burgundy at Sun's admission, and I release a low hum under my breath, smiling at the two of them. It's not until I catch Ryan staring at me, his brows furrowed together, that I straighten my shoulders.

Anaya clears her throat, blinking a few times. "Oh, Sun. That's entirely up to Giselle. Though I hope you'd both visit often."

Giselle brings her finger up to Sun's lips before he can answer. "Mom, enough future talk. All I'm currently thinking about is whether or not I'm going to wear the gown we picked out a few weeks ago to the charity gala and also where I want to stop on the way to San Francisco with Luna and Sun."

Ryan turns his curiosity from me to Giselle's aunt. "A charity gala? For what?"

"Fundraising for a non-profit my daughter and her friends are starting to clean up the ocean," Ruby replies. "I have a spare ticket if you'd like to attend. It's tomorrow."

Ryan leans forward. "That sounds great. If you've ever seen a trash island—"

"That's exactly the type of thing we want to get rid of. And you should totally take my aunt up on her offer," Giselle says.

"Luna needs a date since I wasn't expecting Sun to come so early."

Turning his head, Ryan leans closer and looks at me. "Would you like to be my date?"

I smile. "I'd love to."

The rest of dinner is mildly uneventful apart from Sun, who decides it's the perfect time to profess his love of Giselle to her mom and aunt. It's close to ten when Giselle parks outside of Ryan's apartment, and I climb from the backseat of the Mustang.

"Why don't you go ahead without me?" I say, leaning into the window. "I think I'm going to walk home." I hold onto the doorframe and slide out of my heels. "But you can take these."

Sun takes the shoes from me. "I hope you can join us on our adventure up north."

Giselle smacks his arm. "Don't mind him. You two have fun."

Without waiting for a response, Giselle puts her car in gear and drives away, waving her hand once out the window. Ryan closes the distance between us and hugs me for a moment, resting his head on my shoulder.

"That was interesting," he says, pulling back to smile at me. "I wasn't expecting to have dinner with a billionaire."

"A billionaire?" I ask.

"Ruby King."

My mouth forms an O-shape. "Oh, yeah. I guess. I never really thought of it like that. Where I'm from, we don't define someone by that kind of thing. Mostly by their talents."

He smiles. "This is another reason why I like you, but I do have to ask..."

"What?" I ask when he's not quick to spit out his question.

"Are you royalty? Hiding out in La Tortuga Point or something? Sun kept referring to you as Princess Luna and not in the nickname sort of way." His face remains serious, and I realize he's not joking.

"I—" I'm so caught off guard that my hesitation makes his eyes widen.

"Really?"

I shake my head. "No, it's—" I sigh, taking a deep breath. "It's complicated. But I'm not royalty in the way you think."

"I'm not sure I'm following."

Tilting my head back, I peer toward the sky. "I'm sorry. I should get home." Because I can't explain anything to him or uncomplicate things. I pull away from him, strolling toward the street that'll take me back to the beach.

"Luna, wait." Ryan rushes to my side, grabbing my hand. "It's okay. You don't have to explain anything."

I pout my bottom lip. "I want to, I do. It's just—I'll understand if you don't want to go to the gala with me tomorrow."

"Luna—"

"I had a nice time, Ryan. Thank you for coming with me."

Ryan closes the small amount of distance between us, hooking his hands around my waist. He kisses me, cutting off anything else I can say while also begging me to stay without saying a word. His hands travel from my hips to around my back, his body pressing into mine.

He doesn't stop kissing me until my tight muscles relax. "Hang out a while longer. I can light a fire pit."

I don't respond right away as I consider what to do. I've admitted to having a huge secret, and my secret can only last so long now that Ryan knows I'm keeping something from him. Hiding a part of my life goes against everything inside me when it comes to him, but his safety is important to me. But telling him I'm a real mermaid? That could change things between us in a bad way. He doesn't even love me yet. He doesn't feel the bond between us like I do.

"Please," he says, kissing me. "I won't ask about the whole princess thing again. It doesn't matter. I won't tell anyone anything. Just please, stay."

"Are you sure?" I ask. "I know how hard secrets can be, but I can't tell you. Not yet."

"Because you'll have to kill me?" He smiles as he says it.

I don't. "What? Oh, Ocean, I—"

He laughs. "Even if that were the case, I can handle myself. I grew up on the sea, remember? I'm familiar with dangerous waters."

But I'm not so sure he is. I'm afraid that if it came down to him or the sea, I'd have no choice but to pick the sea. If only he were familiar with mermaid waters.

"You can trust me," he adds.

I nod. It's all I can hope for.

SECRETS

AVA CLASPS TOGETHER THE necklace I made from the sea glass and pearls around my neck. It sparkles against my collarbone, the sea glass turning the white pearls green. I help Ava with the one I made her, and we smile at each other in the mirror.

"Hey, mermaid royalty, Sun brought these ashore for you," Giselle says, spinning two dainty crowns from the throne room in Pearlestria. "I insist you make my boyfriend happy and wear them. What better place than a gala?"

Ava raises an eyebrow. "Only if you can make it look more like a hair accessory."

My cheeks flush. "I can't wear it. I'm sorry."

Giselle and Ava both look at me. I've never denied a thoughtful gift before, and it pains me that I have to. Because really, even if Ryan says I don't have to explain myself or that he can live without knowing the whole truth about me, he won't be able to resist prying more once he sees the crown.

I shrug, trying to keep myself from panicking as my friends stare me down, waiting for me to explain myself. "I messed up last night with Ryan. Sun kept calling me princess at dinner, and when Ryan asked about it, I couldn't think of a response fast enough. Now he thinks I'm some princess in hiding."

Giselle tips her head back and laughs. "You should've just told him the truth."

"That I'm a mermaid princess?"

She nods. "He already thinks we're kidding about the whole mermaid thing. It would've made him think we were all still joking."

I groan, rubbing my fingers across the shiny metal. The crown belonged to my mother, a piece my father thought would make her happy because it came from the land in a time far too long ago to imagine. "It's too late. So, sorry, no I'm not wearing it."

Rushing forward, Giselle snatches the crown from my fingers and places it on my head anyway. It sparkles with aquamarine stones the same color as the surface above Pearlestria, reminding me of home. I don't even have time to protest before she braids strands of my hair around the thin metal, securing it in place. I'd have to mess up my hair to get it off, and now that I see myself in the mirror…it looks so pretty.

"Perfect," Ava says, smiling. She steps closer and pulls a few strands of hair forward to frame my face. "It doesn't even look like a crown. People are going to ask you to add hair jewelry to your Princess Luna collection."

I wring my hands together, staring at my reflection in the mirror again. I almost feel like a part of myself clicks back into place seeing something I've worn hundreds of times over the years on my head. But instead of standing silently as the perfect princess daughter during a traditional mermaid ceremony like a coupling or celebrating the solstice, I'm about to hop in a limo with my intended mate. And though tonight might be fun, I hope it ends quickly enough. I need one last swim before I'm in a car for at least two days, since Giselle plans to make the most of her spring break on the way to find the last human of my land pod. I wish it wouldn't be weird to invite Ryan along. I'm dying to do so.

My land pod. Shaking my head, I push the thought away. I'm nervous enough that I can't think about my cousin and what it means for me.

After helping Giselle put on her pearl necklace, I fluff my long hair over my shoulders, slip into low-heeled glittering strappy sandals Ava brought, and grab the boutonniere I've spent the morning creating for Ryan to match my jewelry. It's my most favorite piece I've ever made from one of the biggest pearls I've ever found in an oyster.

"Luna, you can't give that to Ryan," Ava says, inspecting the boutonniere. "I'm pretty sure a pearl this size costs in the tens of thousands of dollars."

I frown. "It's not my only one." I don't care how much humans think a pearl is worth. The only value I see in it is that I get to give it to Ryan and how perfect it'll look on him.

She sighs. "Okay, fine. Since he thinks you're a princess anyway. But I want you to be careful until you're certain about Ryan. It's easier to get swept away with things on land than it is in the sea."

I hug her. "I appreciate you looking out for me."

Smiling once more in the mirror, I follow Ava and Giselle out of the house to where a stretch limo idles in the parking lot. Carter and Sun stand near the driver, looking handsome in their tuxes, both their gazes locked on their mates. Ryan peeks his head out from the limo, where voices sound through the air, and he comes out to meet me.

He hugs me and leans into me for a sweet kiss. "You look incredible. Beautiful. I almost can't believe you're real and in front of me."

"Carter, man, sounds like you have some competition in the romance department," a masculine voice says from the limo. Matty, a friend of Ava and Giselle, who also dates Giselle's cousin Sapphire, waves from the door of the limo.

Sapphire yanks him back, rolling her eyes, and we all get in to head to the gala held in Azure Waters. Excitement buzzes through the air, and I clink my champagne glass with Ryan while smiling at the rest of my friends. Logan sits between Daisy and Chloe, who talk about spending all of their spring break surfing.

Ryan sips his champagne. "Should be a fun night, huh?"

"I hope so," I say. "Oh, and I almost forgot. I have something for you."

Giselle takes my glass of champagne and drinks it for me while I tug out the boutonniere to pin to Ryan's breast pocket. His eyes widen at the sight of it, his mouth slightly opening, and I can't stop the smile lighting my face because he doesn't even have to say anything for me to know he likes it.

"Just a small treasure I found diving," I add.

The limo pulls to a stop, and everyone quickly finishes their drinks. The driver opens the limo door, and we all pile out to bright flashes from the paparazzi waiting to glimpse one of the many celebrities attending tonight.

Sapphire makes us pose a few times on the blue carpet leading to the hotel, and Ryan holds out his arm to lead me inside. I trail behind my friends, smiling at a few familiar faces. Ava and Carter stroll off to meet Ava's land family, and I wave to her sister Bailey and her mate, Wes. Giselle and the others immerse themselves in the crowd, leaving me alone with Ryan. I'm not a part of their land bonds, but they always make me feel welcome regardless.

"Are you okay?" Ryan asks, pulling me to look at a few art pieces up for auction made by talented artists using human-made things found in the sea.

Forcing my mouth to smile, I nod. "Yeah, but this isn't something I like to do often. I feel like an outsider when I'm around so many hu—people."

"You don't look like an outsider," he says, trailing his gaze from the crown on my head to my shoes. He smiles and pushes my hair back to kiss my cheek. "You look perfect."

I shrug. "You look like you fit in better here than me."

He chuckles. "Not how I see it. But for me, it has taken practice. I've grown accustomed to adapting to any social scene. Now come on. Let's thank the hosts, grab something to eat, and if you'd like, maybe dance." Funny how he mentions adapting to any social scene. I can't stop myself from thinking about how easy it might be for him to follow me into the sea.

"I've never danced outside my condo," I respond to him, suddenly nervous that I'll really stand out when all I want is to fit in now. Something I haven't cared about until seeing how easy it is for Ryan.

He tugs my hand, pulling me forward into the crowd. "Think of this as an adventure. That's how I handle my nerves."

"You and your adventures," I say, smirking.

"Our adventures. It's one after another with you."

"But this isn't exactly an adventure."

"We'll make it one." Ryan spins me on my feet before pulling me against him, our bodies touching like they were meant to stay close. His green eyes hold mine for a second, and he tilts his head forward, resting it on mine without kissing me, just swaying me to the music though no one else dances around us.

"Life shouldn't be any other way," he whispers into my lips.

I let him spin me again and stop in front of him, pressing my hands to his chest. "I'm used to things being simple, though." I don't know why I say it, but I want to open myself up and be as honest as I can with Ryan. I hope doing so will help when I reveal the secret that's been dangling in front of him all along about who I am.

"I guess I'm going to have to change that," he says.

I brush my lips against his, sliding my hands around his neck. "You already have."

Ryan pulls his truck into his apartment complex well past midnight. Instead of following the others to Ava and Carter's for a small after party, I've decided to spend a few hours with Ryan before I leave with Giselle tomorrow afternoon.

"You want to stay here? I'll be quick to change," he says, leaving the engine running.

I nod. "Sure, I don't want to bother your aunt."

He brushes his thumb across my hand. "She wouldn't be bothered. She's dying to meet you. Always up late, anyway."

"Okay, I'll come. I'd love to meet your family." Something about Ryan mentioning that his aunt wants to meet me makes my heart all sorts of happy. For one, it means I'm special enough that he talks about me with someone he's close with. And second, meeting one of the only people he shares a bond with takes our relationship to another level. It took Giselle over two months to even mention to her mom that she was courting a merman, though I can see how our situations differ.

Ryan shuts off the engine and strolls around to help me from his truck. He hugs me close as we walk toward the stairs leading to the second story apartments. I take in everything I can about the place—from the seashell wind chime to the collection of succulents on a small glass table near a patio chair.

The TV hums from inside when he unlocks the door, and I catch sight of the woman from the beach cleanup. Her dark hair hangs loosely around her shoulders, and she wears white and teal floral print pajamas.

"Oh, Ryan. You're home earlier than I expected," she says, standing from her spot on a plush recliner. "And you brought Luna. It's so good to meet you. You're all Ryan has talked about for days. I'm Sherry."

My heart flutters, and I flick my gaze to Ryan, who smiles at me in my peripheral vision. "It's nice to meet you."

"Back at ya. Make yourself comfortable," she says.

Ryan gives me a quick kiss on the cheek and motions for me to sit on the couch. His aunt follows him from the living room, whispering something too soft for me to hear. When Ryan emerges from the hall, dressed in board shorts and a hoodie, he doesn't look as happy as he did a moment ago.

"What's wrong?" I ask. I can't help wondering if maybe I haven't lived up to his aunt's expectations. I thought I did everything I was supposed to meeting someone new, but maybe I missed something.

Ryan blinks and then smiles, softening his features. Reaching down, he pulls me up from the couch, holding my hands in his. "Family drama. My dad called to check on me but no worries. Everything's fine."

I rub my lips together, relieved his frown wasn't about me, but I still wish his smile hadn't been stolen by his dad. "Sorry," I say, because I'm not sure how else to respond. Humans usually apologize for everything, even if it's out of their control. So when all else fails, I either apologize or laugh and nod, depending on the circumstances.

"I'll be back later, Aunt Sherry. Don't wait up," Ryan calls out.

"Have fun, you two!" his aunt yells from the hallway.

Picking up his wallet and keys from a table near the door, he slides into his shoes and meets my gaze again. "I almost forgot." He pulls out the boutonniere from his pocket. "Thanks for letting me wear this."

"Oh, that's yours to keep. I made it for you."

He bites his bottom lip, looking at it in his hand. I'm almost afraid he didn't like it and only wore it to be polite. "Well, how about you hold onto it for me? I'm afraid I'll lose it. You should see my room. It's a disaster."

I smile at his thoughtfulness and drop the boutonniere in my purse. "Okay, I can do that."

Guiding me out the door, Ryan leads me back to the parking lot and to his truck so that we can drive to my condo. A low whistle sounds through the air, drawing my attention away from Ryan. He stiffens the same time I do, and an unfamiliar man strolls from the shadow of one of the buildings in our direction.

The man meanders past us, and I suppress the strange dread blossoming in my heart. It's the same type of panic I sometimes get from boats on the surface of the water. It's hard to shake, but the man disappears, and Ryan slams the door of his truck shut with me inside.

Ryan taps on the window, drawing my attention from the direction the man disappeared in to him. "I forgot something. I'll be right back."

The doors automatically lock, and I sit back in my seat and peer through the windshield as Ryan jogs toward his apartment, but he doesn't climb the stairs. He glances over his shoulder, raising his finger to me, and turns around the side of the building.

I watch the digital clock on my phone, the minutes ticking by fast enough to send worry through me. He's taking too long. Something's wrong. I can feel it in my essence. It's the same pull that draws me to Ryan, but the urge to find him turns nearly unbearable with my racing heart.

Sucking in a deep breath, I unlock the door and climb out of the truck. The misty sea air drifts around me, making me shiver. But it's more than the chill of the night. Muffled voices sound from the direction Ryan left in, and even though panic squeezes my chest, I force myself to follow my instincts.

The strange man shoves Ryan against the side of the building, gripping the front of Ryan's hoodie in his hands. "It's been long enough."

"I told you I'm not going back," Ryan says, through clenched teeth. "Tell my dad he can have his damn money back, but I'm done with him. I'm trying to start a life here."

"Because of the girl?"

Ryan doesn't answer.

"You're making a mistake. You don't turn your back on family, kid," he snaps.

Again, Ryan doesn't answer.

His silence ignites something dark in the man, and the man's whole face twists into a scowl. He shoves Ryan into the building a few times, not letting go of his hoodie. Like he knows he's being watched, Ryan's gaze flicks to mine, his green eyes screaming a thousand silent words in my direction.

I take an automatic step back, using the corner of the building to hide behind.

"You have tonight, Ryan," the man says. "You got it? To-night."

The man swings his fist out, hitting Ryan in the face, split-ting his lip. Ryan jerks out his own arm, but the man punches him again, knocking his head back, sending Ryan to his knees. The man kicks him in the stomach, and Ryan coughs and spits out blood on the sidewalk.

Something comes over me. I know better than to put my-self in the middle of some demented human twisted enough to harm another person, but my feet dash me forward, my spark lighting the world in quick flashes only I can see through the night.

I swing my bag out and whack the man upside the head so hard he stumbles back and trips over the edge of the sidewalk and falls to the grass. Before I can take another step closer, Ryan rushes me, dragging me away and back to his truck. He pushes me up on the driver's side, and I slide over the seat to let him in.

The man rushes from the shadows in our direction, but Ryan stomps the throttle and reverses, sending a cloud of smoke into the air. The man only has a chance to smack the side of the truck with his hands to watch us leave.

"You're bleeding," I say, yanking up the hem of my gown to press it to Ryan's bloody lip.

He doesn't look at me, speeding to the street and away from his complex. "Luna, I'm sorry. This was a mistake. I should've never—" He snaps his mouth closed without finishing.

My lip quivers. "Never what?"

"I'm sorry," he whispers.

"Ryan. What's going on? Who was that? What kind of trouble are you in?" A thousand thoughts swirl through my mind. That man wasn't part of the human authority. I've seen the community helpers of La Tortuga Point, and they don't wear jeans and flannel. They don't carry blades on their belts.

Releasing a small yell, he smacks his hand on his steering wheel, startling me. A strange wildness takes over his soft eyes, and panic tightens my chest, but not because of Ryan. I can nearly feel the fury of his emotions radiating from him. "I have to leave, Luna. I'm sorry. I'm so sorry."

"What?" I can't believe what I'm hearing. I can't believe how quickly he's changed his mind about staying permanently in La Tortuga Point.

"I'm not safe to be around," he says, lowering his shoulders, keeping his eyes trained on the road ahead of us. He refuses to look at me like doing so pains him.

Tears blur my vision at his words, the air between us suddenly pressing against me like the ocean does the second I transform from a mermaid and into a human in need of air. "Ryan."

"I'm sorry," he repeats, his voice shaking. "I need to leave town. I was stupid for thinking it was even a good idea to talk to you. You're this amazing person, and I—"

"Come with me to San Francisco," I blurt, shifting in my seat, feeling like his words are enough to sink me into the darkest depths of the ocean if he continues. Because I've heard words similar to that on TV when people think they're doing the right thing by letting the one they love go because of something out of their control. And those scenes break my heart every time. He's breaking my heart now.

Ryan doesn't respond right away, thinking over my words. I know he doesn't believe he's made a mistake by talking to me.

"Please, Ryan. Come with me. Whatever you're dealing with, we can figure it out. I—" I wring my hands together. "I don't want to lose you, and I'm not afraid of whoever it is you're dealing with or whatever kind of trouble you're in. I can handle it."

Turning his truck into my complex, he parks in the space outside my door and shuts off the engine. He shifts in his seat to face me, taking my hands in his. "It's all so complicated, Luna. You have this amazing life here with great people, I—you shouldn't have to handle anything. I already hate myself that I put you in this position."

"Just come with me to San Francisco. You'll be safe with me there," I say. "Please. I want to help you. I can help you."

"Are you sure?"

"Yeah. Remember how you said you weren't going to let me get away so easily?"

Something shifts in his eyes, his pout pursing with a small smile. "I still don't want to."

"I'm not letting you get away so easily, either."

He releases a small breath and hugs me, nearly pulling me into his lap. Leaning away, he says, "Before I agree, I have to tell you something. I want to be honest about everything with you."

I grasp his hand, pulling it toward my chest to hold against me. My heartbeat thrums with anticipation against his hand. I doubt his secrets could be any worse than mine. "Okay, go on."

"I don't have an inheritance from my mom. I stole the money from my dad."

CALL OF THE OCEAN

I SIT ON THE edge of the couch, covering my face with my hands, taking a few deep breaths of air. All I want to do is run out the backdoor and to the sea, to swim and clear my head, to take Ryan with me to an island no one could ever find him—but in doing so, it'll change the life on land I just got.

"I don't understand," I whisper.

Ryan rubs his hand along my shoulder blades. "I swear I'm not a bad person. I was just—the situation was bad. I wasn't even planning to stay here more than a day or two, but then I saw you. I can't even explain what went through my head."

Pursuing mates on land wasn't common among merpeople.

The sea presented many mates to each other across the colonies. But mine wasn't in the sea. Neither was Carter's, nor Sun's. It's proving a shift is occurring. Uniting the land and sea will help the colonies flourish and thrive beyond the depths.

But I'm not sure how to deal with this. My mind screams danger while my heart wants me to shut up and be brave. There's a reason I washed ashore and met Ryan on the beach before he could abandon La Tortuga Point. There's a reason the ocean tested us on our first date. But now? I need to know why. Finding my true love was supposed to be many nights of fun and romance, not running in fear for his safety.

"Luna, say something," he says, grasping my hand. "Even if it's to ask me to go. I can't stand your silence and not knowing what you're thinking about me."

Pulling myself together, I straighten my shoulders and meet Ryan's gaze. "I don't want you to go, and I know you're not a bad person. I'm just trying to wrap my head around things—I'm scared for you."

He sighs. "If I leave everything with my aunt and lie low for a while, my dad will get over it. He always does. This isn't the first time I've left my family. I just—we don't want the same things."

"And if he doesn't, I know people who can help you," I say. Finding a different life for Ryan—for me even—isn't im-possible. I might even have a better chance to do so for the both of us once I meet my cousin in San Francisco. "Did you know money can buy almost anything on land? Even a new identity?"

He chuckles, giving me an irresistible smile I want to kiss. "Does this mean your real name isn't Luna Stevens?"

I smirk, crinkling my nose. "Well, my name is Luna, just not Stevens. That's Carter's last name."

"You're not related?"

I shake my head. "No, but we're still family."

"So, what's your real last name?" he asks. Something about the secret of his past he shared with me, how he trusted me enough to share a part of his life he regrets, makes me want to tell him everything. But I don't. Not yet.

Shifting on the couch, I reach over and grab the envelope with the information about my cousin in San Francisco to show him instead of trying to make up a story to explain why I don't know my last name. "That's why we're going to San Francisco. To find out."

His eyes dart over the contents of the envelope, including the picture of my mom and great-grandfather. "This must be so weird for you."

I shrug. "It's probably the most normal part of my life, to be honest. I had no idea I had anymore family apart from my dad, and then..." I smile at the paper. "I'm both excited and scared. I doubt they know who I am, and I'm not even sure they'll want anything to do with me. But, I just can't sit here and not try to fill in the missing pieces, you know."

"I'm happy you want to share it with me, even under these weird circumstances. I am sorry I dragged you into this."

I brush my fingers over his pouty cheek, staring into his

bright eyes. He'll blame himself even if I know it wasn't his fault. I'm here because he's my intended mate. I don't think there is any place I could be. "You didn't drag me into anything. I'm choosing to be here to face whatever it is I have to. I feel so connected to you that it's all I can think about. And after I saw that man hurt you, I—"

Ryan interrupts me with a kiss, gently caressing his lips to mine. He inhales a tiny breath, and I pull away and bring my cool fingers up to touch the cut on his lip. We stare at each other for a long moment, and I wish I could open my mind to him like I could if we were both in the water as merpeople. Because even though he admits to stealing from his dad and told me his dad is angry with him, he's still a mystery to me.

"You're my hero, you know," Ryan says, grinning. "I don't think I've ever seen someone knock down Titus before."

I rest my head on his shoulder, hiding my face and the fear blossoming from the memory. "Like I said. I'll keep you safe."

"And I'll try to stay out of trouble, so you don't have to."

The backdoor slides open, drawing us away from each other as Giselle saunters inside, dripping seawater onto the tiles. She shivers, bouncing up and down, while Sun grabs a towel from the chest to wrap around her shoulders. He stands unfazed by the cold, completely nude. Giselle turns her attention to us and releases a loud laugh. I glance at Ryan, who stares at the ceiling.

"I'm sorry, Ryan," Giselle says, throwing her towel at Sun. "I didn't know you'd still be here."

Sun steps closer into the room with Giselle. "He's in need of a healer, my love."

Giselle's smile morph's into a frown. "Oh, no. What happened?" She flicks her gaze to the blood on my dress from trying to stop Ryan's lip from bleeding on the way over. "Are you two okay?"

Ryan responds yes while I shake my head no.

We look at each other, both frowning. Giselle moves forward to get a better look at me, searching my eyes to try to peek into my mind because I'm too slow to tell her why nothing about this situation is okay.

"Ryan's in trouble," I finally say, tightening my fingers around Ryan's to stop my hands from trembling. Saying the words out loud makes them feel so real.

Ryan sighs and hides his face on my shoulder, not wanting me to say anything more. "Luna."

I whip my head back and forth. "No, Giselle and Sun are my po—family. They should know since you're coming with us to San Francisco. We don't keep secrets between each other, and I don't want you to feel like you have to either. They're not going to judge you."

"Princess Luna, what kind of trouble is your mate in? Do I need to summon the guards?" And by guards, he means the sea-chosen warriors of the deep, much like himself. The guards protect the colonies from any threats, but there hasn't been a need for them. The only danger we face now isn't in the sea.

"The guards?" Ryan asks, his brows puckering in confusion. "Like royal guards?"

"It's not like that, Sun," I say, trying to ignore Ryan's question. I can tell things aren't going to add up with me soon. "Ryan and his dad had a falling out, and he wants him to come home."

"You're nineteen, Ryan. Your dad can't make you do anything," Giselle says, speaking up.

Ryan glances at me. "I stole a lot of money from him."

Giselle doesn't react, her face not saying anything on her mind. Sun stands quietly behind her, crossing his arms over his broad chest. He, on the other hand, looks ready to say something. It takes me subtly shaking my head to get him to remain quiet. Because mermen take anything that could put someone in danger seriously, and even though merpeople don't steal or do anything to jeopardize the colonies, Sun is aware of the repercussions on land. We pass information through our thoughts. Learning and quickly adapting is our greatest advantage as a species.

"But I'm giving it back," Ryan adds, shrinking under Sun's gaze.

Giselle bobs her head. "Okay, but are you in trouble with the law? We can't draw a bunch of attention to ourselves. Luna's..." She doesn't know how to explain my situation without revealing I'm a mermaid, either. But now I'm definitely afraid to reveal my secret. At least, until everything works out.

"I'm not supposed to be here," I say.

"No, my dad wouldn't get the police involved," Ryan says.

"He likes to handle things his own way."

"Like sending scary men to threaten him," I say. "But I handled him."

Giselle pales while Sun stiffens.

"Well, I hit him with my bag." I clarify, realizing how my words could be interpreted. I might be the daughter of a shunned king, but I'm not ruthless like him.

"Oh, Luna," Giselle says.

I link my fingers with Ryan's. "Please, Gi. We just need to leave. We'll figure it all out."

She closes her eyes, sucking in a breath. "I've dealt with worse. I've dealt with worse. I've dealt with worse." She chants the words to herself and opens her eyes. "We'll leave tonight. But Luna, you know what will happen if things get out of hand, and you want to keep Ryan in your life."

"It won't come to that." Because I can't imagine leaving the land I've yearned to live on ever since I was a merbabe. And not only that, I can't fathom ever taking Ryan to Celestiana Cove, the magically protected island merpeople frequent to adjust to land. It'd have to be a last resort. I had only planned on taking my possible future mate there after the transition into the merpeople life. Not like this. Especially not now.

Giselle reaches out and touches my shoulder, a smile now lighting her face. "I know it won't. Things always work out." If it weren't for her positivity, I might get swept out to sea on my doubt. Because it doesn't feel like it will.

"I hope so," Ryan says, his voice low like he's mostly talking to himself.

Giselle places her hands on her hips. "They will, especially with Luna by your side." She shifts to look at me. "I should probably tell Ava and Carter."

"Would you mind if I did?" I ask, getting up from the couch. "I could use a swim."

"You're going to swim?" Ryan asks. "Now?"

I press my lips together. "It helps me clear my head."

He seems more surprised that I swim in the sea at night than at the idea of being some runaway princess. "But—"

Giselle shifts her weight between her feet, hugging her towel around her. "I think you're forgetting, Ryan. We don't call Luna a mermaid for nothing."

Sun smirks at me. "A princess one at that." His teasing voice lightens the mood. Giselle must've told him about how his use of my title doesn't exactly work on land, though he still refuses to say my name without it.

Ryan laughs and groans at the same time, reclining back on the couch. I lean over, brushing my lips to his cheek before heading to the back slider. I can't waste any more time trying to seem ordinary. We're all beyond normal now, which might be a good thing.

I shimmy out of my gown right at the door and dash onto the beach without changing into a bikini. I always thought it was funny that humans are okay with bathing suits but not bras and underwear, like there is much of a difference.

A sudden, unrelenting desire to leave La Tortuga Point to

get Ryan as far away as possible cascades over me, making me kick faster through the sand. It's something inside my very essence begging me to listen to it. It feels like I'll die otherwise, like the same feeling that comes with resisting the call of the moon.

Diving into the cold water, I swim through the waves until I'm deep enough to transform. The chilly current warms with my breath of the ocean, and I spin around, listening to the sound of silence brought with the muting water.

Tipping my head back, I stare at the rippling moon overhead, mirroring the surface so I can see my reflection. My dark blue eyes sparkle silver with pale light, and I can't help thinking what it would be like to see Ryan as I am. He'd be as handsome as any merman.

"Luna?" a voice calls telepathically through the sea. "We thought you'd be out swimming. Would you like to join us? It's been a while since you have."

The current shifts, and I twirl on a wave of Ava's making as she turns me around to face her and Carter. She swims forward with Carter right on her back like they're one entity in the sea. Ava's cerulean tail shimmers through the water, her expansive caudal fin fanning, though Carter holds her in place.

I smile through the water, releasing a small bubble to travel to the surface. "I was about to swim to you, but I can't stay long. We're leaving."

"Now?"

Swimming forward, I press my lips to Ava's, sending all the

events from tonight from my mind to hers in the best way I know how. She then shares them with Carter, and they meet me with eyes crinkling with concern.

"You're doing the right thing," Ava says after a moment. "I only wish we could follow you, but—"

I take her hand. "I know the colonies are more important. It's okay."

She frowns. "Everyone's important to me, especially your chosen mate."

"You think he is?" I don't know why I ask to hear her confirmation. I know it already deep inside me.

She nods. "You wouldn't risk losing the land for him otherwise. Trust yourself, okay? Starla and Mateo will be joining us in Coralista, so if you need somewhere to stay, you can use their apartment. They'd be happy to have you even when they return."

"Giselle was arranging everything but thanks," I say. "I'll keep it in mind. I just want to let things settle."

She brushes my floating hair out of the space between us. "They will. We'll work it all out when we get back. Just enjoy your time up north."

I hope there isn't anything to work out when they get back. I hope Ryan is right about his dad backing off. I don't say it though. "Okay," I say instead.

"And don't forget your phone. I'll call you." Ava and Carter hug me together, swimming me back a few feet in the water. Something about this moment, about this goodbye, seems incredibly important and scary, like it's more final than it should be. I know the call of the sea could never keep me away from my friends, but what if I can't come back here? I've grown used to seeing them every day.

I force myself to smile.

"What else is on your mind, Luna?" Ava asks, seeing my hesitation in my inability to turn to swim away.

"I think I might have lost my ability to see what the ocean has planned for me. I don't feel as connected to the sea. It scares me. I feel like I need to tell him soon about being a mermaid, but I'm terrified of what might happen and where all of this will lead. I like Ryan, but this might be too much for him. What if he freaks out about our secret?"

"Then tell him now and get it out there," Ava says.

I puff a bubble through my lips. "But I just met him."

Carter peers at Ava for a moment as they share a silent thought. "That's the only way you'll know for sure, and you seem pretty set already."

Panic speeds up my spark, and it creates a strobe light from my chest in the water. "But the ocean—"

"Knows you can handle it." Ava pulls me close and hugs me again. "*I* know you can handle it. You're the bravest person I know and one of the few who stood against your dad when you didn't have to."

"But I did have to," I say, recalling a time when merpeople weren't given a real chance to explore the shores. "I feel it as much as I feel the need to get Ryan out of here and to keep him safe."

Carter smiles. "Sounds like he might be more than your potential mate, Luna."

I fiddle with my flowing hair, twining it in my fingers. "Oh, Ocean. Give me a sign."

Ava waves her hand, creating a current strong enough to catch me in it to take me back to shore. She blows me a kiss through the water, and I drift toward the shore until the current releases me.

"This is your sign, Luna," Ava says into my mind. "I'm making it for you."

She and Carter disappear into the deep, leaving me bobbing in the shallows near shore. I break through the surface and spit out water to take a few deep breaths of air. Water drips from my face, hazing my eyes, and I catch sight of a figure standing in the sand, staring at the sea.

"Luna?" Ryan calls to me. He jogs into the water, heading in my direction.

Dipping under, I transform back into my human form, racing to put on my underwear before he realizes I'm half naked, though in the dark ocean, he can't see. Not like I can.

I watch him spin in a circle, trying to catch sight of me from the surface. Kicking my legs, I swim toward him and pop up in front of him, clearing my lungs of seawater. He closes the distance, wrapping his arms around me, his teeth chattering from the cold.

"You found me," I say, peering at the shore toward my

condo a good distance from where I'm swimming.

He releases a breath. "I—it's the strangest thing. It was like I knew you'd be here."

Ava was right. I'm more certain than ever that Ryan is my mate. I never imagined a future with him could ever start this way, but here we are, treading water in the surf under the waxing moon.

I stare into his green eyes, drenched in moonlight, searching for answers. It could be so easy to dip under and transform, to show him what I truly am, but he kisses me. His warm lips against mine pushes the thought away. All I want to do is to return to shore with him. To stand on my two legs.

"That's the call of the sea," I whisper into his lips. "It's what brought you to me."

DEEP BREATHS

THE OCEAN BREEZE PLAYS with my hair, twirling it off my neck and behind me. As much as I wanted to spend the entire day traveling to San Francisco, I've agreed to go along with Giselle's original plan. Spending a night in a beachfront hotel in Santa Barbara is pretty amazing. It helps that the rooms are under the alias her mom uses because of her sister, Ruby King, and the fortune tied to the King's name. Giselle refuses to treat our situation as anything other than a vacation, and spring break explains our sudden departure from La Tortuga Point without looking suspicious. And it was easy. Because I don't exist on land and the man who threatened Ryan wouldn't be able to track me to him. Giselle, either.

We abandoned Ryan's truck in the parking lot of the marina, where the *Sea Princess* remains docked. Ryan not only stole money from his dad, but he took the boat from him, too. He would've been long gone by now had our paths never crossed. I hate the thought of how things could've been so different. I can't think about it now. Things are still different. But I'll make the best of it. I can't live on the land like it's only temporary.

"You shouldn't worry about me," Ryan says. "Even if my dad does find me, it's not the end of the world. We just don't agree on a lot of things."

"Like what?" I ask.

He hugs me. "Life in general. He's about making money and business."

"And you're about the adventure and doing good for the ocean," I say, smirking at the sea.

"Is it so wrong if I care about more than money and business?" he asks. "Every time I'm in the water with you, ignoring everything else, I—it's a good place to be."

"It is, isn't it?" I ask. Because the sea is in my heart. I might be a mermaid who has found a place on land, but the ocean is my home. What if all along my desire to break the surface to transform into a human was all for this moment, standing here, looking into Ryan's sea glass green eyes and the ocean stretching to the horizon to hear him admit his love of being in the sea with me?

"You, me, and wherever the waves take us," he whispers.

My heart crashes against my ribcage, a strange sensation crawling from my toes to my torso, stretching up to my heart. I gasp, bending over. Fear blossoms through me at the sudden realization that my thoughts of the sea, of Ryan, of how our life could be, triggered my very nature to show itself.

I'm transforming.

I can't stop it.

I drop to my knees, the edges of my vision shadowing. Closing my eyes, I suck in breath after breath, struggling to breathe in the salty air around us. Ryan touches my shoulder, saying my name, but I can't respond to him. All I can do is crawl forward into the sand and away from the patio of our beachfront hotel room.

"What's wrong?" Ryan asks, pulling me up from the sand. He holds me in front of him and stares at me. His eyes widen, a strange look crossing his face, but he doesn't let me go, though fear morphs his expression.

"I'm transforming into a mermaid," I say, my voice cracking. There's no point in trying to hide it. I can't stop it mid-transformation. All I can do is go into the water, take a breath of the sea, and hope Ryan doesn't run away forever, leaving me feeling like my heart went with him. "Please, help me to the water."

He opens and closes his mouth, surprise paralyzing him in place. I groan, my back arching again. The ocean swells in front of me, threatening to collide into shore to wash me away. But it doesn't have to. Ryan blinks, gives me a once over, and rushes through the sand and to the surf.

"Oh, shit," he whispers under his breath but close enough to my ear to hear.

"I'm so sorry," I say, groaning. "This wasn't how I wanted to show you."

"Shit," he says again, the ocean crashing around us. I realize my pectoral fins have erupted from my skin and rub against his arm. My skin shimmers under the moonlight, now pearlescent as I struggle to slow down the process to take minutes instead of the seconds it usually does.

I expect Ryan to drop me into the water, to push me away to run back to shore, but he rushes to unbutton my jeans and yank them down. He trudges deeper into the sea, still cradling me in his arms.

"Luna, what do I do?" he asks, panic raising his usually deep voice. "Your skin. It's—"

"You have to let me go," I say, keeping my eyes trained away from his. I'm afraid if our gazes meet, then it'll be over.

"But—"

I press my hands into his chest, feeling the beat of his rapid heart against my palms. "Please, I need the sea. I need to go."

He touches my chin, begging me to look at him, so I do. His wide eyes search my face for a moment, and then he leans in and kisses me. I gasp against his mouth, the muscle spasms turning painful the longer I resist the sea. But I'm as afraid to dive under as I'm afraid to let him see me in my true form.

"Don't leave me," he whispers into my lips. "Please, don't

leave. There has to be something I can do."

I link my hands with his, holding him tighter. "Do you trust me?"

He nods, loosening his grip on my legs to submerge them in the water. He keeps our fingers linked, holding me against him, staring at me in the soft moonlight. He looks prepared to follow me into the sea.

So I decide to let him.

"Take a deep breath."

Holding Ryan's hand, I dive us under, completing my transformation. The night ocean glows around us with glittering sand and thousands of tiny bubbles that cling to Ryan's face. He releases a bubble through his lips, his eyes squeezed tight, his fingers gripping mine hard enough to numb my hand.

I don't stop swimming until we're far enough from shore where my caudal fin doesn't fan across the sandy bottom of the shallows. Propelling us to the surface, I expel my lungs of water, and Ryan gasps, swiping his hand across his eyes to clear his face of seawater. His chest heaves as he catches his breath, and I tread in place for the both of us, keeping his head above water as his eyes dart across my skin, now only lit in the moonlight shining from overhead.

Without saying a word, he reaches up and grazes his fingers below the gills on my neck trailing down to my pectoral fins and the tiny webs of skin between my fingers.

"Please, say something," I whisper, staring into his eyes that hold a thousand thoughts locked from me.

He rubs his lips together. "Luna, I—"

"I'm sorry I showed you like this. It was an accident," I say.

"I can't believe—"

"That I'm a mermaid?" I finish for him.

He releases a breathless laugh, hooking his hands to my shoulders. "It's amazing. You're incredible. Can I see all of you?"

"You're not scared?" I don't know what I was expecting, maybe more fear than anything, but his bright eyes, his curiosity, make my spark light up through the water, glowing the sea around us.

He startles and peers down. "Whoa. You're glowing."

Surprise washes over me. "You can see my essence?"

"I wish I could see more. I can't explain it. I just—whoa." He smiles at me, his whole face lit from my spark, his sea glass green eyes refusing to let me out of his sight, like the moment he blinks, I'll disappear.

I lean back, floating horizontally with the surface, and he trails his eyes over my tail, glittering gold even in the white moonlight. He reaches up and hovers his fingers over it without touching it, and I reach out and press my hand on top of his to tell him it's okay to feel my tail.

"I have so many questions," he says, grazing his fingers over my scales, sending warmth blossoming over my skin.

"Ask me anything," I say.

"Are your friends?"

I smile. "Some of them."

"What are you doing on land? How many of you are there? Your dad?"

I cut him off with a kiss and show him the answers to his questions instead of saying them. My mind opens for him, revealing all the important moments of my life from my home in Pearlestria, to my mom and dad, and even to my conversation with Ava and Carter before we left.

Ryan slowly tugs away when my mind flashes to him in this moment treading water in front of me. "You think I'm your chosen mate?"

Out of all the questions in need of clarification, that one wasn't one of them I thought he would mention. The way he says it, the question hanging in the air like he can't wrap his mind around it or believe it, sends doubt cascading through me. It wasn't the reaction I was hoping for because he's not certain. But how could he be? He's human.

Instead of answering him, I dip under the water, sucking the sea into my lungs. Ryan links his hands under my arms and pulls me back to the surface. I hide behind a veil of my black hair, blurring the world around me. I wish he'd let me pull myself together.

"You don't think you are," I manage to say, trying to suppress my disappointment.

He doesn't respond right away, searching my face like I can somehow prove to him what I feel in my mermaid essence. But I can't. There's nothing I can say or show him that would make him understand or believe me.

Combing strands of hair from my face, he says, "Luna, I like you. I mean, I really like you and everything about this situation is crazy insane in the best possible way, but I don't think the ocean would be so cruel to make me your mate."

I duck underwater again to hide my tears, letting sea water drip down my face when I surface. "What's cruel is you doubt part of my essence." My voice shakes, my heart bringing me pain worse than him telling me he had to leave, because even then, I had the chance to convince him to stay with me, to see where this leads.

Now? It takes everything in me not to dive under and swim away.

He frowns, his own face reflecting my heartbreak back to me. How he could even feel that the ocean was cruel to put us together, feel even a tiny ounce undeserving of my affection, is agony. More so than not loving me at all. "Luna."

I shake my head. "It's fine. You're right. The ocean is playing a cruel joke, and I guess I got my answer."

Tilting his head back, he glances at the sky, his eyes shining under the moon. I wish I didn't swim him so far from shore so he could swim himself back to the beach, and I could disappear into the deep, maybe even return to Pearlestria for a while.

"I should get you back to shore," I finally say. "Now take a deep breath."

Without giving him a chance to argue, I wrap my arms around him and flick my tail, propelling to the shallow ocean shore to follow it to land. I release him in the shallow surf and make sure he reaches air, but I don't surface. I can't. I remain underwater until he swims toward the sand and disappears onto the beach.

I lose myself to the sea.

❧ 10 ❧

UNCHARTED WATERS

STORM CLOUDS HANG ON the horizon, blocking the light of morning from brightening another day. I want so badly to return to shore, but I'm afraid to face the land. I don't understand how Ryan could hurt me like he did. He claims the ocean was cruel, but the ocean is only ever truly brutal to those undeserving of its magic, and even then, it still shows mercy for many. It'd never be cruel to me—not when it comes to the matters of my mermaid essence.

Lightning flashes in the distance and the sky opens to rain a torrential downpour over me, slickening my black hair to my cheeks. Waves rise against the rocks I perch on and splash over my tail, trying to force me to move. But I can withstand any storm the sky has to offer. I'm not scared of rising waves and rough waters. What I'm terrified of is that Ryan might never realize how perfect he is for me.

"Luna?" a masculine voice calls through the air, igniting a different kind of storm within me. My heart battles my mind at the sound of Ryan yelling my name in a place far enough from shore he's putting himself in danger to reach me.

I shift on the rock, slapping my tail against the churning tide. "You shouldn't be here. You could get hurt."

Ryan paddles to me on a surfboard, bobbing over the swelling current. "I'm not afraid of the ocean. I couldn't stay on land another minute, either. I've been waiting for you all night, and I was starting to think you might never return to shore, and I..."

"I'll always return to shore," I whisper, my voice getting lost on the roar of the sea and the whistling of the wind, rocking Ryan hard enough that he grips the surfboard.

"I handled things badly last night. I'm sorry." His eyes crinkle with the same sadness flowing through me.

"But it doesn't change things. I realize how much of a fantasy world I've been living in, and it was unfair of me to put you in this position so soon after we've met." I know my way of life in the ocean doesn't reflect the land. They're two different places. We're two different species. Though our differences shouldn't push us away. We complement each other. "You were right. You aren't intended to be anything to me, because you get that choice. I can see it's not what you want right now."

I jump from my rock to close the space between us. I tug his surfboard with me as I swim back to the rocks, afraid for him in these conditions. As much as I need space to think, I need to fill the space with him so I feel like I can breathe in the salty air around us.

He hooks his fingers to the rock to pull himself out of the water. I help him with his board, positioning it so the waves can't drag it around while it's tethered to him. Sitting close to me, he presses his leg into my tail and slides his arm around my back, his cool skin absorbing my warmth.

Silence falls between us, neither of us knowing what to say. I've never been good with my voice or my thoughts on land. I can't speak from my heart—my essence—the way I do in the sea. Humans don't get it. They can't feel what we feel, at least, not in the same way. Because I know Ryan feels something. He wouldn't be here if he didn't. But instead of accepting what his being wants, he denies that such magic is possible.

His gaze trails over my tail, glittering like gold dusts over it, and he gingerly reaches out his fingers. "Can I?"

I nod without a word.

Ever so gently, Ryan caresses my tail, running his hand down toward my caudal fin. Intrigue lights his eyes as he takes in the smooth yet strong texture of my scales. This is the first time someone apart from my close friends has looked at me as I am—touched me in my true form—and I remain utterly still, nervous to move. Because if I do, Ryan might pull away. He might recoil. I worry he's in denial because I'm not the human he thought I was.

"This is so strange," he whispers.

"I know it's not as nice as my legs," I say, wishing he'd let me sink back under to change.

Pulling his hand away, he reaches up and touches my shoulder to get me to look at him. "Are you kidding me? This is amazing. Unbelievable. I mean—I like your legs, they're hot, but your tail? It's beautiful—you're beautiful."

I can't stop the smile crossing my face despite the heavy ache dulling the spark in my chest. Because Ryan continues to treat me as he did even before his confession about not believing in the fate the ocean set before us.

He might not believe it, but I still do. If only the thought didn't drag me deeper into the water to protect myself.

"And you're confusing me, Ryan," I say. "What changed? You were fine coming on this trip with me, but all of a sudden you can't even think about the idea of us being together, yet you put yourself in danger to swim out to me and then you tell me I'm beautiful. I don't understand. What is it you want from me? I need to understand how you want things between us."

He groans in his hands, rubbing them across his face. "I'm sorry, Luna. The last thing I wanted to do was hurt you—and I know I have. I'm having a hard time processing everything and what you are and what it all means. I'm scared."

I swallow the burning in my throat. If only I could jump in the water and take a breath. "Of me?"

He shakes his head, reaching out to hold my hands in his.

"No, of me and my life. You're a mermaid." He exhales. "A *mermaid*. You're something I never imagined possible. You're straight from the stories my mom used to tell me during the weeks we spent at sea. It's incredible. But at the same time, I feel like I'm not good enough for you."

"The ocean thinks you are," I say, shifting.

Ryan adjusts my tail, allowing me to lay it across his lap, where he holds our hands. "Does it talk to you or something?"

I shrug, slapping my fin on the wave, splashing us with cold water. "Not in the way you're thinking. But if it didn't think you were worthy of my mermaid secret, you wouldn't be here."

His eyes widen as he interprets my words to match whatever fear he suddenly creates in his mind.

"The same goes for if you do not deserve me. The ocean wouldn't have let you rescue me if it thought otherwise."

He's silent for a moment, brushing his thumb against my scales. "To think I thought I was your hero."

I rest my head on his shoulder, letting him move to hug me against him, nearly cradling me on his lap. Rainwater pools on my tail to slide into the ocean. "I don't think anyone in the world can say they saved a mermaid from drowning."

He offers me a small smile as he sinks into his own thoughts. I don't try to say anything more to fill the silence. He needs time to process and to realize I speak the truth. The ocean isn't always so clear to me, but in this moment with Ryan, it is. I won't accept it otherwise. It's a sign that he's here. That he stayed and didn't run to land.

"So, did I lose my chance with you?" Ryan asks quietly, drawing his attention away from his thoughts. "Because I'd like to see where this leads."

"Ask the ocean," I say.

Ryan laughs and gets to his feet, cupping his mouth with his hands. "Hey, Ocean! Do I still get a shot at making this amazingly beautiful, talented, caring, breathtaking mermaid fall in love with me? I promise I won't mess it up again."

Warmth blushes my cheeks as he shouts at the sea.

Turning to me, he smiles and unleashes his surfboard from his leg before jumping into the water. He disappears under the rocky surface, his board now set adrift. I slide off the rock and into the waves, dipping under to see Ryan hovering with his eyes open, the sand clouding the sea between us.

I swim closer and stop a few inches from him. Bringing my hand to his face, I cup his cheek, staring into his squinting eyes. He holds his hand over mine, pressing my fingers deeper into his skin. Bubbles cling to his nose, and he releases a small breath, just watching me in the water without kicking to the surface like he wants to take in the sight of me where my heart feels fullest, where I'm most comfortable despite how much I enjoy breathing air.

Closing the space to kiss him, I slide my hands around his back, pressing my body to his. His legs brush my tail, and I flick my fin and jet us to the surface. He takes a breath while I release one of water, and then I kiss him once more, leaving him breathless all over again. His hands twist in my wet hair, and he kisses me deeper, sucking my salty bottom lip into his mouth, exploring my shimmering skin with his fingers.

"The ocean told me you should return to land with me," he whispers into my mouth, pressing his forehead to mine.

I smile, pulling back enough to see his eyes clearly. "Is that so?"

"I made it a promise to keep you safe on shore."

"And I'll keep you safe in the sea."

Steam from the shower fogs the bathroom, and Ryan shifts on his feet in the doorway, looking from the hotel room behind him and back to me. Sand peppers his bare chest, expanding with another long breath, and his Adam's apple bobs in his throat, his eyes trailing down my body before returning to my face.

"What is it? Is something wrong with my body?" I turn to look at myself in the mirror. "I sometimes scrape myself swimming to shore."

He blinks a few times, swallowing again. "No, it's just— I—you're perfect. I'm sorry. I'll wait in the room."

I giggle. "Just come in. You're dripping sandy water everywhere."

Stepping into the bathroom completely, he shuts the door behind him but doesn't close the space between us. I don't think I'll ever get used to how shy some humans are about nudity, but Ryan's extra cute, trying not to be too obvious as he drinks me in.

"It's okay to look at me," I say. "I like that you do."

His embarrassed smirk shifts serious, and he gazes at me with an intensity that blooms tingles from my heart to the rest of me. I step closer under the weight of his stare, drawn to him like his eyes alone are capable of pulling me in, and he gently brushes my sandy, tangled hair from my shoulder to push it to my back.

"You're unlike anyone I've ever met," he says.

I slide my arms around his neck, smiling. "Well, I am a mermaid."

He chuckles. "I don't think it's completely that. Every second feels like uncharted water to me. I don't know what to expect with you. It's—"

"Scary?"

"Nothing about this is scary," he whispers. "It's exciting. I just—can I kiss you?"

I answer him by brushing my lips to his, feeling the coolness of his bare stomach against the heat of mine. Steam clings to our skin, and Ryan nudges me toward the shower. His hands slide down my back, exploring my skin, memorizing me in my human form the way he did with me as a mermaid.

"I like your body," I whisper, running my hands down his chest and to his stomach.

He releases a breathless laugh against my lips, kissing me deeper, brushing his tongue over mine, making my knees shake. Something hot runs through me, igniting the spark in my chest in a way I've never felt before. I gasp, my mind racing, my heart pounding.

Ryan moans into my lips before grazing them to my jaw and then to my neck. Whatever I'm feeling in this moment far exceeds everything I know about finding a mate and coupling. It exceeds the love I've yearned for all my life in finding the perfect person to complete me. In this moment with Ryan, as his body touches mine, his breath mingling with mine, I've never felt so utterly and completely human—something I never thought possible.

He hugs me tighter, pressing his face into the crook of my shoulder. "We should stop before—"

A bang on the bathroom door cuts Ryan off, and the cold air from the hotel room shifts the shower curtain, sending goosebumps over my skin. I peek my head out as Giselle strolls into the bathroom, a strange, almost wild look morphing her usually cheerful expression.

"We have a problem," Giselle says, combing her fingers through her hair. She shifts on her feet, her gaze looking past me at Ryan. "Oh, crap. I'm sorry. I thought you were alone."

"We were just showering," I say, grabbing the towels. "It can wait."

She turns away while we get out. Sun stands in the middle of the hotel room, dressed only in a pair of board shorts. The adjoining door to our room remains open, and I notice a ton of shopping bags on their bed.

Giselle places her hands on her hips. "Someone broke into

the condo."

My eyes widen, a dozen thoughts rushing through my mind. "Oh, no."

She drags her hands down her face, groaning. "They trashed the place. Took everything valuable along with some of our pictures. My mom only noticed because they shattered the frames."

"Why would someone do this?" I ask, turning from Giselle to Ryan. That seems so weird to take something so personal from us.

Ryan's chest still heaves, though his shoulders straighten. The color drains from his face, and he tightens his fingers around mine. Neither of them answers me right away. I can study humans all day long, and I still have trouble grasping why some people do what they do. The land is more complex than the sea.

My heart slides into my stomach, searching my best friend's face. Anger and sadness pinch her expression, stirring grief through me, washing away the intense feeling arisen in me by Ryan. "I'm sorry, Gi. I know how much everything means to you."

She presses her lips together. "It's okay. It's all okay. It was just stuff. We have insurance. We have copies of the pictures. We're all safe." She directs the words to herself like saying them out loud will make her feel better.

I stroll forward and hug her. "You're right. That's what matters."

Releasing a frustrated scream into my shoulder, she fists her hands at her sides. "This is so creepy, Luna. Why would someone want our pictures? My mom wants us to stay away while the police investigate. She wants to hire a bodyguard, but she knows she can't because..." She waves her hands at my legs.

"I will protect you and Princess Luna, my love," Sun says.

She groans without turning to her mate. "I just—I don't want to have the need to be protected. I feel sick."

Sun wraps his arms around Giselle from behind, sandwiching her between us. She releases a small sob into my ear, and then stiffens, composing herself. I refrain from reacting to the idea that someone was in our home, that I'm as scared as she is. If Giselle's struggling to find something positive to hold onto, I know it's bad, and I need to be that something positive for her. She takes care of me on land and has helped me adjust. I will do anything for her. I'll be strong to help us through this.

"You faced scarier things," I say. "You're strong, and we have the whole ocean behind us. If some strange human thinks they can dare take your smile away, they'll realize how mistaken they were to try."

Sucking in her bottom lip, she nods and swipes her hand across her wet cheeks. "I like fierce Luna. She's badass."

I smile. "You've haven't seen me clobber someone with a purse. There's no way I'm going to let some thieves ruin your spring break fun."

"You're right. My mom's handling it, and we're all together," she says.

Sun tugs her away from me. "Come on, my love. I know something that'll return the enchanting smile to your beautiful face."

She pouts her bottom lip before smirking and nodding. Sun guides Giselle to the glass slider that leads to the sand, and they disappear on the beach. I'm sure Sun would swim her to Hawaii to chase rainbows if she'd allow it.

Turning to Ryan, I meet his frown. His jaw tightens as he looks down at the towel wrapped around his hips. He shifts on his feet, turning his gaze to me, drawn to the heaviness of the silence between us. The look he gives me, all pouty and sad, tugs at my heart. He's more upset than I am, but I don't think it's for the same reason.

"I'm sorry, Luna." He holds open his arms for me, and I fall into them, letting him wrap me in an embrace I didn't know I needed.

"They were just things," I say. "I didn't even know what to do with half of them."

He tugs back to peer into my midnight blue eyes. "This happened because of me."

"You don't know that," I say, searching his face. His green eyes crinkle in the corners, guilt stealing the light from his eyes that had set my spark ablaze.

His muscles flex as he hugs me. "I do. This was my dad's doing."

"Why would your dad break into our condo? We have some valuables, but it's not like we were swimming in riches."

"The gala," Ryan says. "There was a lot of media coverage, and I guarantee my dad saw an opportunity, especially if he knows who you associate with. I was probably being followed this whole time."

I grimace, studying his face, trying to understand and make sense of everything he's not quick to explain. His dad is a fisherman. Ryan's the one who stole from him. "Why take our pictures?"

Jerking away from me, he spins to face the wall, clenching his fingers into fists. I take an automatic step back, his anger palpable in the room, though I know it's not directed at me. Something dark clings to him, hiding away all the light emotions I like about Ryan, and I straighten my shoulders, wishing I could summon the royal guards of Pearlestria to shore to show this man he can't mess with Ryan like that.

"He wants to mess with us. Retaliate for what I did." Ryan hangs his head. "I'm sorry for bringing you into this."

"This feels like it's more than that. Seems like a lot of trouble to get back at you, especially since you returned what you had taken," I say. "He's a fisherman. Why would he risk getting in trouble with humans?"

"My dad's not a fisherman, Luna. He's a criminal—a thief. He doesn't care about the law," Ryan says. "I'm sorry I didn't tell you. It's not exactly something I wanted to announce when I was trying to impress you."

I open and close my mouth. "I would never judge you based on your dad's actions. He is not you." I know what it feels like for being the daughter of a shunned king. Some merpeople still look at me with distrust because I visit Dad. It's one of the reasons that pushed me into moving to the land from the sea.

Sauntering up behind him, I slide my hands around his waist, gently digging my fingers into the skin above his navel. I rest my cheek between his shoulder blades, listening to his heart thrumming.

"I know that now," he says. He relaxes under my touch, releasing a breath. "I wish I had never stolen from him."

"You did it to get away." Ryan admitted he came from a bad situation, but I never imagined it was something like this. I can't blame him for stealing to get away from a life where that's what his dad wanted him to do. Ryan's better than such an existence.

"He won't see it like that, and now I brought you into it—your friends. It's the last thing I wanted to happen. I was hoping he'd back off because I returned his money."

"I'm sure he will," I say. "He'll realize he can't mess with us or scare us."

He slowly bobs his head, thinking about my words. "I want you to tell Giselle's mom. Get the police involved."

I press my lips together. "I don't know if that's a good idea. I'm a mermaid, Ryan. I don't have an identity apart from what the sea gave me. If humans get involved, they'll—I can't risk my secret."

"I'm going to figure out how to fix this. It was one thing to mess with me..." His voice trails off, and he spins to face me, drawing his green eyes to me. "I should've never brought you into this. I knew better. But—"

I bring my fingers up to his mouth, cutting him off before he unintentionally says something to hurt my feelings. "I know you can't see things like I do, but there was never a choice for us. The ocean brought me to you for a reason."

"Luna, I—"

"It's okay if you don't believe or can't understand, but you can't blame yourself for the call of the ocean. You said it yourself. It's in your blood." I slowly drop my hand, preparing myself for an argument I can't win against his human rationale.

He hides his lips in a line, his jaw tensing. "I kind of wish it wasn't. Not in the way that it is."

"It'll change. I'll show you."

He leans into me, wrapping his arms around me. "Will you go somewhere with me? I need to make a phone call."

"You can't do it from here?" I ask.

"I'd rather not. I'm going to call my dad and see if I can get him to back off. I'll threaten him if I have to."

A blip of fear erupts in my heart, but all I do is nod my head and allow Ryan to pull me back toward the bathroom to get ready. I don't know how to handle this situation either. Not without putting my secret at risk. I'm supposed to be a nameless face. A human that has no reason or need to be involved in human matters like this. "You don't think I should stay here?"

He brings my hand to his chest, so I feel his heart beating

under my palm. "Please, come with me. I don't want to leave you alone, especially after this. My dad knows what you look like, and I don't even know all that he's capable of."

I exhale a long breath. "Okay, I'll come. We can send your dad a message together."

I hope he listens. Because I'm afraid of what'll happen if he doesn't. I have the ocean behind me, and it doesn't take kindly to those who seek to harm. With the fury of the ocean, even the shallows turn into dangerous waters.

11

FAMILIAL BONDS

RYAN SQUEEZES MY HAND, leaning his back against the wooden railing of the busy pier. The sun sets on the horizon, casting golden light across the rippling sea, turning the water from bluish-green to gray. I search around the pier, shifting my gaze from the sea to the land, because I'm nervous that at any second the man from Ryan's apartment will appear out of no-where. If he did confront us, I'm sure the sea would rise to wash him and this whole pier away.

Cool wind whips through my hair, and I lean closer to Ryan to listen to his dad through the line. I expect him to sound like a terrifying monster with a deep and threatening voice, something memorable, unearthly, but he sounds eerily similar to Ryan.

"You tell the girl about me, son?" the man asks. "I found it funny that you two disappeared overnight."

Ryan presses the phone to his ear, his shoulders tense. "It's spring break. She's on vacation with her roommate."

His dad hums under his voice. "You're with her, aren't you? You can't lie to me. I'm not stupid."

"Leave her out of this." Ryan's sharp voice echoes over the wind as he glowers at the ocean. I bring my hand to his back, rubbing my fingers along his shoulder blades and across his tight muscles.

His dad bellows a laugh through the line, startling me. I don't understand why Ryan being with me is funny. "I have to say, Ry. I'm impressed. Though I'd have gone after the Kings' daughter. That's where you'd get your money from."

Ryan stiffens even under the weight of my hand, his fingers paling the tighter he holds the phone. "I said leave her out of this. It's between me and you, and I want out. I left everything with Sherry. I left my truck and the boat. You can have it all. But stop looking for me. I'm done with you."

"I'm going to need more than that, son. You cost me a job, walking out on me like you did," his dad says. "Compensating for your absence hasn't been easy either. You're my best crew member."

Shifting toward me, Ryan meets my gaze with knitted brows, his eyes gray in the light of the setting sun. "You stole from my girlfriend. Isn't that enough? She won't get the police involved if you call it even."

His dad laughs. The more I listen to him, the less he sounds like Ryan. His dad's deep voice holds something dark in it that I can't put my finger on. But still, I'm not afraid of a voice through the line. "Are you threatening me, Ry?"

"You can keep whatever," I say, speaking up. I can't stand the way he talks to Ryan. "I don't care." Because my land things don't mean anything to me. Stopping whatever Ryan's dad attempts to do, trying to scare him and manipulate him into a life he doesn't want, means far more.

Ryan shakes his head at me, holding his index finger over his lips. The look he gives me, wide-eyed and worried, makes me regret opening my mouth. But it's so hard to stand here and listen without standing up for Ryan.

His dad hums in the phone again. "So, she is with you. Let me talk to her. I'd like to get to know the one you feel is worth destroying your good life and relationship with your dear old dad."

Nerves tighten my stomach, and I clear my throat to respond, but Ryan turns away from me, so I can't grab the phone from his hand. He glances at me from over his shoulder, shaking his head at me again.

"Not happening," Ryan says, nearly yelling.

"You better listen up, Ryan. That girl of yours had a surprising collection of pearls and gemstones just sitting around in her apartment. I also saw something interesting on that tux of yours that wasn't in the apartment. I want it."

Ryan takes a few more steps from me, pacing in a small circle. I lock my fingers to the back of his shirt, stopping him from answering his dad by denying him what he wants. Ryan's silent thoughts shine as clear as the fiery sky in front of us, and I can tell he wants to hang up.

I spin him to face me, begging him to listen to me with my eyes. "Say yes," I mouth.

He whips his head back and forth, his eyes narrowing at the thought. I know he doesn't want to give in to his dad, but I'll do anything to try to pull Ryan from the situation. I can feel in my heart how much torment he carries even talking to his dad on the phone, but Ryan hasn't shared anything more with me about his life, and all I can imagine is the worst.

"Say yes," I repeat, whispering the words. "It's a pearl. There is an abundance of them in the sea."

Ryan studies my eyes for what feels like forever. But I'm not trapped in his gaze. I think he's more lost in mine than anything, trying to figure out the best way to do right by me. Because he already thinks he's undeserving of my attention, and having his dad do something like this makes him feel worse, except I have experience with unreasonable dads.

"Just the boutonniere? Then you'll leave me alone?" Ryan finally asks.

His dad sighs, and the mumbling voice of someone else sounds through the line, but I can't hear them clearly like something covers the microphone on the other end of the line.

"Breaking my heart, kid. Turning your back on family for a girl."

Anger rushes through me. "He's not—"

Ryan reaches out and presses his fingers to my lips, cutting off my words. "Answer my question, Dad."

His dad grumbles a few swear words under his breath and then says, "Whatever you want, son, because I know you'll come back to me. She'll see you for what you are."

"I'll overnight the pearl to you, all right?" Ryan says, ignoring his dad's comment.

"What? You don't want to see me?"

"Bye, Dad."

Hanging up the phone, Ryan releases a breath and turns to hug me. We hold each other until the sun fades into the horizon, leaving us in the artificial lights glowing along the railing of the pier. The hum of the waves draws my attention to the night-darkened sea, and I step back from Ryan only to pull him with me to head to the sand.

"You know what always makes me feel better?" I ask, touching my bare foot into the chilly water.

Ryan's hard features soften at the sound of my voice through the air. He hugs me again, burying his face in my hair, breathing into the crook of my neck. "It's freezing."

"When has that ever stopped you? We can go back to the hotel and grab a wetsuit. I promise to keep you warm," I say, smirking even though he can't see my face.

He pulls away and laces his hands behind his head, staring

at the stretch of dark water lit by the light reflecting from the pier. "I don't know. I can't stop thinking about my dad. He says he'll leave us alone, but I know him better than that."

"It's a pearl. I'm willing to try for you." I close the space between us again. "He's just one man."

"Who's made my life miserable," he says. "He's doing this on purpose, trying to make me look like an awful person to you."

I pout at his self-doubt again. I don't know what I can do to make him see that his dad doesn't define him or could ever change my idea of who Ryan is to me. "You could never be."

"How do you know?" he asks.

I shift to stand in front of him, pressing my hands into his shirt over his heart. "Because I can feel it."

He sighs.

"I mean it," I whisper, sliding my hands around his waist, standing on my tiptoes to rest my chin on his shoulder. "Now, let's go back to the room and grab your wetsuit. Because I think you could use some time with the ocean. Let me take your mind off things."

"You, me, and the sea," he murmurs. "How could I resist?"

I grin and graze my lips across his jaw. "You can't."

He hugs me tighter. "I think you're right."

My stomach hits the soft beach, and I flip over on my back, tilting my head into the sand to peer at the glittering sky. Ryan turns onto his side, sliding his arm under my head. He pulls me up to meet him for a kiss, and saltwater drips from his forehead to mine.

"I can't wait to do that in the day when I can see something," he says into my shoulder, resting his weight on me enough to press me into the sand.

I smirk. "I see fine. The night ocean is amazing. You get a lot of curious creatures that emerge from the abyss."

His eyes widen. "Have you explored the deepest parts?"

I nod, biting my lip between my teeth, smiling. "I've swum everywhere. I've had a lot of time on my hands before I was given my sea stone ring to come to land."

The moon reflects in his eyes as he stares at me. "I wish I could see things for myself."

I almost tell him that he can, but I hold myself back. I don't want to push him away when his human rationale still controls him. He feels our connection, feels the pull between us, but until he can explain it to himself, I'm not going to mention the transformation ceremony anytime soon. Giselle even gets nervous at the thought of it, and she's been immersed in the merpeople world for months. Twice as long as I've been living on land.

"I'll show you as much as I can," I say instead, running my finger through the sand next to me. There are a lot of places I can take him without even having to wear scuba gear, which would be too dangerous to drag him around in at the speed I swim. It's safer for him to hold his breath.

"Like your home?"

"Pearlestria?" I ask. I hadn't even thought about doing something like that. I couldn't take him all the way, but there's a lot to see even halfway from the surface.

"Yeah. I saw it in that mind thing you did."

I bob my head. "I'll have to do some planning, but it might be possible."

"I'd like that."

Ryan shifts and pulls me from the sand, hooking his fingers to my side, so I fall into step next to him. Cool air wraps around us from the AC unit humming under the window, and he jogs to the bathroom to grab a towel to bring to me.

"Why don't you shower first?" I ask, wringing out my sopping hair on the patio before stepping inside. "I need to talk to Giselle."

He wraps the towel around my shoulders, using it to pull me closer so that our bodies touch. "It can't wait 'til after?" His lips hover a few inches from mine as he stares down at me.

I purse my lips. "That's one way you'll get used to my body. Maybe you'll stop blushing all the time, though you're cute when you do. You don't need to be shy."

He smiles, his cheeks flushing with color. "I don't even know how to respond to you, Luna. But I'm pretty sure I'm not shy."

I tip my chin up to close the space between our lips even more, feeling the heat of his breath against my skin. "Then what is it?"

He chuckles, his cheeks reddening without me even doing

anything. "I feel like I'm going to corrupt you by saying it."

My heart races, and I inhale a small breath. "I might lack experience, but I understand the different kinds of bonds between people. You're as attracted to me as much as I'm attracted to you."

He licks his lips, searching my face. "It's more than attraction. You turn me—it's human desire."

I open my mouth, excitement washing over me, because I'm sure that's what I was feeling kissing him earlier today. It was a feeling different from love. Rawer. Almost overwhelming. When two merpeople couple, all of those emotions wrap together as one, but as I'm standing here on two legs, I know it's different with humans. It's separate. I also know it can be together. "I thought I felt something different this morning. It was the first time I felt that way. I liked it."

He chuckles. "I..."

Nervous laughter bubbles in my throat, and I cover my face with my hands. "I'm being weird, aren't I? I'm sorry. Giselle says I sometimes over-share. I—"

He cuts off my words with a kiss, pulling me against him. "I like your honesty, and I definitely like the way you make me feel."

"But you're nervous about your feelings, too," I say. "Which is fine. I understand how confusing things can be."

He releases a breathless laugh. "More cautious than nervous. I don't want to mess this up or get ahead of myself. I don't know anything about dating a mermaid."

It's my turn to laugh. Because I'm constantly telling myself to not get ahead of myself. With Ryan, I'm standing at the edge of the cliff overlooking the sea, ready to jump, but then every time I bend my knees to dive in, the ocean yanks back the tide, leaving only rocks to break my fall. "I'm pretty sure I'm already in front of you."

"I think I'm catching up. It's just—everything with my dad." He groans, leaning his head on my shoulder. So much for the cold water stealing his worried thoughts away.

I hug him, the intensity of his desire lightening as his mind wanders from me and to the rest of his life. I cup his face, begging for him to stay with me in this moment that feels incredibly important. He's holding out his heart to me, letting me glimpse inside his head in a similar way that I've done for him through my kiss. But it's a one-way signal. I can't see what's on his mind but can only hear it from him. And I don't like that it's shifting.

"We'll take care of it and give him what he wants, and then you'll be free to enjoy this adventure with me," I say. "If you still want to."

"Oh, I want to." He kisses my neck. "You have no idea."

"I do. I'll show you."

I meet him for another kiss, opening my mind to him in a way I never imagined possible without him being a merman. Ryan's fingers dig deeper into the skin on my sides, his lips devouring my kiss as I show him a glimpse of a moment between us from this morning. He breathes my name into my lips, kissing me like he's never kissed me before, throwing his caution away as our waves of desire crash into each other.

He pulls back first, gasping, his chest rising and falling against mine. "Whoa, I—that was—damn."

I grin, cupping his face, brushing the now dry sand from his cheeks. "Want me to show you more?"

He bites his lip. "How does it work? I want to try."

I shrug. I don't know how to explain feeling his connection and using it to link myself to him. "I open myself up and let you in. It's hard to explain. All merpeople can do it."

Ryan closes the distance, brushing his lips to mine. "Did it work?"

I puff out my lips and shake my head. "No."

Sucking in a deep breath, he kisses me harder, more fervently, hungrily. He scoops me into his arms, and I wrap my legs around his waist, letting him carry me toward the bed where he sits on the edge, sliding his hands up my back.

I open my mind to him, letting him see himself through my eyes, holding me to him. Ryan kisses me deeper, brushing his tongue over mine, kissing me in such a way that lust blossoms in my spark to travel through the rest of me.

And then something happens.

I no longer see Ryan in my mind.

I see me through his eyes. But not me in this moment. He's thinking of me as a mermaid, and about him as a merman. It's not a moment that's happened, but one he wishes will. He's thinking about our future together.

And it feels so certain, like fate. I know Ryan feels what I feel. He's not thinking like a human. He's thinking like my intended mate. Like my destiny.

I pull away, gasping, touching my mouth. "Ryan."

He cups my face. "Did it work?"

I blink the surprise from my eyes and nod. "You and me in the water."

"Is that even possible?" he asks, bringing my hands up to his heart.

All I can do is nod.

He smiles. "I hope that's where this adventure leads."

12

BRAZEN MERPEOPLE

"SO, LET ME GET this straight," Giselle says from behind the wheel of the rental car we picked up this morning, leaving her Mustang at the hotel for her cousin to retrieve to drive home. "Your dad was responsible for breaking into our apartment, and you waited until now to tell me?"

Ryan leans on his elbows, meeting her gaze in the rearview mirror. "Yeah, sorry. I—"

I touch his knee, knowing how badly he feels already. And Giselle, while the most giving and compassionate human I know, is also the most vocal. I never have to wonder what's on her mind. "We handled it, Gi. You were stressed enough already. I didn't want you to freak because his dad—"

"Is the actual thief," she says, more just repeating what Ryan told her rather than questioning it. "But why target us?"

"He's trying to sabotage my chance with Luna," he says, still looking at Giselle in the rearview mirror, though her gaze trains on the road.

"Obviously it isn't going to work, but are you sure he's not going to try anything else? I like where I live. And he could cause some serious problems." She flicks on the blinker and switches lanes. "How do you feel about abandoning him on a deserted island?"

"I—"

I groan and rub my eyes with the balls of my hand, hating that I've already thought about her suggestion a dozen times since last night. "Ava said never again if we can help it. Plus, it's Ryan's dad. They share a bond whether it's good for them or not. We've already sent the boutonniere, so can we not talk about this anymore?"

"Only if we talk about the fact that you transformed into a mermaid in front of Ryan and didn't tell me. Or how I caught you guys making out in the shower," she says, giggling. "Way better topics than disgruntled, psycho dads, which I must add you both have in common. The ocean sure knows how to pair people."

Ryan blushes, and I doubt it was because of the dad remark.

Giselle laughs again, tapping her hands on the steering

wheel. She sits up straighter to meet my gaze in the mirror. I narrow my eyes, pursing my lips, and then resort to smiling. I can't help it. I've been dying to talk about everything with her to get her human opinion.

Sun shifts in his seat to look at us. "Hot showers are awesome, aren't they?"

"I'm pretty sure it wasn't the hot shower he thought was awesome," Giselle says, grinning at me again in the rearview mirror. "You brazen merpeople don't even realize how you affect our poor, unsuspecting human emotions."

"I'm well aware, my love," Sun says, smiling. "Your poor, unsuspecting human emotions ignite an intense passion inside me that even a swim to the Arctic can't cool."

She smiles, shaking her head. "We'll call it even then."

Slinking lower in his seat, Ryan shifts and bumps his knees into mine. I grin at Sun and Giselle before smiling at him, loving how the flush of Ryan's face brightens the green of his eyes. His dark hair falls on his forehead, and he combs it back with his fingers.

Giselle's laughter sounds over the music as Sun whispers something to her I can't hear, and she pulls the sedan into the valet of a six-story, red brick hotel with a view of the water. A man in a vest with a bowtie opens my door for me, and I meet Ryan on the carpet leading to a revolving door entrance of the hotel Giselle's mom arranged for us.

Giselle glances at the pier across the street and then to me. "Why don't you scope the area for a somewhat easy access to the water while I get us checked in?"

I nod. "Okay."

"Don't forget your purse. I added extra cash to what you had from the jewelry you made for Chloe's mom and my credit card if you need more. Ryan could use a few more things while you're out. Pick out something formal. We're finally going to enjoy our vacation."

Ryan shakes his head. "I'm good, Giselle. I'm not completely broke."

She shrugs. "Okay but know as Luna's boyfriend, you're now in the secret mermaid society, and we take care of each other any way we can."

He nods, tilting his head, probably trying to decipher if she's joking about her made up society. "I appreciate everything you've already done by allowing me to come with you."

Reaching out, she half hugs him to whisper, "You know, all you have to do is say the word about your dad and he—"

I flick Giselle's arm, glaring. "No one's getting dropped off on an island."

She releases a breath, blowing her hair from her face, only responding by glaring right back at me, hiding her smile through her pursed lips. Hugging me once, she waves us away as she and Sun head inside the hotel. Ryan slides his fingers through mine, and he tugs me toward the busy street leading to a row of shops with everything from clothing to jewelry, beach sports supplies, and a few restaurants.

Twilight steals away the sun, lighting up the city around

us. People go about their lives, the sound of traffic muting the familiar noise of the sea I'm so in-tune to hearing, even at its calmest in a bay.

"This feels so normal," Ryan muses, smiling at me in his peripheral vision. He brushes his thumb along the side of my finger, holding my hand.

I laugh, swinging our arms for a moment before a familiar couple catches my attention coming from around the corner at the end of the block. I wasn't expecting to see Carter's parents on our trip, because they were supposed to have left already to Coralista, and now they're nearly running this way.

I slow our step, bracing myself. "Not for long. Have I mentioned Carter's parents live here? They must've been waiting for us to arrive, and I think you're about to get interrogated in three, two—"

"Luna! You're exactly the person we were on our way to see. We postponed our trip a day to make sure you got here safely." Starla opens her arms, pulling both Ryan and me into a hug, which he surprisingly accepts without stiffening or anything. She rocks us back and forth for a moment, her teal gaze lighting when they fall on Ryan. "And you brought such a handsome boy with you. Welcome to San Francisco, Ryan."

Carter must've told his parents everything. I don't think they'd still be here if he hadn't.

Mateo scoops me up and spins me around next, making me laugh. "He'll make a fine merman," he whispers in my ear.

My heart nearly bursts at his assuring thoughts.

Starla smiles, tugging Mateo away from me. "Did you two get settled at the hotel? You know you're welcome to stay with us if you want. You're family. We finally converted Carter's room into the guest room now that he and Ava have their own place."

"Giselle's already planned our entire stay. Thanks, though," I say. "I'll keep it in mind if I decide to stay past spring break. It all depends on..." I let my voice trail off. It depends on a lot of things—my cousin, Ryan's dad, if it's even safe to go back to the condo.

Mateo nods his head, tightening his jaw for a moment, but he doesn't clue me in on everything he knows. "Well, the offer stands," Mateo says. "And you're welcome in our home too, Ryan. If there's anything you need—"

"Food," I say, cutting him off before he says anything strange or makes Ryan nervous. Mateo might have lived on land for all of my life, but he's always been ready to serve the ocean as one of its finest warriors. "We're starving and tired from the drive."

"Oh, perfect. I think we can stay a few more hours to catch up. There's this great little restaurant around the corner. Why don't you call Giselle and have her and Sun meet us?" she asks.

I glance at Ryan. "That would be great."

Starla motions us to walk with her. "Well, come on then. We'd love to get to know Ryan."

He nods. "Ask me anything you'd like."

"When should we expect the coupling ceremony, Princess Luna?" Mateo asks, leaning back in his seat.

It didn't take long for Starla and Mateo to learn that I revealed our secret to Ryan once Sun and Giselle arrived. Secrets are rare in the colonies and news travels fast. I'm sure the whole ocean will know soon enough that I found my intended mate on land.

But something holds me back from telling them where Ryan comes from. Giselle's quick to keep Sun quiet as well.

"A coupling ceremony?" Ryan asks. "Is that like marriage?" His voice remains even, unfazed by the sudden attention Starla and Mateo give him. I nearly fall out of my chair at his question, though. Not because of the idea of marriage but because how easy it is for him to ask. He's not shifting or looking for an escape at all.

Starla flicks her attention to me before returning it to Ryan. "A bonding of souls. A piece of paper with legal weight does not define the promise of love where we come from."

Ryan nods his head. "Well, I—we just met."

I swallow. His nerves hitch his voice now, but I can't blame him.

"But don't you want to know Luna in a way that'll fulfill your existence? The human world no longer matters when—"

My mouth drops open. Is that what I sound like? I feel bad for all the times I've even mentioned a coupling ceremony to Giselle. Something about hearing Starla question Ryan nearly sends me running on his behalf. It's got to be a lot to take in.

He's just accepted the idea that we're together.

"Starla, reel it in," Giselle says, holding her finger up. "Traditions are changing, remember?"

Starla groans and looks to me to take her side, but I remain quiet. The only side I'm on is Ryan's and following whatever it is he wants. "But this one—"

"Is incredibly important, I know, but it's a huge decision for those of us who have to end our human lives to go through with it." Giselle leans into Sun and pouts her bottom lip at him. "It's scary."

Ryan pales from next to me, and I watch his eyes flick back and forth as he tries to process a conversation Starla and Mateo speak of so casually. It's different for them because they were born in the sea.

"Please, you two. It's been a day since I've shown Ryan what I am. I haven't had time to tell him any of this. You're going to scare him away," I say.

Mateo huffs. "There is nothing scary about—"

Standing up, I pull Ryan to his feet, stopping Mateo from saying anything more. "Thank you both for the lovely dinner, but we need to go. I wanted to look up my cousin's address tonight and come up with a plan to introduce myself tomorrow. You two have a long trip ahead of you anyway."

Starla stands up and hugs me. "Oh, Princess Luna. I was so wrapped up in getting to know your handsome mate that I forgot the reason you've come. Your mom would be so thrilled for you. This was the life I know she imagined for you."

Tears blur my eyes at the mention of my mom. I used to never cry over her, because she's been gone since I was a merbabe, but now knowing she renounced her mermaid essence to save humans my dad thought undeserving of life as a way to protect the colonies gets to me. I feel closer to her with her memories. She did it for me, so I could have a life of my making because she thought the world was a beautiful, exciting place both on land and in the sea.

Ryan slides his arm around my back, hugging me without saying anything. Starla and Mateo send us off with good luck wishes and remind us of their offer about staying with them, though I don't know if I could handle being around Starla through my courting with Ryan.

Giselle and Sun remain with them to finish dinner instead of following. I think they can tell I need this moment alone with Ryan after the tidal wave of information Starla and Mateo cast at him.

Cool night air gusts around us, sending my hair off my shoulders. Ryan holds me against him the entire way to the hotel, our steps identical, probably even our breathing is in sync. He fills the silence by pointing out things in the windows of a few shops and stops inside a bakery to buy us each a chocolate cupcake.

"Dessert is my favorite," I say, licking the frosting off my finger. "I had no idea anything could taste like this."

He chuckles. "You make everything, even eating a cupcake, exciting."

"Because everything is exciting," I say.

Ryan kisses me on the sidewalk, his lips as sweet as the dessert he finished. I suck his sugary lip between mine, an image from earlier flitting through my head, and he releases a low moan in his throat.

Slowly pulling away, he says, "I hope I never get used to that."

I laugh and tug him through the revolving door of the hotel. "We'll just have to create new memories so that it doesn't."

"Now?"

Smiling, I shake my head. "As soon as I see my cousin's house for myself."

He grabs my hand and pulls me toward the elevator. "Then we better hurry."

13

THE CELESTIANA

I STARE AT THE security booth outside the chain-link gate that separates the private marina from the row of restaurants and shops bustling with life. I don't know what I was expecting, but it wasn't this. Starla never mentioned that my cousin lived on a boat.

"This makes sense," Ryan says, peering at the row of boats along the dock. "If your great-grandfather loved a mermaid, he loved the sea. His brother probably did, too."

"And they passed down that love," I muse out loud. It reminds me of how Ryan claims the sea is in his blood.

"It also looks like your cousin's not here." He points to the empty slip where the boat should be docked.

My heart slides into my stomach, and I stare at the spot like I can summon a boat to appear, but nothing changes. "Oh, no."

Shifting in front of me, Ryan blocks my view of the empty spot and pulls me into a hug. "Hey, it's okay."

"What if they never come back?" Who knows how current the information is that Starla and Mateo found. What if my cousin hasn't been here for a while? There would be no possible way to track my land family if they're at sea. I can't summon some magical bond out of thin air. There are merpeople gifted with tracking bonds, but they must be established, and it's never completely accurate. They can only pinpoint the vicinity to search with the help of others, and that's not on the surface.

Ryan releases a breath against my hair. "They will."

I sigh. "I just—I don't want to wait. If I knew more about the boat, I could try to find them."

Ryan steps away from me, holding his finger up. "Give me a minute."

"What—"

He smiles and spins away, strolling toward the guardhouse where I spot a man sitting and watching TV next to a monitor with what looks like a video of the boats. Ryan points at the dock and then to me, saying something to the man I can't hear.

I wave, and the security guard smiles at me before turning to his desk to type something into his computer. Ryan leans over, looking at the screen with the security guard and nods. He shakes the security guard's hand before heading back in my direction.

A smile lights his whole face, and I jog the short distance to close the space between us. "What did you do?"

"I asked him when the owner of slip five was coming back," he says. "He asked how I knew Talia Torres, so I told him we were friends passing through."

My mouth drops open as I repeat my cousin's name in my mind. Ryan made talking to the security guard look so easy. I'd have been a mess trying to explain my situation. "Did he say anything else?"

Ryan's smile brightens. "That she takes her boat out a few nights a week."

"So, she's close?"

He nods. "And guess what?"

I stare at him without answering, waiting for him to say more.

"He referred to the boat as the *Celestiana*."

Surprise widens my eyes, and I throw my arms around him. "Oh, Ocean. This is a sign. Would it be crazy if we waited here all night?" Because I'm ready to plop down on this sidewalk and stare at the empty dock until I'm told to leave or the boat I'm looking for appears.

Ryan slowly nods. "I had another idea."

I stretch on my tiptoes, hooking my fingers through the fence. "What?"

He doesn't let me grip the links for long, gently prying my

hands away to twine his fingers through mine. Without answering me, he tugs me away from the private marina, bumping my shoulder every time I glance back at the docks until I can't see them any longer and our hotel comes back into view.

I stop in my tracks, pursing my lips. "If you plan to distract me until—"

He chuckles. "Now that you mention it."

"Ryan," I say, puffing out a breath through my mouth.

"I'm kidding, sort of."

I step back and place my hands on my hips. "Well, why did you bring me all the way here? I thought you had an idea."

He nods. "I do. Coming here was for me. I was afraid if I told you at the marina, you wouldn't have given me a chance to change into a wetsuit."

"Huh?"

"You're a mermaid, Luna. We don't have to wait on shore. We can swim. Apparently, she enjoys the view of the land from the bay. He recommended we ask her to show us her favorite place near the Golden Gate Bridge."

"You make talking to humans and finding out information so easy," I say in awe. I'd have never been able to gather the type of information he did in such a short conversation.

He grins, guiding me into the hotel. "It's a gift of mine."

I stop and kiss him in the lobby. "So you'll swim with me to find her boat?"

"I'll swim with you anywhere," he says.

When we reach our room, I pack a small waterproof bag,

and Ryan changes into a wetsuit before heading back out. We stroll toward a beach access with a pier that stretches out into the bay. A few people huddle around a tall table on the patio of a bar, but apart from them, the sand is empty this time of night because of the drop in temperature.

City lights dance across the rippling surface of the water like stars brought to earth. Ryan guides me away from the lights of the pier and into the shadows of a building closed for the night. He bounces on his bare feet in the sand, rubbing his hands together more in anticipation than the cold.

"You sure you're up to this?" I ask, rubbing my hands up and down his arms to summon more warmth for him.

Jumping into the bay at this temperature will be a bit of a shock, but I naturally radiate heat from my spark as a mermaid.

His serious expression morphs into a smile. "Yup."

I inch closer, moving my hands from his arms to rub over his back, feeling him slightly tremble. "You're nervous."

He releases a low laugh. "Not gonna lie, Luna. The dark water is frickin' scary to me. It's like being propelled into an abyss with no sense of direction or idea of what's going on around me. I don't dive in low visibility because of the danger. But in pitch black, my brain automatically thinks man-eating monsters."

I puff out my bottom lip, feeling a bit bad that he doesn't find a night swim as pleasant as I do. I never even considered he'd be afraid of ocean predators, because they never bother merpeople, and they definitely wouldn't bother Ryan with me.

"But you're willing to go for me?" I ask.

He nods, bouncing on his feet. "I like to think I'm a tough guy."

I smile. "You don't have to be a tough guy."

"It helps that you promised to keep me safe in the water," he adds, brushing his lips to mine. "But don't tell anyone I need the idea of a mermaid princess protecting me to get me to jump into the deep."

I laugh into his lips. "I still think you're incredibly brave."

He rubs his hands over his face, smirking. "As I stand here shaking."

"Well, it *is* cold."

He releases a loud laugh. "Thanks for that."

Slowly tugging myself away, I slip my sundress over my head and hand it to Ryan to put in my bag. His eyes trail over me in my bikini, my skin lit by the soft light of the moon peeking through the marine layer rolling in.

I step into the water first, cold from the drop in temperature of the spring night, and Ryan rolls his shoulders a few times before rushing ahead of me to dive under. He pops to the surface, releasing a yelp, shaking water from his face.

"Think about the hot shower you'll get after," I say, grinning.

He presses his cool body to mine. "I think I need another reminder."

Scooping me into his arms, he kisses me while carrying me into the bay until he can no longer touch the bottom. He dips under with me, his eyes closed, oxygen clinging to his face. I untie my bottoms and change, arching back with dull muscle spasms. Swimming as fast as I can around Ryan, I catch him in my current, pushing away my desire to kiss him, and jet us to the surface.

He gasps a breath, water trickling down his face. His legs slide against my tail, and he brushes strands of wet hair from my face, looking into my eyes like I'm all there is in the vast ocean.

"So worth the cold to see you like this," he whispers. "But maybe we can visit tropical waters next."

"We can go anywhere."

He smiles. "I love this. Making plans with you. I never thought I'd be making any real plans after leaving my family. I was just going without a destination, and it all led right to you."

A wave of warmth washes over me with his words. I haven't thought much about my future, only that I knew I wanted it to be with the person who completed me. And a future exploring the world, the land and sea, is something I never knew I wanted so much until this moment. I love La Tortuga Point, and I love my life there with my friends, but there's something about doing more than just living that ignites a desire as intense as the one Ryan elicits from inside me.

I hug him, stopping him from shivering in the cold. "We'll make lots. But first, take a deep breath."

Diving us under, I swim along the shallows, peering over Ryan's shoulder while he embraces me, keeping his face tilted into the crook of my shoulder. I barely notice the extra weight, him fitting perfectly against me like he's a part of me. His hands slide along the ridge of my tail separating the skin of my stomach from my scales to trail along my short dorsal fin until he reaches my shoulders. Without even an inch of water between us, I concentrate on the drum of his heartbeat against mine.

He releases some of his air, sending bubbles above. Flicking my tail, I ascend toward the mirror-like surface. I usually let Giselle go to swim for air alone while waiting below, but with Ryan, I pop us both through and listen for his intake of breath.

Flipping over, I swim with my back inches above the bay's floor. I pass a bat ray grazing for prey, its expansive body gracefully cutting through the calm water. The ocean life crowds the sea around us, and I carefully swim past a few fish, making sure nothing touches Ryan. Sea grass tickles my skin, and an octopus shoots past us, nearly tangling in my loose hair. I release a laugh, sending bubbles into Ryan's neck, and he hugs me tighter.

I swim toward the surface again and pop through to spit out water. Ryan gasps, heaving a breath, and then he rests his head on my shoulder, preparing for me to dive back under. Instead, I spin in place, taking in the bay around us from over him. A few boats glide across the surface, and the Golden Gate Bridge glows, reflecting sparkling light on the water. City lights pepper the shores, and I absorb the beauty of land meeting sea.

"Do you ever worry about people seeing you?" Ryan asks, his warm breath tickling my shoulder. "There are a lot of boats out."

He motions toward a large vessel heading toward the bridge, leaving a glittering trail in its wake. Music hums through the air, and I catch sight of humans dancing on the sundeck, enjoying their night.

"Sometimes, but I don't think about it as much as I used to," I say. "It's dark anyway."

"What about underwater? Scuba divers? Researchers? Underwater cameras?" he asks.

I bring his hand up to my chest, pressing it into my heart. "My mermaid spark protects me—and you. If anything, they'll think I'm an animal. We don't exactly swim face-to-face, though more and more merpeople are leaving the colonies."

"I can only imagine what would happen..." His voice trails off. He doesn't have the same faith in the ocean I do. I've seen its mercy and wrath. Its strength and magic can wipe out entire towns. It's protective.

"It wouldn't fare well for those humans who are out to do us harm." I lean back and meet his gaze. "But stop worrying about that. A mermaid has never been caught and never will be."

He bobs his head, snuggling against me in the cold water. I spin around again and search the surface. Most of the vessels scattered around are too large to dock at the private marina we visited earlier.

"Luna, look," Ryan says, letting go of my neck to point.

I shift sideways with him to peer in the direction of his finger. A small yacht hovers on the water, facing the bridge. A figure with long black hair rests her elbows on the railing, staring off into the distance.

I suck in a small breath, a strange feeling washing over me, drawing me closer to the boat. It's the same feeling I get with my dad from our familial bond. It doesn't allow me to find him anywhere like a bond with my forever mate would, but it's still there, like my essence suddenly recognizes my distant cousin.

"That's the boat," Ryan says. "It has your mom's name."

Like my cousin can feel the weight of my gaze, she slowly turns in our direction. Panic blossoms in my heart, and I drag Ryan under with me, not giving him much time to inhale a long breath. I swim a few dozen feet, hoping she doesn't walk toward the stern, and slowly pop back up.

From this spot, I can't see her. I release a breath, burying my face into Ryan's shoulder. He rubs his hand along my back, rubbing his fingers across my small dorsal fin, pushing away the trembles from my body the best he can.

"I want to swim closer, but I'm afraid," I whisper.

"Of what?"

"I don't know. I just—oh, Ocean."

I let go of Ryan for a minute and swim a circle around him, close enough that he can still see me and run his hand across my body but with enough space that I'm not dragging him around with me. My thoughts cloud my mind into a jumbled mess. All my life, I thought I was alone with my dad, abandoned by my mom, with no prospects for mates in all the five oceans. But now, here I am swimming with a guy I want to plan my future with while staring at a human who connects me to the land.

Ryan grabs my hand, pulling me from the current I created around him. He lifts me back toward the surface and combs away the dark hair veiling my face. Locking me in his gaze, he cups my cheeks in his hands, studying my face, trailing his stare from my eyes to my lips.

He kisses me, tasting of salt with a hint of sweetness from the cupcakes we ate earlier. "I think we should swim closer."

"I don't want to break the surface so close. She's staring at the water."

"Maybe she's searching for mermaids," he says, releasing a laugh.

I groan.

He kisses the frown off my face before it can overtake my expression. "I think you'll regret it if we don't. I can hold my breath long enough."

I don't respond for a long moment, just reading my mom's name painted across my cousin's boat over and over again. Ryan hugs me closer, pressing his chin into my shoulder and breathes his warm breath against my skin.

"Don't think about it. Just do it," he whispers.

I bob my head, squeezing him tighter against me. At the sound of his intake of breath, I dive us under and swim a few dozen feet below the surface. The closer we swim toward the bridge, the deeper the water gets. From what Carter told me when I was learning to swim with Giselle, I know I can dive several hundred feet safely with a human. As long as a human intakes air from the surface and not compressed air from a machine, there shouldn't be any issues, and I haven't experienced anything as of yet. It helps that Ryan's an experienced diver compared to Giselle, though I know Sun works on it more with her when he's around.

Hovering in the water, I tilt my head up and stare at the bottom of the boat, fanning my tail to keep us in place while I peer through the rippling surface. Slowly swimming up a few feet, I stare at my cousin's blurry face peering into the water. She's younger than I expected, maybe a few years older than me, but we both have blue, almond-shaped eyes, hers being a few shades lighter than mine, and they sparkle ocean blue against her tan skin. I can see her as clear as I could in the daylight with my mermaid vision lighting the world aglow.

She glares down at me, surprising me, and I sink deeper until the rippling water distorts her face. It's impossible that she can see me from the surface, but seeing her narrow her eyes at the sea sends a mixture of emotions through me. I'm not scared, but the sudden urge to break the surface engulfs my being, and I can't swim away fast enough before I follow through.

It takes Ryan digging his fingers into my back to remind me that I can't keep swimming the bottom and back to the beach without allowing him to intake a breath of air. I flick my tail, pushing us toward the surface and let him rise for a breath without me. He peers around and looks down at me, and takes another breath, realizing I'm not planning to emerge. We swim the rest of the way to shore stopping a few times to let him breathe. I only surface in the shallows when I'm ready to transform into my human form.

Ryan holds out my bottoms to me, letting me brace against him to change, and he swims me to shore for once, letting me clutch onto his back until we both hit the sand. He links his fingers with mine, holding my hand while lying next to me, both our chests heaving as we catch our breaths.

"What happened? You swam away so fast," he says, propping himself up on his elbow.

I lick my lips, trying to remember how to speak as my thoughts consume me. "She was beautiful. I—" Snapping my mouth shut, I sit up and stare at the small waves lapping the shore for a moment. "I almost swam us to the surface. I could barely control myself, so I had to leave."

Tears rim my eyes, and I sniffle, wiping water from my face. Seeing my cousin from below, just staring into her eyes the same color as my mom's, felt as important as the moment I laid my eyes on Ryan, like we're supposed to be together—she as my family and he as my mate.

Ryan hugs me to him, pulling me into his lap. He wraps a towel from my waterproof bag around us, rubbing away the chill of the water and spring night the best he can. He embraces me without saying a word until my eyes stop leaking so many tears that if I were in the water, the sea would rise.

"I'm sorry," I say with a breath. "You're probably so cold."

"I'm fine," he whispers. "Just breathe. It was a lot to take in."

I nod. "I know I'm crying, but I'm not sad. I'm so incredibly happy. Like I've been waiting my whole life for tonight."

He runs the towel over my cheeks, drying my tears and the droplets of sea trickling from my hair. "I'm happy I could share it with you, Luna."

"I hope she's there in the morning," I murmur. "I can't wait to meet her."

Ryan nudges my chin, so I turn my gaze back to the water. "Look."

I gasp a small breath, catching the sight of my cousin's boat now gliding across the water in the distance, heading toward the marina.

"We can go now," he says, pulling me to my feet.

I shake my head. "First thing in the morning. I can wait. I don't want to meet her looking like I came straight from the sea."

He nods and guides me to the beach. "Good, because I'm looking forward to that hot shower you promised."

14

STRANGE FEELING

GISELLE LIES NEXT TO me on my bed, her bronze hair spilling over the extra large pillow. "You know, Ava always complained I was an early riser, but you merpeople wake up before the sun more often than not."

I laugh and shift on my side. "Mermen like to hunt first thing."

She laughs. "Ryan's face was priceless when Sun insisted he join him on a hunt for breakfast."

I snicker at the memory. "I told Ryan to insist they pick up something hot and sweet."

"God, I love you, Luna," she says, pressing into the pillow.

"I'm so glad we're here."

Shifting on my side, I meet her gaze. "I saw my cousin last night. Her name is Talia Torres. She lives on a boat." I can't get the words out fast enough. Giselle and Sun were out when we got back to the hotel last night, and I feel like I haven't even had a moment to catch up with Giselle.

Giselle sits up, her eyes wider than her grin. "What? Really?"

I nod. "I thought we could all go meet her after breakfast. I just watched her from the water."

She claps her hands. "Yes! Yes. This is so exciting. Are you sure you want me and Sun to come?"

"Yeah, I'm so nervous. You're great at talking to people. I thought you could help to make sure I don't come off weird. I don't want to scare her." Because I know I don't always say things like a human would. I can see it on Ryan's face, though he humors me. Giselle, too.

"For one, you're never that weird. Honest? Yes. Innocent? Definitely. Scary? No way. You're as scary as a guppy, Luna," she says. "But I'm here for you for whatever you want or need."

I fling my arms around her and hug her, bouncing as she bobs in excitement. She always knows what to say to make me feel better. And putting myself out there to meet a long-lost relative is terrifying. What if she doesn't want anything to do with me? Bonds are incredibly important in the sea, but on land? People survive fine without any real connections. Some prefer it.

The hotel room door beeps and swings open, cutting off my thoughts. Sun strolls in, greeting Giselle with a huge smile lighting his whole face like he hasn't seen her in months, though it hasn't even been an hour. It's the kind of look I hope to get from Ryan every time we're together.

"Breakfast fit for two enchanting lovelies," Sun says, holding out a paper bag. "And just as hot and sweet. My love, I hope you like berry crepes, brown sugar muffins, and a delicious smelling cheese Danish. I've never had one."

I frown, realizing Ryan isn't with him. "Where's Ryan?"

Sun sets the paper bag on the table, still holding his smile for Giselle, though he brings his gaze to me. "He saw someone he knew and told me I shouldn't keep you two waiting for breakfast while he stopped to say hello."

I grimace at Giselle. "I have a strange feeling. I didn't think Ryan knew anyone here."

Giselle lifts and drops her shoulders. "You don't think it's..."

"Would you like me to return to your mate, princess?" Sun asks, crossing his arms over his chest.

I whip my head back and forth, letting my hair hit my cheeks, and roll out of bed. My chest tightens, making it hard to breathe. All I can think about is getting out of here to make sure Ryan's okay, to get some fresh air into my lungs while I'm at it. "No, it's okay. I'll be right back. Stay with Giselle."

The sudden urge to find Ryan intensifies the second I step onto the elevator to go to the lobby. People bustle through the hotel, guests checking out and talking to the concierge. My bare feet slap against the slick floor the faster I move, concentrating on not breaking into a full-blown sprint to exit. I probably already look a mess, still in the cotton shorts and tank top I slept in with my hair unkempt from sleeping with it loose.

I push through the revolving door to exit the hotel and peer around the crowded street now lined with morning traffic. A few cars honk, and a bicyclist flies down the bike lane. I shade my eyes from the sun, trying to remember the direction of the coffee shop I saw on the bag Sun brought in. We passed by it sometime yesterday. I just can't remember when.

Closing my eyes, I push the noise of the outside world away and map the area in my mind, relying on my photographic memory that works a lot better if I'm in my mermaid form. My legs automatically step forward, and I open my eyes, the pull tugging at my spark, not unlike the ocean on the night of the full moon.

I jog to the end of the block and turn, searching the crowded sidewalk in front of a café. Hands grab my shoulders, startling me, and I jerk away and spin. Ryan steps back with his hands raised into the air for a second before taking me into his arms.

"Are you okay?" I ask, my breath panting as I try to suppress the uncomfortable, dark feeling still coursing through my essence.

His serious expression gives nothing away before he says, "Yeah, are you? You're trembling."

I swallow, my hands shaking with nerves. "I—I don't know."

"Did anyone stop at the hotel and try to talk to you?" he asks.

I shake my head, resting on his shoulder, letting him hug me while I pull myself together enough to talk. "Sun said you stopped to talk to a friend, but I didn't think you knew anyone in San Francisco. I couldn't shake the strange feeling that made me need to find you. I just—it was an awful feeling. Are you sure you're okay? Why would someone stop at the hotel?"

Ryan slides his arms around me tighter, petting my hair while hugging the nerves that shake my voice away. "I only wanted to make sure. But it's okay. I'm okay. It's nothing."

"Nothing?" A frown pinches my eyebrows. This doesn't feel like nothing. It feels like Ryan doesn't want to tell me what's going on.

"Come on. We should go back." He glances around and strides us in the opposite direction I came from. We'd have to go around the whole block to get back to the hotel.

"Ryan..." I can't let it go. Knowing that something happened that he doesn't want to tell me about makes me feel awful.

He nudges me to keep moving. "I'll explain when we get back."

Inhaling a deep breath, I concentrate on calming myself down. If Ryan isn't panicking or rushing me away, I should trust that it's not as bad as my feelings are making it out to be.

"Why are we heading in the wrong direction?"

His jaw tightens. "Precaution. I don't want anyone to know where we're staying."

I swallow the fear tightening my throat. "What?"

"I swore to you I'd always protect you on land, remember?" He picks up his pace, nearly carrying me with him.

"Oh, Ocean," I whisper, realizing why he's acting so strange. He acted like this the night we left La Tortuga Point to come here after his dad sent that man to threaten him. "This is about your dad."

Ryan peers at me in his peripheral vision but keeps searching the street. "It's fine. He received the pearl and wanted to let me know. I'm being cautious just in case."

"How did he know we were here?" I ask.

"I bought us the cupcakes last night. I shouldn't have put it past him to track my bank account," he says.

I twist my lips, confusion pushing away my panic. "What? He can do that?"

"Money buys a lot of things, and my dad is a thief. He takes a lot of it. Knows a lot of people. But he's not here, so I don't want you to worry."

I knew this. I've seen what money can do, experienced it myself with Giselle and Ava. With their families. But I never dreamed of something like this. It ignites fear in my heart, making me want to run back to the bay and head out to sea. "How do you know he isn't?"

"He'd let me know." Ryan turns us into an alley to cut

through the block and back toward the street with our hotel. "Please, try not to worry. I know you're still scared about the other night, but I've been handling my dad for years. He got what he wanted, so we're good. Now he's just messing around."

My mind races with all the possible things that can happen if Ryan's dad knows we're here or the fact that he wanted us to know he knew. He was supposed to leave us alone. The boutonniere was supposed to be enough to get him to stop.

My worry turns into fury, and angry tears burn my eyes. "How dare he—"

Ryan stops in his tracks and spins me around. "I handled it. We're okay. Today's supposed to be an exciting day. You're going to meet your cousin—"

"I think we should leave," I blurt, rubbing my hands over my cheeks to push my hair from my face.

He frowns. "Luna, no. I'm not going to let anyone, especially my dad, ruin this for you. He was only sending a message. Paid someone to tell me. Don't worry, okay?"

"That's easy for you to say," I snap. I cover my mouth with my hand, shock coursing through me at the tone of my voice. "I—I'm sorry, Ryan."

He pulls me along. "No, I'm sorry. And you should yell at me for all this. It'd be weird if you didn't."

"But I—"

"I've messed up. Made some mistakes," he says. "I'm pissed at myself that you even have to deal with this. So, please. Yell at me a lot. I deserve it."

I scrunch my nose. "I'm letting it go because I don't like feeling this way."

His face softens, and he stops to pull me into another hug. "I'm going to make it up to you."

"You don't have to do that," I say.

"But I want to," he says.

I smile, blinking to clear my vision. "How?"

"You'll see tonight. Today, it's about meeting your pod."

I laugh. "You're learning my language. Did Sun teach you that?"

"That merman was incredibly insightful. He promised to teach me everything there is to know about how to court a mermaid."

I raise my eyebrows. "Oh, really?" I shouldn't have expected anything less from Sun. It's tradition for mermen to help each other.

He kisses me, humming in his throat. "Really. You'll see."

I release a happy sigh. "I can't wait."

15

WARRIOR POTENTIAL

I TWIST BLACK STRANDS of hair in my fingers, tying them into a braid as we walk in the direction of the private marina a few blocks from the hotel. It'd be faster to drive, but there's something about strolling near the bay, breathing the briny air into my lungs, and hearing the chatty birds along the shore that relaxes my nerves.

"Do I look okay?" I ask no one in particular.

Giselle smiles over her shoulder. "Hot."

Sun gives Ryan a nod, drawing my attention to them. Giselle's eyes glass over, and she releases a laugh like the three of them share some kind of inside joke.

Ryan clears his throat. "You're more beautiful than the sunset glittering across the vast ocean on this mesmerizing spring day."

My cheeks warm at his compliment, and I can't stop the smile overtaking my face, hurting my cheeks because I can't control it.

"And twice as hot," he adds.

Ryan outstretches his hand to Sun, and they bump their knuckles together.

Giselle cracks up. "That was the most ridiculous, grossly romantic thing I've ever heard, but damn I can tell how much Luna loved it. I'll only make fun of you a little."

Ryan chuckles and slides his arm around my waist. "There's more where that came from."

"Be careful, Ryan. Say anything else like that and I'm pretty sure she's going to melt and drift back to sea," Giselle says, looking me up and down.

Ryan presses his lips to my temple. "It's a good thing I'm an excellent swimmer."

"I was quite impressed," Sun says. "You have warrior potential. Right, princess? But I don't expect anything less from the mate of a royal."

I nod, words lost to me. I don't know if it's the nerves of the marina coming into view or that Ryan surprised me by saying something about me that my heart can't stop racing about, but now I feel like my brain turned to mush. Giselle was right about me drifting out to sea.

Giselle laughs again, snapping her fingers in my face. "I think that might've been too much for her innocently romantic mermaid heart."

I bat her hand away and roll my eyes. "It was perfect and surprising and..."

"Cheesy," Giselle says.

"Look, there she is." The sight of my cousin emerging from her boat cuts off all my thoughts of Ryan and his cute attempt to follow Sun's guidance on appealing to my mermaid essence.

"Oh, my God. You look like sisters," Giselle whispers, grabbing and shaking my arm.

"The bond is there," Sun says.

My cousin yanks a net bag along with some snorkeling gear from a storage compartment. She jumps onto the dock and strides to the gate, waving to the security guard in the booth. Without thinking, I jog away from everyone as my cousin reaches a pathway that winds toward the same beach Ryan and I used to enter the water last night.

"Luna, wait up," Ryan calls.

He sprints up next to me and clasps my hand, trying to slow me down.

"I'm going to lose her," I say, dragging him faster. I peer over my shoulder at Sun and Giselle. "Hurry up."

Giselle waves me away, and I run down the cement path with Ryan. When we reach the sand, I spin around, trailing my gaze over the few people on the beach. Panic grips my heart because my cousin's gone. I missed my chance.

"Where did she go?" I ask, disappointment coursing through me. "It's like the ocean is purposely keeping me away. Because why else would I miss her twice now?"

Ryan rubs his hand over the scruff on his face, peering around the water. "I don't think it's that, Luna."

Brushing my fingers through my hair, I push it out of my face. "Then what else could it be? It brought us together."

"Could be a bunch of different things. It's not like we know her schedule or much about her," Ryan says.

"How could she vanish?" I ask. No one is left on the beach now.

Ryan slides his arms around my shoulders. "You sure she's not a mermaid?"

I shift and stare at him with startled eyes. "I know every merperson in all the seas."

"You sure?"

I nod. "Yes, I'm sure. If she were a mermaid, I'd know."

"If she's not on the beach, then she went in the water," Ryan says. "Why don't we go back to the marina and wait for her."

I pout. I can't help it.

"Or we could go for a swim..."

"I—"

Without warning, Ryan lifts me off my feet and props me onto his shoulder, jogging me deeper into the water. "No more thinking about it. You want to meet Talia, then we're going to find her and meet her, even if we have to comb the whole bay."

I laugh as he spins me around. "I didn't want to meet her looking like I came from the sea."

"But you have, and I'm pretty sure she'll appreciate it," he says.

"I'm trying to be a human."

He twirls me once more and sets me on my feet. "Well, I'm pretty sure she's trying to be a mermaid. Look."

I twist in Ryan's arms, following his line of sight. Bubbles erupt on the surface, and a figure pops out of the water. My cousin flips her hair, shooting a stream of saltwater through the air, and she adjusts the net bag on her arm.

On the front of her wetsuit, a small metallic mermaid silhouette logo sparkles in the sunlight beaming from overhead. I smile from her to Ryan at the sight. She wipes water from her face, trudging through the surf with her head bowed to stare at the ground. After a few feet, she freezes. Bending over, she reaches into the water and picks up something shiny, tucking it into her bag. She's collecting things from the sea.

"Talia," I say, my mouth saying her name before my mind can catch up.

She jerks her head up to look at me, her smile disappearing, her mouth falling open. Taking a few steps away, she splashes through the waves and puts space between us. She doesn't say anything, just keeping her eyes locked onto mine, continuing to move away.

I kick a few feet through the water toward her, holding my hand up. "Hey, it's—"

Releasing a loud scream, Talia spins away from me completely, dropping her bag. Ryan grabs my hand and yanks me toward him, stopping me from chasing her. Talia rushes down the beach, peering over her shoulder a few times to look at me.

"Let me go, Ryan. I need to stop her," I say.

He doesn't let me go. Instead, he spins me around and hugs me. "You can't. Did you see how scared she was? If you chase her she might call the police or something."

"But why was she afraid?" I ask.

He frowns. "I..."

He doesn't know how to answer my question, but I do. I don't know why it didn't occur to me until this moment. The only reason a human would be afraid of me is if they knew what I was—but not as who I am today. Because it wasn't long ago that humans who discovered the mermaid secret were taken by the sea. It was a death sentence. One of the ruthless laws my dad set as the king, because he trusted no human.

But he's been shunned by the sea.

Times have changed, and I'm free to live on the land. I'm free to share my secret with those I know who are worthy of it.

I groan, trying my best not to cry, though I desperately want to. I'd like to sink into the waves and transform so I can hover amid the water where tears can't burn my eyes because they blend with the sea. "She ran because she knows I'm a mermaid."

Ryan grimaces. "But why be afraid?"

I let out a small breath. "Because she isn't aware that times have changed. The ocean is a much kinder place with my dad bound to land."

"Oh," is all he says.

Huffing a breath, I stroll to the water and scoop up Talia's bag. "Come on. Let's go back to the hotel."

"You sure?" he asks. "I know you were so excited. We can try another approach."

"What's the point? I'm already ruined for her. She's not going to want to attempt to form a relationship with me even if we share a bond."

From the look Ryan gives me, glassy eyes, twisted lips, his forehead wrinkling with a pout, I'd have thought I said something to hurt his feelings. "Luna, you're not ruined. You—"

I press my fingers to his lips. "You wouldn't understand."

One of the reasons I left the ocean to live on land was because I couldn't get away from my dad's shadow or the hard feelings all the colonies now have for their shunned king no longer gifted with ocean magic. The colonies were always sheltered, so few emerging from the depths, but everyone knew the consequence for revealing the mermaid secret to someone not intended to be a mate. I bet my great-grandfather knew and passed the information to his family. It's why my mom fought to create a haven to protect humans without my dad's knowledge. I always assumed it was for the human she loved, but now I realize it was more. A backup plan to keep our human family safe.

Ryan swipes his fingers across my cheeks to smear the tears

dripping from my eyelashes, pulling me from my thoughts. "But I do understand."

"How?"

"Because I was pretty certain I was ruined for you."

Sea lions call for me from the dock they sunbathe on at the end of the busy pier. Giselle insisted that if I wasn't going to agree to a stakeout to wait for Talia to return that I had to do something touristy with her, so we took a trolley to Fisherman's Wharf to explore and shop.

Ryan watches the sea lions from next to me while we wait for Giselle and Sun to catch up to us. I'm pretty sure Giselle's going to have to rent a truck to drive back to La Tortuga Point to bring everything she's bought so far. She claims that the robbery at our condo was more of a gift because she has an excuse to buy whatever she wants. Sun might now have a bigger land wardrobe than I do.

A sea lion splashes into the water and swims closer. It barks at me, bobbing up and down, nearly begging me to jump over the railing to swim with it. But I'm not in the mood to play or go into the water at all. I can't stop the sorrow raining on me, reminding me that Talia might never get to the place where she's brave enough to approach me or let me approach her. I thought about leaving a note with the security guard at the marina, but she might not trust it and suddenly take off. I could lose her forever.

And I didn't come here to mess up her life.

I wave my hand, shooing the sea lion away as it jumps from the water, trying to splash me. "Go back to your colony," I say. "I'm not jumping in to play with you in front of all these people."

The sea lion barks again and darts away to the docks where too many sea lions to count have made their home.

Ryan leans forward over the railing to glance at the green water and then to me. "You can talk to animals? I guess I should've considered it a possibility since you are a mermaid."

I draw my gaze from the sea lions and to him, a smirk pulling at my mouth. "Oh, all the time. You should hear how loud the ocean is. Everyone always talking and chatting." I point my finger to one of the sea lions. "That one's planning to splash that group of people over there at any minute."

Ryan's mouth drops open.

I laugh, tipping my head back. "I'm kidding."

Ryan fake glares at me and chuckles. "You're lucky I love how much you teasing me brings a smile to your face. I've missed it all morning."

I smile wider, letting my hair fall into my face to veil the world between us. "You have?"

He turns me away from the water, standing in front of me instead of beside me. His hands grasp the railing on both sides of me, caging me in, so he has my undivided attention I'm happy to give him. "I didn't realize how important your smile was to me until you stopped, though your pouty lips make you incredibly kissable."

I laugh again, touching my hands to his chest to slide them up to his shoulders. "Why's that?"

"Because when I kiss them, you smile," he whispers, leaning into me.

I giggle against his lips, knowing he's purposefully excessive in his compliments to make me laugh. I can almost see Giselle rolling her eyes now while Sun puffs his chest out, proud that his new protégé makes my knees weak.

"Careful, Ryan," I whisper into his lips. "Keep talking like that and I might ask you to swim away with me."

"I hope you do."

His kiss whispers against my mouth, teasing me while making me yearn for him to give me another. I sink against him, pressing my chest to his, feeling our hearts beat against each other's through our shirts.

"Think we'll be missed if we left now?" Ryan asks.

I shake my head. "Definitely not."

He smiles into my lips, kissing me once more, and turns to tug me down the pier and in the direction of the giant wheel-shaped sign with a bright red crab in the middle of it. We pass a small building near one of the boating companies, which take tourists out on the water, and I slow down at the sound of a soft voice humming from the window cutout.

The side door swings open and out walks Talia, wearing a polo shirt and khakis. My heart nearly escapes from my chest, the shock of seeing my cousin so close and out of the water enough to make me step back into Ryan's arms.

Her marine blue eyes turn from who she's talking to inside the building to me. She glances around the pier, taking in the crowd. Something in her wide eyes shifts, and she struts forward, her finger outstretched to me and Ryan.

"I can't believe you're here," we both say at the same time.

Her surprise morphs into anger, and I take an automatic step back, pushing Ryan with me. He slides his arm across my chest protectively, adding more space between me and Talia. She keeps strutting at us until Ryan's back hits the wall of another building.

He raises his hand up, motioning her to stay back, but I shrug from his hug and close the space between us.

"I—"

"Don't talk or come any closer," Talia says, shifting to glance at the few tourists meandering behind us. "You need to leave me alone. You promised."

I open my mouth to respond, but she pokes my chest, startling me. Her words are so strange. How could I promise something when this is the first time we've ever met?

"I mean it. I remember who you are, and I haven't done anything wrong or said anything like you asked. Just go home and don't come back here or I'll—"

"Hey," Ryan says, speaking up for me. "You need to—"

"Stop or I'll make a scene. I mean it. The last time you— just go back to wherever you came from and leave me alone. I don't want you here. I don't need you. It's not worth the risk of him coming back." Spinning on her feet, she turns and strides away, leaving me standing in shock in Ryan's arms.

My mind whirls at her words, but I can't make sense of anything.

Talia peers at us from over her shoulder and then turns to a woman wearing the same uniform she is. She points at us, saying something I can't hear, and the woman frowns. Ryan tugs me back and into the crowd. He doesn't stop until I finally get my legs to function properly on their own, and he picks up his pace even more.

"She has some serious issues," Ryan mutters, only slowing down when we're back on the sidewalk and a block away from the Fisherman's Wharf. "We didn't even do anything."

"She's going to think I'm stalking her," I say, groaning. "To keep showing up wherever someone is can be seen as unacceptable behavior on land even if it's by accident. She'll assume this was on purpose instead of fate." Giselle told me this particular rule before my first outing in the world when I was determined to search for my mate. I never thought it could apply to my distant cousin, even if I'm not stalking her.

Ryan tilts his head and smirks at me. "Or a coincidence."

I release a breathless laugh. "I don't think so. The ocean sees to it that it puts people with bonds together."

"Like how we kept crossing paths after we met?" he asks, finally stopping at a corner to wait for the signal to change.

I huff, blowing hair from my face. "Yeah, except you liked it."

He wraps his arms around me, breathing into my neck.

"You're definitely right about that. So much so, I couldn't stay away myself."

"But with Talia..." I clench my fingers into fists against his chest. "We should do as she asked and leave. She was saying some strange things, and I don't know how to interpret them without her even giving me a chance to use my voice. I don't think anyone outside my dad has ever showered me with so much anger."

"You want to give up on her so easily?" he asks like he can't believe what I'm saying.

"No, of course not. But I'm scared."

"And when has that stopped you?"

I bring my eyes to his and glare. "You're different. You're my mate."

I cringe, saying the words out loud, especially how deep and important that little admission is to me. I'm afraid he'll react as he did the night I revealed to him I was a mermaid, and then I'll need to return to the water, because I don't think I could handle another rejection. Especially not from him.

Stupid mermaid spark. Why can't I act and think like a normal human?

Quickly pulling myself away, I don't give Ryan a chance to respond to save ourselves from any awkwardness. He calls out my name, but I keep running, and then I lose myself in the crowd. I need a moment to think, to not have to worry about the land and everything that comes with it.

My phone rings from my bag, and I pull it out and see the

picture of Ryan Giselle programmed in it. It nearly makes me stop in my tracks and turn around. If only the land weren't so overwhelming and complicated. It's so easy when I'm submerged in the sea with him.

"Luna, please come back," he says into the line, his voice low and pleading.

It takes everything in me to keep my legs going. "Can you meet me back at the hotel?"

He groans. "Please. I need to talk to you."

But I don't want to talk. I want to swim.

Cramps rush through my legs, stealing my breath as my mermaid transformation begins without my permission. I was too careless letting my guard down. I knew better than to let my heart wander to the sea. But I couldn't help myself. My emotions are a jumbled mess, and there's only one place everything seems perfectly clear.

I race toward the beach, my lungs already burning with the need to inhale a breath of ocean. I jog into the water, not even caring who sees me, and dive in. And I swim. I swim until my feet can't touch the bottom and the shore grows smaller.

Dipping under, I undress and stop resisting the spasms pulsing through my muscles. I suck in a breath of the bay, letting it fill me with everything I need in this moment, but it still doesn't feel good. Nothing feels right.

I transform back just as quickly, treading water in my human form.

I break the surface and clear my lungs, expecting to hear

the world shouting about the mermaid in the water, but no one pays attention. No one saw.

Ryan pops up next to me, sending a wave of water over my head, startling me. "What's the matter? What did I say wrong?"

I squeeze my eyes shut, kicking to stay afloat. It's a lot more effort without my expansive tail. "It wasn't you. It's every-thing. I know how you feel about the whole mermaid mate thing, and I didn't mean to—"

Ryan swims closer, splashing my face with the sea at the movement, cutting off my words. He runs his thumbs across my forehead to stop the water from streaming in my eyes. "You can call me whatever you want, Luna. I don't care anymore. All I care about is you, okay? Now please, return to shore with me."

I slowly nod. "I'm sorry. I didn't mean to accidentally transform. You could've waited on shore."

"And risk you disappearing into the deep?" he asks.

I rub my salty lips together, twining my fingers through his so we stay afloat together. "I'd never."

He sucks in a breath. "It's okay if that's what you want, but can I ask you a favor?"

I nod.

"Take me with you if you do."

My heart soars and breaks at once. I don't think he under-stands what he's asking of me. But I'm also afraid to tell him what his words mean. I'm afraid to hear him change his mind.

All I do is nod again.

"I mean it," he says, pulling me to swim back toward the

beach. "I don't want to lose you to the ocean. It's supposed to be me, you, and the sea, remember?"

I smile. "I'd never forget."

16

SIMPLE LIFE

GISELLE STANDS UNDER THE sign for the Fisherman's Wharf with Sun next to her holding an armful of bags on his arms. She crinkles her nose, glancing at us up and down. Ryan and I look at each other and release a laugh. Neither of us was dressed for swimming, and we leave a seawater trail behind us.

"What the hell? Did the sea lions lure you into the water to play?" She places her hands on her hips. "I thought Ava was bad, but you both are ridiculous. We have at least a dozen more places to go to."

"I saw my cousin," I blurt. "She works on one of the excursion tours."

"Oh, my God. That's crazy. Do you think Starla and Mateo knew she was so close? She could've been living here all this time."

I shrug. "My mom did live here, but I don't think she'd have told anyone if she knew."

"Oh, I guess so."

I cross my arms over my chest, steeling myself to the hurtful memory of Talia yelling at me. "It doesn't matter, though. Talia told me to leave her alone."

Giselle's pout shifts into a scowl and she places her hands on her hips, looking ready to run back to the pier to find Talia to give her a piece of her mind. She probably would if she knew I wouldn't stop her. "That makes me so mad. What if I talk to her from one mermaid secret holder to another?"

I throw my arms around her, knowing how much she cares about me, but she didn't see Talia react. She'd probably call the police right away if she knew Giselle was there on my behalf. She'd assume she was a mermaid, too. "You are the best, you know. But this is my problem. I should learn how to handle my life on land if I'm going to remain here." If only the ocean didn't beckon me to return to the deep so often where I know it's safe. Where it's a simple life of living and loving. Of just existing for my mate while my mate exists for me.

I sniffle, my heart aching at the thought. I never imagined such a life wouldn't sound so perfect anymore. Because I've realized what a big world it is outside of my mermaid colony. Outside of my condo on land. It's meant to be explored, and I want to do so with Ryan. But I'm afraid it'll never be possible. I'm afraid I'm not cut out for the land.

Turning to Sun, she adds, "I guess I'm no longer needed to help Luna with land things. My little mermaid's growing into a human."

I laugh and flick her arm. "It's a good thing your mate needs you."

She smirks. "My life would be so incomplete without him."

The look Sun gives her makes even my heart race, and I don't think Giselle realizes how much her words affect her merman mate. He scoops her into his arms and showers her with kisses. She tilts her head back to peer at me upside down, the smile lighting her face comparable to the grin on Sun's.

"Oh, my bronze-haired jewel, you just made me the happiest merman in all the seas," Sun says.

"Well, I'm here for you for whatever you need, Luna," Giselle says, twisting in Sun's arms. "You're one of my best friends."

"And I'm here for when—"

"Don't even say it," she says, fake glaring.

I laugh. "It's just a thought."

"Yeah, and you're probably thinking about..." She glances at Ryan and Sun, who listen to us.

I laugh again. "Not right now. I just got to land, remember? I want to enjoy it."

She releases a breath. "It would be something, wouldn't it?" Her gaze flicks to Sun's again like he's the only one she wants to look at. I know she's referring to a double coupling ceremony, but she would never dare say it out loud yet. She clings desperately to her humanity, though I can already tell she's starting to shift her mind. "But enough talking about all this mushy far, far, extremely far in the future stuff and think about what's going to happen the rest of the day. No more water for you."

I link my fingers to Ryan's. "Definitely not. How about you and Sun finish up here, and we can all meet for dinner?"

"In something formal," she says.

I laugh. "Whatever you want."

She claps her hands. "Perfect." She grabs a bag from Sun. "Because I bought you both something to wear."

Ryan clears his throat.

Giselle holds out her hand. "No arguing. I've dressed so many merpeople that I can already judge your size, so I know it fits, and you'll look handsome. It's all settled. You guys owe me this."

"It might be fun," I say, running my hand along his arm.

"I suppose you're right, and it looks like Luna wants to, so we're in. Anything for my mate." The corners of his lips pull up, making me take a breath and appreciate how he's trying to do things the merpeople way. I know this whole mermaid thing is a lot for any normal human to handle. *But he's not normal. He's your intended mate.*

Giselle and I both sigh at the same time and then laugh. She'll never admit to loving romance and will be the first to roll her eyes, but I think she's coming around. She can't help it being around merpeople all the time.

Sun grins at Ryan and holds out his fist, and they bump them together.

"Oh, my God. I'm going to die if this turns into a romance competition," Giselle says.

"It's not a competition. It's life," Sun says. "And you love it."

She full on giggles. "You're right. Now come on. Time to hunt for a restaurant."

Sun strolls off with her, still holding her in his arms, and I watch them disappear into the Fisherman's Wharf.

Ryan chuckles, lacing his fingers with mine and watching them stroll away. He draws my attention back to him and away from the crowd. He studies my face for a long moment, and neither of us says anything, though I can see a dozen thoughts swirl through his eyes.

"I'm sorry for such a weird day. It's usually not like—"

Ryan kisses me, cutting off my words. I sink into him, devouring the interruption I had no idea I wanted and needed. The feeling of him gliding his hands over my wet hair and to my waist, pulling our bodies close enough that the water of my clothes soaks into his already drying shirt, sends my thoughts away from all the little things that make me feel like a land failure. I haven't scared Ryan away and it's important for me not to lose my heart to the sea while he's still here before me as a human on land.

"I know you think you made things weird for me, but I

wanted to make sure you know again that you didn't, Luna," he says, resting his head against mine. "If anything, you've helped me realize that you are right."

"I am?"

He chuckles. "You're this incredible gir—merm—" Pausing, he reaches up to push my hair from my face. "You're this incredible *being*, and I would be stupid to let something like an idea of how things are supposed to go in our relationship make me hesitate or pull back from what I feel right here."

He drops his hand to his chest and pats it. My breath catches, feeling the wave of emotions suddenly breaking from him to wash into me. It happens for a split second before I lose myself in my own emotions.

I knew what to expect from coupling. I knew we'd know each other on a deep emotional level with the ability to find each other no matter what. I knew our hearts would beat the same, our life essence together yet split between us. But what I didn't expect was to feel it as much as I do now, especially on land without Ryan transforming or the traditional ceremony we'd go through. I can only imagine how much more powerful it'll be.

And the way Ryan's eyebrows pucker tells me he might've felt what I did a second ago.

"Whoa," he whispers.

I kiss him. "I have to warn you. It gets more intense."

He embraces me tighter. "This might drive me crazy...in a good way."

I stand on my tiptoes and kiss him again, slipping my tongue over his until he releases a small moan from his throat. "It's supposed to," I whisper. "Wait until you can hear my thoughts."

Raising his eyebrows, he pulls away and chuckles. "You'll hear mine, too?"

I nod. "Why are you laughing?"

He flushes. "Because that's dangerous territory right now."

I release a small gasp, feeling his sudden desire wash over me, and I can't stop my body from reacting. "Oh," I whisper.

His Adam's apple bobs in his throat. "I think we need to get out of here."

"I think you're right."

17

COUPLING, COURTING, AND HUMAN DATING

"YOU'LL TELL ME IF I'm moving too fast," Ryan whispers into my neck, smelling of the citrus soap from the shower. "Because I need you to guide me through this. I don't want to mess up. I don't know how it works in the ocean or if... Am I getting ahead of myself?"

Heat washes over my collarbone as he trails kisses along the skin above my bikini top. "You're not. This is perfect. It's unheard of for mates not to get to know each other's bodies before a coupling ceremony, but you don't have to think about that."

Even though that's where my mind wanders since Giselle mentioned it. Because once the decision to couple is made, pretty instantly, it's basically the purpose of our simple life in the sea. It's so ingrained in me from my nature and sheltered existence that I can't stop myself from jumping all in.

"And how long is the whole mermaid courting process?" he asks, running his fingers over my stomach. "Sun said it's more of a tradition than anything and that merpeople already know they'll bond with whoever your essence draws you to."

"In the sea, anywhere from days to months. I've never known courting to last more than a year between two merpeople. It always happens on a full moon, too."

He turns his attention to my face. "And between a mermaid and human?"

I shrug. "However much time it takes to be certain for a human to want to give themselves completely to the sea, but even then—" I frown at the thought.

"What?"

"The sea has to choose you."

He blinks a few times, letting my thoughts settle into his mind. There are few human-born merpeople for several reasons—for one, not many merpeople have ventured to land until recently. And two, giving their last breath to their intended mate is scary for humans, and if they didn't, well, my mom created a sanctuary for humans for a reason. But things have changed. We're adapting and uniting the land and sea.

I brush my fingers into his hair as he shifts to rest his head on my chest, pressing his ear to my skin, listening to my heart. "You don't have to go through with anything," I add. "Apparently, my great-grandfather remained human. I didn't realize he was the reason my great-grandmother finished her life on land. My grandma finished her life on land, too. My mom grew up here, but she chose the sea. I never thought much about my pod, because they were gone before I was born. It's always been me and my dad until recently."

Thinking about the mermaids who came before me and ended up on land reminds me how lucky I am to be able to do so now. But I can't imagine it's easy to feel like your heart is apart from you while your mate remains on land. It's what kept drawing my grandmother and mother to land after my great-grandmother. Part of it was in their blood. I don't tell Ryan that my great-grandfather was the exception until recently. It doesn't matter now.

Ryan releases a small breath of air, tickling my skin. "I can't imagine not choosing to go through with it one day. The idea of exploring the ocean with you is a life I never knew I wanted until I realized it was a possibility."

My heart races. "Really?"

He turns and meets my eyes again. "It feels crazy saying this out loud because of how short of time I've known you, but I feel like if I don't, I'll regret it."

The whole world freezes around me at his words, and I hold my breath.

"I think I'm—" His eyes search my face, his brows

scrunched, his hand trembling against my stomach. "I'm falling in love with you."

"You're falling in love with me?" The words take me aback for a second.

Propping up on his elbow, he nods. "You sound surprised."

Because I am. I had prepared myself for the longest courtship in all of existence. I've been told hundreds of times not to get ahead of myself, that humans are different, that I shouldn't wear my heart on display and to be careful.

"I'm sorry," I say. "It was unexpected."

He chuckles. "Don't apologize. I caught you off guard."

"I just—" I close my mouth, not even knowing what to say. I didn't think it was possible for Ryan to admit to loving me so soon. I knew in my heart he was shifting his behavior to connect with me, but I had no idea he was throwing his human caution out to sea to truly be with me. And I'm conflicted on how to react, if I should throw my own caution with his to mingle together and open up completely to him. What if he changes his mind?

I push the thought away. Too many emotions run through me that I can't think a moment longer about things I'll never be able to control. I can't do anything but show him how much his words mean to me and pray to the ocean he'll treat me with care.

For Ryan, it's a risk I'm willing to take.

I kiss him instead of responding.

I kiss him with every one of the hot emotions pouring

through me, igniting my spark for him. He moans against my lips, his desire crashing into mine in a way I don't have to feel it radiating from him to know it's there. But the harder he kisses me, the faster his hands brush my skin, the more dominant the bond we've created flourishes, and our minds automatically open to each other as a response. The scattered images disappear in a fleeting moment as Ryan focuses solely on me in the present and me on him.

I caress my tongue to his, combing my fingers through his hair, our breaths blending in quick gasps. I've never felt like this, my body humming with warmth, and it's like everything suddenly makes sense, and I realize why merpeople couple so quickly. Because even glimpsing a tiny bit of Ryan's essence touching mine explodes a wave of pure love and happiness into my heart. It's something I know I can survive on if it's all I have left regardless of the land or sea.

Ryan rolls on top of me, deepening our kiss while sliding his hand under me to pull the tie on my bikini top. He hesitates and leans back, playing with the strings for a moment.

He slowly tugs my top off completely, his breath panting.

And for the first time, he looks at me. Not as the boy trying to suppress his attraction to me but as the mate who wants to drown in the desire I stir in him. I smile, reaching up to draw him closer. Something about how his eyes darken and light up at the same time, the way he releases a small breath, looking past my body to see me as his mate elicits indescribable, incredible feelings from my essence. I never want him to look at me any other way.

Tingles rush through my body, sending goosebumps over my skin that he kisses away inch by inch as he familiarizes himself with me in my human form.

His lips trail away from mine, working down my neck, making me gasp. I glide my fingers over his shoulders, down his back, and to his waist to pull his shirt over his head. Our bare stomachs touch, and feeling his skin against mine, his legs between mine, sets off a deep-seated need within me.

I freeze for a second, nervous I'll suddenly transform and ruin this moment, but the tingles rushing through me aren't the call of the ocean. It's Ryan. It's his human essence, his lust, his love all entangled inside him as I sink deeper into his kiss, wanting to get to know him on a level I never thought about until this moment. This far exceeds everything I thought I knew about coupling and courting, about human dating. I'm losing myself in unfamiliar territory, and it's exciting and terrifying at once.

I feel utterly and completely human.

"I love you," I whisper against his lips as he leans into me for another kiss, one that devours my words, stealing my breath away.

Ryan pulls back, his chest heaving, and he drinks in the sight of me again, trailing his fingers down to my bottoms. My heart thuds against my ribcage, threatening to launch itself at Ryan to set his heart aglow with my spark.

"Is this still okay?" he asks, leaning back down to kiss me.

I nod, my breath trembling with anticipation and nerves. "Mmmhmm."

Locking his gaze with mine to study my face, he says, "And this?" His question comes out a breathless, shaky whisper, reflecting my own nerves. He slows down, his fingers gliding over my bikini bottom ties without undressing me completely.

"You're nervous," I say, shifting so Ryan lies next to me. We face each other, laying on our sides close enough that my knees rest between his but far enough that I'd have to stretch to kiss him.

He releases a breath. "That obvious?"

I purse my lips, smirking. "It's okay. I'm nervous, too. I've only had legs for a few months now and haven't done anything like this before."

"Me either but not about the legs."

"Really?" I wish I could take back the word and hide my surprise. Giselle told me that unlike in the sea, some humans get to know each other on casual terms. She said they don't see someone and just know. I was prepared for the possibility that Ryan has been with other people, but I never thought much about it because he's with me. He looks at me like I'm the most amazing person in the world, and it's all that matters.

He smiles, releasing a whisper of a laugh. "Yeah. I grew up on a boat and not around a lot of people. I just—I want to take my time and make sure everything's perfect for you. I thought I knew what I was doing, but you're different."

I bite my bottom lip. "I'd like that. I know I'm a little

strange sometimes."

"You're not strange. You're honest and incredible and—I meant you're different in the best possible way. You're an adventure I'm enjoying every second being on." Ryan shifts, trailing his gaze and fingers along the curves of my body, gently yet purposefully.

I smile and slide my arms around him. "You sound like a merman, you know."

He chuckles. "Hopefully one day."

I smile against his mouth. "When you're ready."

He nods. "You'll be the first to know."

Giselle and Sun stroll in front of us down the cement walkway leading to a cute restaurant lit aglow in twinkling lights. Soft music hums from inside, and Ryan pulls me closer, digging his fingers into my hip just hard enough to make my skin buzz all over. He hasn't stopped touching me since we left the hotel, either hugging me or holding my hand, reminding me of how close mated couples act. It makes this feel more real and incredible than I could have ever imagined.

When our eyes meet, we both smile. Warmth blossoms from my chest to crawl up my neck at the memory of today. Things went from awful to amazing, and it'll only get better after dinner, because Ryan asked me to take him on a swim after hearing Giselle and Sun talk about it.

"You're smiling an awful lot," Giselle says, peering at me from over her shoulder.

Sun leans in and whispers something to her, and her eyes widen before she grins. She stops and spins, and Ryan pulls me back before I crash into her at her sudden change in direction. Giving me a once over, she narrows her eyes searching for something.

She glances at Sun. "How the hell can you tell?"

He chuckles. "Instinct, I guess."

"You merpeople and your superpowers," she says. "That's so weird and kind of creepy. Too much information."

Ryan scrunches his face and turns to me. "Am I missing something?"

Giselle laughs. "Apparently you've made things pretty official between you two."

Ryan blushes. "I don't even know how to respond. I—"

"You don't," I say, flicking Giselle. "Giselle's just being her human self."

"How else am I to act?" she asks, grinning. "This is something to celebrate, right?"

I didn't think Ryan's skin could deepen in color anymore. Reaching up, I brush my fingers along his jaw, smiling at him again.

"Well, I did make you that bracelet after you and Sun—"

She brings her hand up to her mouth, hiding her shock at the same time her whole face turns redder than Ryan's. He slides his arms around her waist from behind, grinning at me from over her shoulder.

"You knew? You said it was a gift just because," she says,

waving her hand to fan her face. She laughs again, her eyes widening. "I can't deal with you mermaids and all your weird traditions. Ava didn't—"

"Ava gave you that surfboard," I say, holding back my smile, though my eyes squint against my best effort to remain expressionless.

"You guys are—"

"The best friends ever?" I ask.

She tips her head back and laughs, her voice echoing through the night. Sun beams a smile at her and scoops her up to carry her away before she can say anything more to me. Ryan shifts next to me, staring at the side of my face as I remain in place and listen to Giselle's uncontrollable laughter trail off inside the restaurant.

"I'm sorry she embarrassed you," I say, turning to face him.

He rubs the back of his neck. "It was a little weird, yeah, but I'm glad to see that I'm not the only one still learning the merpeople way, to be honest."

I smile. "Giselle likes to pretend she's not getting swept out to sea by Sun, so I'm subtle with some of the traditions. I just can't ignore them."

"Like gift giving?" he asks. "Sun mentioned it. He offered to teach me to fish merman style."

I smother my laughter with my hand. "He thinks quite highly of you. I'd love to watch."

He chuckles. "Maybe some other time. I'm trying to impress you, not disappoint you when I can't wrangle a fish with my hands in the open water. I thought of something else, though." Reaching into his pocket, he pulls out something he keeps hidden in his palm. "I've been holding onto it since our first date."

I suck in a small breath. "You're giving me something?"

"It's tradition," he says, nodding, his whole face lighting up at the sudden happiness warming my heart at such a surprise.

"Oh, Ocean. It's tradition in the sea, not on land. I don't expect—"

He kisses me, cutting off my words. Because Ryan's given me the gift of himself, I didn't expect anything more. It's enough for any courting mates. "I don't have to be in the sea or a merman to sweep you away, you know."

Spinning me around, he motions for me to lift my hair from my neck. A cool stone rests between my breasts, and I pick it up to stare at the midnight blue piece of sea glass Ryan's wound with fishing line.

"It reminded me of you." He hugs me from behind. "A crescent moon the color of your eyes."

I smile at the necklace, watching blue light bounce across my chest from my flickering spark. "It's perfect."

"Like you."

I turn and slide my arms over his shoulders. "Thank you."

Ryan smiles, tucks my hair behind my ear, and then guides me toward the restaurant. Giselle and Sun wave from a table near a glass wall with a view of city lights sprinkled on the land on the other side of the bay.

A candle glows in the center of the white-clothed table, creating shadows across Giselle's smiling face. She twirls her finger in a circle, spotting the necklace Ryan made and pulls out her phone to snap a picture.

"Ava's going to be so excited," she says, grinning. "Maybe you'll both stop harassing me about—"

"I'll wait forever for you, my love," Sun says.

"Not forever," she says, resting her head on him. "Just not yet."

Ryan laces his fingers through mine under the table, listening to Giselle steer the conversation away from her and to what we should do tomorrow. Ryan mentions taking a tour boat to a place called Alcatraz, but Giselle shoots him down and says she spent last summer imprisoned on an island that she doesn't need the reminder with an island prison.

"Is it just me or is our server taking forever?" Giselle asks, shifting in her seat.

I peer around the busy restaurant. "It does seem longer than usual."

The sound of glass shattering silences most of the chatting patrons, and I turn my gaze in the direction of the kitchen. I squeeze Ryan's fingers, catching sight of a familiar feminine figure haloed in the light of a chandelier, waving her hands at a man in a bowtie.

"Oh, Ocean," I whisper. "That's Talia."

And she sees me. There's no doubt that she doesn't, because she narrows her eyes before turning back to the man.

Reaching behind her, she unties her apron and drops it at the man's feet, storming toward the front door of the restaurant.

"I'm so sorry about the wait," a blond woman says. "What can I get you to drink?"

Something comes over me, and I stand up and push back from the table before anyone can respond to the server. Ryan grabs my hand, but instead of trying to stop me, he gets to his feet.

"We'll be right back," he says.

"Luna, are you sure that's a good idea?" Giselle asks, knowing I want to follow my cousin.

I shrug. "I guess I'll find out."

Pulling Ryan with me, we rush from the restaurant and spot Talia strolling along the walkway in the direction of the private marina where she docks. It takes her getting to the corner to wait for a traffic signal before she turns around to see us.

"Before you accuse me of stalking you, I want you to know I wasn't," I say.

"Yeah. You just happened to pick the restaurant I work at—used to work at—to eat dinner, considering there are tons in this neighborhood," she snaps.

I hold my hands up. "I didn't pick it. I swear."

She shakes her head. "I can't do this. Please, leave me alone."

"Talia," I beg.

The crosswalk signal changes, and Talia runs away from us without stopping. She disappears around a corner, but instead of letting her go, I pull away from Ryan and start to chase her.

"Luna, stop," Ryan calls. "What you're doing is dangerous."

"I want to talk to her. The ocean wouldn't keep putting her in front of me like this for no reason." I head in the direction Talia disappeared, only stopping to kick off the heels Giselle made me wear with my dress.

An arm hooks around my waist, pulling me back, and I hit Ryan's chest. We both fall back, but he envelops me in his arms, taking the brunt of the fall onto him. He huffs, the wind knocking from his lungs. Rolling over to his side, he gently sets me next to him. If he didn't start coughing, I'd scramble to my feet to race away.

Tears burn my eyes. "I'm so sorry, Ryan. I didn't mean for you to get hurt."

He shakes his head, trying to catch his breath.

"And now you're bleeding." I reach for his arm to inspect the blood staining the sleeve of his light blue dress shirt.

"It's nothing," he manages to say.

"I'm sorry," I repeat. "I couldn't help myself. I need to talk to her."

"Not like this." He pulls me closer. "I'm sorry I had to stop you, but I promised I'd keep you safe on land, and you chasing her could've caused a whole lot of trouble."

I groan and rub my hands down my face. "I know I should give up, but—"

A scream rips through the air, cutting off my words. Ryan

glances to me and then to the direction Talia left in. My heart crashes against my ribcage, fear washing over me in an icy wave.

Another scream sounds out before a call for help.

And then silence.

18

SWEPT AWAY

"NO, NO, NO, NO, no," I say, taking the short staircase toward the stretch of beach lit by a yellow streetlamp that does nothing to light the area. I know I heard Talia's scream come from this way, and it only took seconds to get here. "Where is she?"

Ryan peers around the empty sand, tensing next to me. "Luna, when you said the ocean protects mermaids, what did you mean exactly?"

"I've seen the ocean capsize a boat, wash people right from the shore even, but—"

Ryan points his finger. "Look."

My breath catches as I jog closer to where he's pointing. Seawater drips down the steps a dozen feet away, running into the sand to disappear. This is a sign. The ocean snuck up on Talia, surprising her to drag her away like it did with me on my first date with Ryan. But this is different. Talia isn't a mermaid, and the ocean acted on my behalf against what I wanted. "Oh, no. Oh, Ocean."

I charge into the water deep enough to dive under and leave Ryan on shore. If the ocean swept Talia away, there's still a chance I can find her. I refuse to believe I came all this way only to have her taken before I even got the chance to talk to her—to make things right.

I don't believe Talia's a threat to the mermaid existence. If she were, she'd have been swept away long ago and not permitted to remain on land. But what if things are changing with her? Desperation makes people do dangerous and unthinkable things. My dad is proof. So is my mom. If only Talia had listened to me. The ocean wouldn't have forced her into the water to make her stop—to help me control her desperation.

At least, that's what I'm praying for. What the ocean does isn't always so apparent, but it's a force beyond anyone who wields ocean magic's control. If Ava were here, she could tame the waves. But I'm not Ava. I'm the daughter of a shunned king and a mermaid who gave up her ocean magic to help those on land. I'm just a mermaid who wants a union between my love of both. But my cousin? She's too afraid. The ocean doesn't take kindly to those who threaten the ones who protect it.

Peering around the blurry water, I search for a figure floating in the surf. I can't see anything in my human form that dulls all my mermaid senses, especially with the low visibility created by unnatural currents, making the ocean life scatter. I suck in a breath of saltwater, willing my body to react, arching through the spasms pulsing through my muscles. The cold water shifts warm as my body acclimates and my spark heats me from within, and I spin around to get a better view of the glowing sea.

I gasp in more water, my spark pulsing hard enough that I think it might try to escape me.

Ropes of kelp tangle around Talia's legs, trapping her in place, preventing her from swimming to the surface. She stares at me with wide eyes, though she wouldn't be able to see me in the dark current. Her fear of being stuck in the pitch blackness of the ocean I know she loves and fears at the same time is obvious on her scrunched face. Oxygen clings to her skin as she holds her breath, her lips fuller and puffy, but she doesn't move or thrash. Time ticks past a minute at least, yet she remains calm as she works on trying to break through the strands of kelp twisting around her in the whirlpool current.

I jet through the water, stirring up sand while cutting the kelp I pass with my sharp nails, sending it drifting away. Fish flee, darting out of my way, and I close the distance between me and Talia as fast as I can. The water shifts, the temperature cooling more than usual, and I flick my tail harder. But I can't swim any faster. Talia jerks her body, struggling amid the sea as she fights to hold her breath now as she starts suffocating instead of breathing in the sea. If she breathes, she'll drown, and her body is about to make her open her mouth for a breath that won't come in the form she needs.

I fight the current flowing toward me, trying to keep me away from my cousin. No matter how hard I swim, I can't get close enough. The ocean's preventing me from closing the space, warning me to stay away.

My mind whirls with prayers to the ocean, to the land, to anything willing to listen as I fail to save my only familial bond outside my dad. Seconds drift away from me in the current, but I don't give up swimming. I flick my tail to push me harder.

"I won't leave her!" I scream to the ocean, sending my thoughts out in a loud burst I'm sure all the merpeople in the sea heard.

My spark flickers through the water in bursts of light until it shines so brightly it puts a spotlight on my cousin before me. The light radiating from my chest dims, and despair washes over me in an icy waterfall, leaving me freezing in my mermaid form. Talia stops moving, her body slackening enough that the whirlpool sways her around. I stare at her shining eyes in the water, and all I can think about are the small bubbles drifting from her nose and mouth to trickle to the surface.

"Talia!" I scream, my voice muted in the water as I try to say the words out loud.

Her body jerks once more, her saucer eyes darting to mine, and I know she can see me. She outstretches her hand, the ocean swirling her midnight hair around her head.

And then she releases her last breath.

I scream again, sending small bubbles scattering. Talia droops forward, her outstretched hand drifting back.

The current keeping me away from her calms, and I suddenly fly forward through the bay. I swim in circles around her, cutting the kelp ropes from her legs and arms, and her body floats a few feet away to sink lower into the water toward the bottom.

I close the distance between us, panic clenching my chest. "Talia." I don't say the words out loud. Instead, I project them from my mind and into the sea. "Please, don't leave me."

But I'm too late. Her vibrant blue eyes no longer shine with life.

She's gone.

"Please, no," I say, praying to the ocean. "How could you? You didn't give me enough of a chance. I thought you wanted me on land? I don't understand."

The ocean doesn't respond. It doesn't give me a sign or the answers I seek.

Something comes over me, my spark flickering in quick successions, lighting the bay around us again instead of dimming with my grief. I cup my cousin's face between my hands, both our dark hair veiling the sea between us. As I stare at her body, feel the bond we have through blood, the anchor she creates that draws me to land like the mermaids before me, I realize I can't let her go. I can't allow the ocean to take her from me no matter the reason. Our bond will not be severed.

Leaning forward, I press my lips to hers, willing with everything inside me that I can bring life back to her and share my breath, give her the spark in my chest, use my very essence to keep her with me. Heat travels through me, trailing from my heart and up my throat, warming my lips.

But as quickly as the sensation courses through my body, it disappears. And with it, the ocean sweeps us in a new current, breaking us apart. The water jerks my body, and I grab onto strands of kelp to stop myself from getting swept back to sea, the ocean bashing at me in hot waves.

All I can do is wait out the rough waters that keep me in place—a sea now angry I tried to give up part of my life to save someone not intended for me.

My eyes burn, though my tears blend with the saltwater around me. Talia's body disappears, and I grip the kelp in shock, my chest heaving, my spark still blinking so quickly the water around me flashes.

It feels like an hour passes before the current settles, but it couldn't have been more than seconds, just long enough for the sea to take the only family I have left apart from my dad from me. Maybe a union between the land and sea isn't part of the ocean's plan. I wasn't chosen for such a life like Ava and Carter. If I had been, I'd wield the magic of my parents. Instead, I've been gifted with the ability to navigate all the oceans, create everything the colonies need in the water. Maybe it was wrong of me ever to emerge.

But then I'd have never found Ryan.

"What do you want from me?" I think to the sea, begging it to give me the answers it keeps denying me. Answers it only ever gives in strange signs I can no longer decipher.

I pop up to the surface, expelling the sea from my lungs, needing air instead of water to clear my head. A sob rips from me, ringing through the night, and I cover my mouth with my hand, afraid someone might hear my cries. I swim a few feet on the surface in the direction of the shore.

But I'm afraid to go back, afraid to face Ryan. Because I'm so confused and conflicted. I was prepared to give up my one chance to transform a human on someone who wouldn't even give me a minute to explain myself. I was willing to give up my one opportunity to couple with the boy of my dreams, my perfect mate, everything—all for a moment longer with my cousin.

In that split second, I would've ruined everything.

And the part that gets to me the most is that I don't regret it. I'd try all over again. I'd try harder. I'd make the ocean give me my cousin no matter the consequences it'd have on my life and being. I'd bind myself to someone who might hate me for turning her into something she's spent all her life fearing just to give her the chance to live. I'd figure out how to make a life on land work with Ryan even if it means I'd have to renounce my mermaid essence to do so. Because I can't live a life split and torn in between. I can't.

I suck in a breath of sea air and pull myself together. Turning my gaze to the beach, I spot Ryan kneeling in the sand.

He's not alone.

I sink back under, flicking my tail, swimming as fast as I can. I don't even stop to transform. Using the cresting wave, I slide up into the sand in my mermaid form. Ryan performs chest compressions on Talia, counting under his breath, only pausing to lower his head to listen to see if she's breathing.

I sniffle and touch his shoulder. "The ocean took her."

Ryan begins chest compressions again without looking at me. "And we're taking her back. Why else would she wash right onto the beach at my feet?"

"I already tried to sa—"

Talia jerks and Ryan shifts her as she throws up seawater, clearing her lungs. She heaves a breath, a sound I never thought could be so beautiful, and coughs some more.

"Talia? Talia? Can you hear me?" I ask.

"Try to keep her conscious," Ryan says. "I'm getting help."

He rushes up the steps, and I hold Talia in my arms, fanning my caudal fin to stop the waves from crashing over us. I push the hair from her face and release a heaving breath against her shoulder, my heart breaking and coming together at once. I hug her to me, whispering silent thanks to Ryan, who I had no idea had the capabilities of a healer. I relish in feeling Talia so close. I can feel the familial bond between us with everything in my being.

Her eyes roll for a moment before she focuses on me, puffing her lips as she breathes a dozen breaths I've never been so grateful for. A tear trickles down my cheek with the seawater dripping from my hair, and a stream splashes her forehead, making her blink. She gasps over and over, catching her breath, but doesn't say anything.

"I'm so sorry, Talia. I didn't mean for this to happen. I just—" I sniffle and wipe my face with my arm. "It was a mistake coming here. I should've listened to you and left. Your life would've never been put in danger, but I was selfish. I wanted so badly to get to know you. You're my family."

"You haven't changed since I was a little girl, Celestiana," she whispers. "But you said you'd never come back because of the king. Was this his doing? Did you lead him to me because you couldn't stay away? You told me what could happen if you didn't. Why put me at risk again? You know what the king did to my father."

I blink, hearing her say my mom's name while speaking of my dad. "You knew my mom?"

Sirens ring in the distance, drawing my attention away from Talia. Panic washes over me because I'm still in my mermaid form where anyone could come running up to see me at any time. I wouldn't put it past the ocean to sweep more people away.

"Luna! Luna, we have to go," Ryan says, kicking up sand as he runs to me. He bends forward to move Talia into the sand. "An ambulance is on the way."

I frown. "I can't leave her."

"Even if you transform back into a human, they'll ask too many questions. Your dress is ripped. You're bleeding," he says.

Talia inhales another breath. "Go."

I release a low sob, my chest aching, everything in me hurting at having to leave, but Ryan's right. I can't stay. I can't draw attention to myself. I can't risk Talia coming to her senses and accusing me of stalking her and nearly drowning her—even if it was the ocean—it still did it because of me.

Ryan scoops me into his arms, hoisting me up the best he can with my heavy tail. The sirens grow louder, and flashing lights cut through the night. Ryan submerges me in water deep enough that I can swim myself back into the surf.

With one more look over my shoulder at Talia, I take Ryan's hand and dive into a wave with him, swimming us away. We break the surface together far enough from shore that someone would need a spotlight to notice us.

Ryan hugs me. "She's going to be okay."

I lick my salty lips and swallow. "I hope so."

"She is."

If only I could say the same thing about me.

19

PERFECTLY CLEAR

GISELLE AND SUN WAIT outside the hotel. Sun leans his back on the red bricks while Giselle paces in circles, wringing her hands together. Water drips from my ripped dress, now covered by Ryan's dress shirt, leaving him in a white T-shirt with his slacks. Ryan carries both of our shoes in one hand and holds me with the other like I'll sink to the ground at any second, which I might.

"Oh, God. What the hell happened? We went looking for you. It was total chaos on the beach."

I hang my head, letting my tangled hair shield me. "I nearly cost my cousin her life. Ryan saved her and called an ambulance to make sure she was okay."

On the way back to the room, I spill my heart to Giselle. Sun and Ryan listen as I cry through my words, skipping over how I tried to change Talia to save her, but the ocean wouldn't let me. It hurts to even think about, especially with the way Ryan looks at me now.

"I want to go to the hospital and make sure she's okay," I say.

Ryan and Giselle look at each other, but it's Sun who says, "Princess Luna, that isn't wise. Allow me to look in on Talia. She doesn't know who I am or that I'm a merman. I'll be quick."

Giselle reaches out and grabs my hand. "I'll go with him. We won't talk to her or anything. It might be too much for her after what you've told me."

I can only nod. "I'm going to write her a letter to leave with the security guard in the morning. After that, I think we should go."

Nodding, Giselle says, "How about we finish spring break in LA with Sapphire? Go to Hollywood. Check out the beaches there? Maybe we can go to the OC and visit Disneyland. You can meet another mermaid princess."

I smile, a laugh escaping my lips at the thought. "I'd like that."

Giselle and Sun exit our room, leaving me with Ryan. He tugs me toward the bathroom, hugging me from behind, and instead of turning on the shower, he fills the spa tub, adding in a miniature bottle of soap until bubbles nearly spill over the side.

"So, can a mermaid survive in a bubble bath? Yes or no?" he asks, trying to shift my mind away from the events of the night.

I laugh. "I've never had one, but I don't think it'd be possible unless you dragged me from the sea. Even then, I don't think I could just lay there. Confined spaces drive me crazy. I once spent the night in a sea cave and—"

"Human in the tub it is," he says, smirking while unzipping the back of my dress.

Sliding it off my shoulders, he trails his hands along my sides, pulling it down until it drops to the floor. He shifts my hair off my neck to kiss my shoulder, pressing his damp shirt into my back for a minute.

I turn in his arms. "I like this kind of distraction."

He grins and meets me for a kiss, still tasting of the sea. "As much as I want to continue to distract you, I also want to take care of the cuts on your arms and legs. They look like they hurt."

I shrug. "I'll heal in a few hours."

"Well, until you do, I'm taking care of you." He kisses me once more and spins me back toward the tub and helps me in.

I last all of five minutes, because even though the water smells amazing, and the warmth eases the aches blossoming on my bruised skin from rushing onto shore in my mermaid form, it feels confining. I like the shower because I'm not submerged.

But the tub? It makes me want to swim.

And I'm furious with the ocean.

Getting out of the tub, I dry off with a towel and wrap myself in the fluffy robe hanging on the door. I pad across the cool tiles and into the room, where Ryan left his wet clothes in a heap on the floor. He's gone downstairs in search of bandages.

I stroll to the balcony and push open the curtains to look at the twinkling lights of the city sprinkled on the land in the distance from across the bay. Light traffic sets the street below aglow, and I watch a few people strolling along, enjoying their night.

Stepping outside, I suck in a breath of fresh air and shiver as it dries my damp hair. The hum of the city mutes the sounds of the bay, and I close my eyes for a moment to focus on the human world and all the cacophonous noise that comes with it. Unlike the quiet of the sea, the land wraps me in excitement and wonder instead of the calm I've lived in all my life.

A car honks, drawing my attention to the street below. I frown at the sight of a line of vehicles swerving around a black sedan idling in the lane instead of pulling into the hotel valet to park. A guy stands in the street next to the car, pointing into the passenger's side window. Fear creeps into me, and I can't believe what I see. Ryan steps back from the car, shaking his head, and then peers up at the building.

Our eyes meet, and a frown tilts Ryan's lips downward. A cop car flashes its lights from down the block, and then the car peels off, speeding away to cut down another street to disappear. The now heavy traffic prevents the cop from going after whoever was in the car, and Ryan's already gone from the sidewalk.

As if my night couldn't get any worse. Something about the car, about how Ryan looked at me, sends alarm bells ringing in my mind. I've been so distracted by my own personal matters with Talia that I haven't thought much about Ryan's.

And now I feel guilty.

The door to the room beeps, but I remain on the balcony, staring off into the night. I listen to Ryan move around the room for a minute without calling out to me. As much as I want to run inside and ask him what that was all about, I keep my mouth shut and my hands firmly gripping the rail.

Ryan comes up behind me, caging me against the balcony to rest his chin on my shoulder. "Why aren't you storming to me to find out what's going on?"

"Because I figured you'd tell me," I say. "It was obvious you weren't buying a first aid kit from some random person on the street."

He tugs me from the balcony and guides me back into the room. "The concierge had one along with a message for me. Sorry I didn't come right back. I thought you'd be in the tub longer and didn't want you to worry."

I remain expressionless. "I realized I hate baths."

Releasing a small breath, he slides his hands around my waist and buries his face into the soft fabric of the robe. "I should've figured."

Ryan falls silent, still hugging me, and I let him until I can't handle the silence anymore. I pull him toward the chair at a small table, and he sits down, pulling me into his lap. I hang my legs over the armrest, letting him trail his fingers over the still bleeding scrapes on my skin.

"Was that your dad?" I ask, finally relenting to one of the million questions in my mind.

Ryan hums his confirmation while cleaning one of my cuts before sticking a bandage on it. "Same old stuff. He wants me to come home."

I frown. "He was supposed to leave you alone."

Ryan sighs. "I know. It's complicated."

"Maybe we've gone about this all wrong with him. He's your dad. It's a bond you can't deny no matter how much you want to," I say. I should know. I'm embarrassed by my dad's actions when he was king, but I still love him.

"He's—" Ryan shifts me on his lap to gaze into my eyes. "I don't even know how to explain him to you except that he's probably someone the ocean would wash away."

"So did he want anything else besides asking you to come home?" I ask. "I can find another pearl if it'll make him happy."

He presses his lips together. "No way, Luna. It'll make it worse. He already wants to meet you. But that's not happening. We'll be out of here in the morning."

"Maybe I should meet him," I say. "You're my mate, and when we make things official one day, he'll be my family. Even if you two don't see things on the same page, I'll inherit your bond."

"Really?"

I nod. "You'll inherit mine, too."

"Kind of like in-laws."

"I think it's a little different."

"I still don't think it's a good idea," he says. "I promised to protect you on land, and my dad is—"

The landline on the dresser rings, startling us, and I get up from his lap to answer it, motioning for him to hold his thought. He automatically follows me, like he doesn't want even a foot of space between us.

"Hello?" I ask into the line.

Ryan leans closer to listen.

"I think Talia refused care," Giselle says on the other line. "She's not here."

"What?" I ask.

She breathes into the phone. "Yeah, she's not on record anywhere. I called around for any near-drowning victims."

"She must've gone home," I say. "I think I'll head over there."

"We'll meet you," Giselle says. "And remind me to get you a new phone in the morning."

"Okay."

I hang up the phone and turn to Ryan, meeting his cute pouty face. Reaching up, I run my fingers along the scruff on his cheek. He covers my hand with his to press my fingers deeper into his skin.

"As soon as we check on Talia, we'll figure out the situation with your dad," I say. "Maybe we can leave the rental car here and swim to another city to get a new one. Instead of LA, I can take you to an island for a few days where no one can find you and make him think we've vanished."

It's not ideal, but it might help get Ryan's dad to back off. We can wait things out until Ava and Carter return. Because I don't know how else to handle his father, and I don't want to risk him causing problems.

He smiles at me, the frown vanishing with my words. "A deserted island?"

"Semi-deserted. My dad lives there with a few others."

"So, instead of meeting my dad, I'll meet your dad?" he asks, smirking. "Should I be worried?"

"He can no longer summon the sea, so no. He can't leave the island, either. It's big enough that you wouldn't have to see him if you didn't want to."

"I honestly don't know if I do."

"I understand. I'm the only one who ever does."

Grabbing my bikini from my bag, I drop the conversation with my robe, and Ryan's smirk shifts as desire crosses his face. I smile at him, turning away to pull my sundress over my head, even though the temperature has dropped since dinner.

"I'm officially looking forward to this island getaway with you," he says, offering me one of his hoodies.

I slide it over my head, smelling the scent of the citrus body wash. "It's not exactly luxurious. It's a simple lifestyle, living on the land, though it's come a long way. Merpeople are fast learners and have built a nice community."

"Still sounds like an adventure," he says, kissing me sweetly.

I never thought taking Ryan to Celestiana Cove was something I wanted until now. "I can't wait."

"Maybe we can leave after you see Talia tonight."

"I need the night to prepare," I say. "I can only handle a short swim with you, so we need a boat and some supplies. I also wanted to write my letter to Talia. I'll do it when we get back from checking on her. I don't want to waste time doing it now."

"Okay," he says, hugging me, releasing a shaky breath.

I meet his gaze. "Are you sure about all this? You look nervous."

He nods. "I'm not nervous about leaving with you. It's staying. It's—let's just go."

"We're going to be fine, okay? Trust me." Out of everything in the world, it's the one thing I'm certain of.

"I do trust you. It's the rest of the world I worry about."

"It's a good thing we can handle the rest of the world. You have the land. I have the sea. We have each other."

Ryan pulls me to the door, stopping in front of it to look at me once more. "I love you, you know."

I smile. Because his love is now perfectly clear. "And I love you."

20

LIFE ISN'T FAIR

"TALIA'S BOAT IS GONE," I say, tugging Ryan with me as I close the space to the fence keeping us from the dock. "Think she went out to cruise the bay and will be back?" I don't know why I ask. Seems doubtful after what happened.

He runs his fingers through his hair, pushing it out of his face. "I'd think that's the last place she'd want to be after tonight." I hate that he voices my doubts aloud.

Fear sneaks into my heart, tightening my chest with each breath. "No, being here is. I think she left because of me."

I turn away from the dock and cover my face with my hands. I was afraid this would happen. I knew it was a possibility. But I was hoping I'd have more time to try to talk some sense into her. To tell her I'd leave her alone. I wanted to lay my heart out for her the best I could and let her decide if she wanted to see me, knowing things have changed in the sea, but after the ocean swept her away, I'm not so sure she'd believe me. I'm not so sure things have actually changed. My dad controlled the ocean with his magic before he lost it, but the ocean is now free. And the sea is a force I can't control, not that I'd want to.

Ryan stares at the dark bay beyond the docks. "We can try to track her boat. She can't be far."

"If she left the bay, it might be impossible unless the ocean wanted us to reunite. And even then..."

"We'll scare her," he says, finishing my thought for me. "So, we have to approach things a different way. A human way."

I scrunch my face. "I don't know how to do that."

"Good thing I do." Lacing his fingers through mine, he pulls me down the block and toward the pathway that'll lead to the beach. "Unless Talia has a ton of money, which I'm not so sure she does since she was working two jobs, she's going to need to at least contact her employer for her last check. We can give them the letter for her."

My sadness floats out to sea with his idea. "You think it'd work?"

He shrugs. "Doesn't hurt to try."

I release a small cry of joy, flinging my arms around Ryan to bury my face in his chest. He chuckles into my hair, squeezing me tighter to him. He slides his hand past my waist and lifts me up, so I wrap my legs around him. He strolls forward without letting me go, still laughing as I shower his neck with kisses.

"Are you still up for that swim?" Ryan asks, kicking through the sand and toward the water. "Or we could go back to the room and..."

I inhale a breath of the salty air, smiling at him. "We could do both, but we'll have to go back for your wetsuit."

He kisses me. "You'll keep me warm."

I laugh as he splashes into the water, letting me take his shirt off along the way. Goosebumps prickle over his skin, and I brush my lips across his bare shoulder, kissing his skin and making him tremble.

"You sure?" I ask, rubbing my hands on his arms. "You're shivering."

"Not because of the cold," he whispers. "Sort of."

Strolling us deeper, he shifts my weight to one of his arms and uses his free hand to untie the bottoms of my bikini. I pull my dress over my head, wrapping it around my arm with his shirt, and he inhales a long, shuddering breath when I press my skin to his.

I hold his face in my hands, kissing him long enough to make him moan. "Take a deep breath."

He fills his lungs with the cold air and jumps back, taking us both underwater. I hook my arms around his sides, inhaling a breath of the sea to transform. His hands slide down my back, brushing my short fin until he reaches the ridge between my skin and scales and back up again.

I flick us both to the surface, and Ryan kisses me the second I take a breath of air. His mind opens to me, and a dozen images of myself flash through my mind. It's strange seeing how I look to him in his mind compared to how I see myself. It's a spark-lighting rush that makes me kiss him harder.

"Princess Luna." A familiar voice trickles into my mind, drawing my attention away from Ryan's lips.

Slowly pulling away, I meet Ryan's face lit in the silver moonlight shining above us. "I forgot we were meeting Giselle and Sun at the docks."

He chuckles. "Whoops."

"Princess Luna," Sun calls again. "I'm coming up to you now."

I squeeze Ryan tighter, holding him in place, and a wave of water crashes over us. Ryan startles, but I don't let him get far, swimming with him. Sun spits water next to me, and Giselle heaves a breath, releasing a small scream.

"Oh, crap that was fast," she says, hugging onto Sun while burying her face in his neck.

Sun chuckles and kisses Giselle's cheek. "I'm sorry, my love, but we're in a hurry." Sun turns to me. "We saw Talia set sail and followed her out of the bay. I can take you to her."

I shake my head and tell them about our plan. "I don't want to make things worse."

Giselle frowns. "Your plan won't work. Sun said she removed something from a lobster trap that wasn't dinner."

"What?"

"Come on. We can take you, princess. We don't have to contact her, but you should see things for yourself." Sun motions for us to swim.

Ryan nods to me. "You might regret it if you don't."

He's right. I know I will. This whole trip was about finding and meeting my land family. If I've scared Talia so much that she's pulling what I think she is from the sea, then it means she won't reach out to her human ties. She plans to disappear.

"I will swim us, Princess Luna," Sun says.

Giselle groans. "Oh, jeez. Brace yourself, Ryan, and hold on tight. My boyfriend is a swimming maniac."

I spin in the water and situate Ryan on my back, linking our hands together. "I won't let you go. I promise."

He rests his chin on the crook of my neck. "I know."

Sun slides his arm through mine, linking us together, and he turns to Ryan. "Keep your cheek against Luna's back and tilt your chin toward your chest or else you'll get water in your nose."

Ryan does as Sun says.

"Take a deep breath," I say.

At the sound of both Ryan and Giselle taking a breath, I dive under with Sun. I flick my tail, matching his speed solely because he's tugging me with him. The glowing sea blurs around us, and dozens of fish scatter.

Ryan's fingers tighten around mine, and I concentrate on the beating of his heart as it slows with him getting used to the sudden acceleration of Sun's powerful tail. After a minute, Sun swims us toward the surface, and we breach together instead of letting go of our mates, only giving them a few seconds to gasp another breath. It's a risky move, but if anyone saw from the surface, it'd have been too dark and fast to have gotten a good enough look—not like they'd automatically assume merpeople.

We reach the open sea in half the time it would have taken me to swim alone, and Sun swims us toward the surface, slowing to break through instead of breaching. He lets go of my arm, and I let go of Ryan only to swim a circle around him to pop up, facing him.

He heaves a breath, treading water, and I slide my arms around his waist, fanning my tail to keep his head above water. His mouth hangs open, and water drips from his hair and into his eyes, making him blink.

I rub my hands up and down his back. "You okay?"

Panting, he says, "A little dizzy, but that was awesome and scary as hell."

"It's better in the day," Giselle says, still gasping.

A splash sounds through the quiet ocean air, and I spin around while still holding Ryan, in the direction the noise came from. From over his shoulder, I spot Talia's boat floating a few hundred feet away, its anchor keeping it in place in the midnight waters.

I swim us a few dozen feet closer. Sun remains by my side with Giselle still clinging to his broad, muscular back. Bubbles pop along the surface near the boat, and I sink under without

Ryan.

A bright light glows in the water, drawing my attention to a scuba diver swimming through the ocean in the direction of a cluster of underwater rocks. Talia holds a spear gun in her hands, along with a flashlight.

I almost can't believe what I'm seeing. For being afraid of merpeople, she's incredibly brave to face the night ocean alone, which means whatever she's searching for is important enough for her to risk her safety.

I break the surface again and spit out water. "Talia's in the water looking for something."

"You should go to her, princess," Sun says. "She won't see you."

"I don't think the ocean will hide me from her, and if she happens to see me, I'm afraid of what will happen. She's armed."

"Armed?" Giselle asks. "What the hell is she doing?"

"Protecting herself," I say. "And I can't blame her."

"So, what do you want to do?" Ryan asks, peering from the boat to me.

I dip under again, listening to my heart beating through the muted water. I inhale another breath of the ocean and watch Talia's light in the distance. Popping back up, I meet the others' gazes. "Would it be crazy if I said we should board? I'll write her something quick and hope for the best. We could be gone before she gets back."

"Or we could wait for her," Ryan says.

"Now that's crazy," I say.

"Is it?" he asks. "Talia's afraid because she knows the merpeople secret, right?"

Hair hangs in my face, and I tilt my head back and let the sea pull it from my forehead to spill behind me. I think about his question for a moment without answering him.

"It wasn't safe for humans before," Sun says, answering for me.

"But it is now," I say. "Only those worthy learn our secret."

"Like me and Giselle," Ryan says.

"Among others," I say. "Which means..." A smile crosses my face, knowing exactly what he's thinking because I'm thinking it too. I've been trying so hard to talk to Talia and to tell her that times have changed, but I should've been focusing on trying to show her.

And I can do that right now.

I close the space to Ryan, meeting him for a kiss. His legs graze my tail, and he breathes against my lips, a smile lighting his whole face under the moon. He hugs me tighter, absorbing the warmth from my skin, just feeling me against him.

"Will you come with us?" I ask Sun and Giselle. "I think it'll be better with you."

Giselle nods. "Anything to get me out of this freezing water."

Sun flips her over his shoulder, pulling her into his arms to hug her against him. With a nod to me, he whispers something in her ear that makes her smile, and they sink under to swim ahead of us toward the boat.

I meet Ryan's green eyes. "Ready?"

He sucks in a deep breath in response, and I dive us under to close the distance to the boat. Sun's already helping Giselle up the small rung ladder from his merman form, and then he sinks back under to transform into a human. Giselle drops something into the water, and Sun emerges wearing underwear instead of the slacks he wore to dinner.

Giselle smiles at Sun as he closes the space between them. "We should do more spontaneous swimming," I hear her tell him before I dip under to transform into a human.

Ryan swims with me to the boat, and Sun reaches down and helps me up first. Ryan follows behind me, and Giselle emerges from the stairs leading to the saloon with a handful of towels she found.

"She has plenty more," Giselle says, shrugging at my frown.

I dry off and wrap the towel around me, keeping my eyes trained toward the water. The glowing ocean remains lifeless around the boat, the fish and other marine life keeping their distance from the commotion caused by us splashing to climb aboard.

Ryan comes up behind me, resting his chin on my shoulder to peer into the water. He points in the distance, catching sight of Talia's flashlight. "I think it'll be better if we wait inside. The last thing we want is for her to attack first if she sees us."

Linking his fingers through mine, he tugs me to the short ladder that'll take us into the boat. I hesitate when we get inside, staring at the small galley to the right with a few dishes in a drying rack. Warm woods and navy blue furnishings decorate the saloon. A queen-sized bed sits up on a platform with the privacy curtain pulled open. Giselle and Sun sit on their towels at a table containing a spread out map with circles and navigation coordinates written in pen on it.

"I think this is a treasure map," Giselle says.

My breath catches, and I step forward to look at Giselle's discovery. She's right. And it's not only this spot marked on—there are at least two dozen more spots scattered across all the oceans. My legs shake, and I rest my palms on the table. My fingers brush against something under the map, and I lift up the edge and spot a dozen envelopes all addressed to Talia, now yellowed with age.

"These are letters," I say, gently picking an envelope up to pull out a sheet of crinkled folded paper.

"Your cousin's a treasure hunter like you," Ryan says from behind me. "Come look at this."

I set the letter down and turn to see Ryan digging through a bag by the door. Seawater pools around it, and he holds up a glittering necklace in the soft light. And I recognize it.

I've made dozens of similar ones over the years using beads I've made from sea glass and other interesting pebbles and pearls I've found. I learned the weave of fishing line from studying one of the necklaces my mom left behind when she fled Pearlestria. Except the necklace Ryan holds isn't one of mine. I've never seen it before.

"That belongs to our lost queen," Sun says, shifting out of his seat to inspect the necklace more closely. "I remember it from a Winter Solstice when I was a merbabe. I liked how the silver pendant matched the queen's tail."

"Oh, Ocean," I whisper. "I don't understand."

Giselle clears her throat from behind me. "Luna, it was a gift to Talia from your mom."

I grimace. "But—"

"All these letters are from Celestiana," she adds, cutting me off.

My head swims with both awe and heartache, seeing unfamiliar writing scrawled across brittle pages. This is the first time I've seen something from my mom created by her in a form I've only seen in glimpses through other people's memories.

I've never known her as a human, doing human things, and something about seeing all the letters, the maps, these memories I'll never know of, brings uncontrollable tears to my eyes—ones of both happiness and sadness.

"I'm sorry," I say, wiping my face with my hands. "I don't mean to cry. I'm just—how can I feel so conflicted. Look at everything my mom did for my cousin, and Talia won't even give me a minute to explain myself. This isn't fair."

Ryan and Giselle rush to my sides. They both hug me at the same time, and I can't stop the small sob from escaping my mouth.

"We're going to figure this out," Giselle says, petting my wet hair. "Talia will—"

"No!" Sun yells.

Ryan slams into me and Giselle, knocking us over, and we spill to the floor. The boat lifts and drops on a swell, sending my stomach crashing into my chest. Something thuds into the wall behind where we were standing, and a feminine voice screams as the boat rocks again.

I scramble to my feet, gripping the wall to face Talia holding onto the ladder leading up with one hand. She squeezes a metal spear in her other hand, aiming it at us. The noise I heard was her chucking the gun itself in our direction.

"Talia, stop!" I scream. "I'm not going to hurt you. I've had enough of you treating me like I'm some monster."

"You are!" she yells back. "Attilonious would've never followed you tonight had you just given up on whatever idea you thought you had. You're the reason my dad is dead."

"I—"

She shakes her head. "Don't even say it. Apologies didn't work then and they still won't. I'm only getting this stuff now because you've messed up my whole life all over again, and I don't know what to do. So you and your pod need to leave. I mean it. I'll—"

The boat rocks again on another swell, and Talia screeches, clutching the ladder tighter. Ryan grabs my wrist, stopping me from tumbling forward and into my cousin. Her fury runs so hotly through her, it's palpable. It makes me step back into Ryan's arms.

"You're going to get me killed," she snaps.

I take a small step forward. "I won't."

She waves the spear. "Everyone I love is dead because of merpeople."

"I'm sorry. I—"

Talia yells, startling me. I don't even have a second to react before she launches at me with the spear. Her ocean eyes meet mine, her whole face contorting with anger, and I brace myself.

Talia screams again.

21

START OVER

THE BOAT RISES ON another swell, knocking Talia sideways. The spear scratches my side with the motion, and I jerk back. I crash into Ryan as Talia falls on top of me, squishing me between them with the force of her weight. My breath heaves from my lungs, sending tears to my eyes. I snatch her wrist, digging my nails into her skin to make her drop the spear before she tries again to impale me.

Sun scoops Talia off me, locking her in his arms only long enough to get her away. She drops to her knees and releases another yell, searching the ground for anything she can use against me.

"Stop, Talia! Listen to me. My name is Luna. I'm not Celestiana or here to hurt you," I say.

"Then why are you here? Why risk my life?" she asks through an angry breath.

"Because you're my family. I've been on land for only a few months, and when I heard that I had a cousin, I—I've been dying to meet you. I had no idea my mom had familial ties to the land. She kept it from everyone."

"She's why I'm alone."

"Things have changed. My dad—"

"You're the king's daughter?" Talia's voice rises through the room.

"He's not my king," Sun says, stepping closer. He's ready to restrain Talia if she tries anything again.

I hold my hand out to him. "He's right. My dad has been shunned and ripped of his magic. My mom renounced the sea and—" Tears burn my eyes again. "You're my family, Talia. I would never let anyone hurt you. Please, let me explain, and if you still want me to leave, then I'll go."

"And them?" She points at the others.

"These are my friends," I say, pointing to Giselle and Sun. "And Ryan's my intended mate. He's human like you. So is Giselle. You have to believe me when I say that you're not in any danger. We're trying to unite the sea and land to help the ocean and our colonies."

The rocky current calms, the ocean no longer rising and falling with the waves, and I pull away from Ryan to close the distance between me and Talia. She covers her mouth with her hand, worry lines scrunching her forehead with a dozen thoughts. She finally relaxes her tense muscles and looks at me, trailing her gaze from my damp hair to my bare feet.

Sitting on the floor, she pulls her knees to her chest, wrapping her arms around herself. "This is a lot to take in. I've spent all my life fearing merpeople."

"Yet you haven't left the coast?" Ryan asks, touching his damp towel to the bleeding scratch on my side.

"I've tried many times, but something keeps drawing me back," she admits. "And I wasn't going to let some nightmare from my childhood ruin the place I love."

I shift on my feet. "I don't know what to say. I know there's nothing I can do now to make up for everything that happened to you, but I'd like to be here for you. Get to know you if you'd let me. My great-grandfather was Charles. I have a picture but it's at the hotel. It's how we're related."

"I know who Charles Torres is. My dad was named after him," she says.

"He was?"

Talia slowly gets to her feet and crosses the room, keeping her eyes on everyone while she shuffles to a storage cabinet above her bed. She reaches in and pulls out a leather book tied closed with string. Unwinding it, she flips the book open to the middle and reads over it.

"This was his journal. Dad thought his Uncle Charles was a storyteller with how he used to call his Aunt Marina his beautiful mermaid because she washed ashore right in his backyard here in San Francisco. But that's all he knew. The journal stops right before they had a daughter."

"Grandmer Misty," I say. "She coupled with my grandpa, and they both moved to land and chose to stay after my mom learned how to remain human as a toddler. My grandparents died on land when my mom was a teen, and my dad convinced her to return to the sea to be his mate."

It's all I know. I don't know how my grandparents died, only that they never returned to the water. My dad hasn't told me much more, because I wasn't supposed to ever have to worry about the land. A king's daughter was meant to remain in the sea.

"Oh, Luna. I had no idea," Giselle says, speaking up.

I realize everyone, including Talia, is staring at me. "I never thought much of it. My mom abandoned me when I was too little to remember. I didn't know she had intended to return for me once I was old enough to remain human until recently. I always thought it was because she was in love with a human before coupling with my dad, but I'm starting to think it was partly because of you, Talia."

She sucks in her bottom lip between her teeth. "Attilonious came for my dad when I was in preschool. He washed him away with our home and ten others in what people claim to be a freak tsunami."

I hold my hand to my heart. "Oh, Ocean. I'm so sorry."

Her eyes shine with tears that she blinks away. "Sounds like you've lost people you love, too. I had no idea Celestiana had a daughter or renounced the sea. She came to me a few days after the tsunami happened and told me all about the vengeful king and made me promise I'd never speak a word of it. She promised to fix things, so I'd never have to worry again, but I was so scared by her stories. I remember crying anytime she came near. Then she disappeared. It wasn't until I turned eighteen that I was contacted in regards to a trust with this boat that belonged to my dad. It's where I found the letters from your mom with the maps."

"With the treasure," I say, motioning to the bag where Ryan found one of my mom's necklaces.

"Among other things. It's like her life scattered in pieces throughout the sea, but I've only ever looked through the ones nearby, and I always returned them just in case except for tonight. I—I needed money to leave."

My head spins at the thought of my mom leaving stuff from her life hidden throughout the world for Talia to find. I sink to the floor, grief washing over me in uncontrollable waves. I no longer feel like I know who I am. My mom hid this huge part of her life from me because of my dad and because I was so young, and my dad kept a huge part of my mom's life from me because he was afraid I'd follow in her footsteps and choose the land, which I have.

But now, sitting on this boat with my cousin, hearing her story about my mom—a story I'll never really know firsthand— leaves a fissure in my heart, and it spreads through the rest of me. A hand touches my shoulder, and I shift, expecting to meet Ryan's gaze, but Talia sits next to me and slides her arm around my back.

I smear my tears with the back of my hand. "I'm sorry. I had these huge expectations when I planned this trip. I was so excited to meet the only part of my pod I have left besides my dad, who is basically in island jail, but I had no idea of anything you had gone through. I'd have done things differently. And then now everything with my mom—I just, she didn't leave me anything. Maybe I was too much of a reminder—"

"I don't think that was true," Talia says, cutting me off.

"Why's that?"

"She addressed them to 'my sweet girls.' I always wondered why it was plural, because she never mentioned any name other than her own. I think the letters were intended for you, too. The locations of her belongings aren't exactly human-friendly."

I shift to look at Ryan. He kneels next to me and hugs me. A smile tugs at my lips. I don't even know how to process all of this. I had envisioned this perfect reunion with Talia, one where we'd hug and connect, get to know each other, and bond how a pod should, but I never knew that with her would come my history I so desperately want to know.

"We're going to give you a few minutes," Giselle says, moving to pull Sun toward the ladder to climb to the deck.

I lace my fingers through Ryan's to keep him from following them. Talia helps me to my feet to motion me toward the table with the maps and letters. Ryan looks at the collection over my shoulder, and I almost can't believe how comfortable I feel, standing here with Talia and Ryan, who I know are the beginning of this magical future I've always dreamed of.

"This is all so amazing," I whisper, sorting through the letters. "Do you mind if I read through them? Or maybe you can make me copies. I don't want to bother you. Maybe we can start over and meet like regular people."

She twists her lips to the side in thought. "I'd like that. I'm sorry for acting like I did, I—"

I meet her eyes, a lighter blue than mine. "I understand. I know things haven't been so great for those who discovered the mermaid secret."

"Thanks for not giving up on me." She turns to Ryan. "And thank you for saving my life tonight."

Ryan hugs me from behind. "I wasn't going to let the ocean take my mate's last human family member."

She touches his shoulder. "So, are you remaining human? You two have a place on land? I feel like I have a lot of catching up to do."

"We'll have plenty of time for that," I say, brushing my fingers along the letters. I have as much time as I want. I can stay in San Francisco with Starla and Mateo.

"I hope so. How long are you staying in San Francisco?" she asks.

"Until tomorrow." I frown at my words. I had almost forgotten we had planned to leave after I figured out how to give Talia a note. But now? I can't stay. Not now. But it's going to be hard to go.

Ryan scrunches his face, peering at me, knowing what I'm thinking. "Maybe we can stay a few more days."

Before I can argue, Talia says, "That would be great. I kind of have some free time since I quit both my jobs."

I grimace again, scrunching my face, trying to be happy but all the little things I've messed up come back at me. "I'm sorry. I didn't mean—"

She bumps her shoulder with mine. "Hey, no. They were just jobs. I'll find another."

Ryan points at the map. "You might not need to."

Leaning forward, Talia searches over the map, trailing her finger from one circle to the next. "It does look like your mom put a great deal of effort into setting this up for us."

"A way for us to live on land like she envisioned," I whisper.

I know my thoughts ring true. I feel it deep in my spark— the spark that led me to Ryan and now to Talia, the spark that'll light our journeys in this world straddling both the land and sea. Because I have land in my blood, but my heart draws me to the ocean. It connects me to these people who'll give me the life of my dreams, and I hope to do the same.

"So, a few more days?" I ask Ryan.

"Anything for you," he whispers.

I've never been happier.

22

DANGEROUS WATERS

SUNLIGHT BEAMS FROM THE open curtain of the balcony, streaking across Ryan's bare stomach as he sleeps half tangled in the downy comforter. I couldn't stay in bed, my mind still whirling with thoughts of Talia and our plans for today. I stood in the shower for over thirty minutes to keep myself from waking Ryan, washing what seems like never-ending salt and sand from my hair even though I had sort of washed it last night—though Ryan distracted me, so I can't be sure.

I stand in front of the mirror, drying my hair with a towel, staring at my reflection. The scratch from the spear is nearly invisible, and all the scrapes and bruises have faded, leaving me feeling a million times better.

I hear a small intake of breath behind me, and I turn and smirk at Ryan, propping up on his elbows. He smiles and waves his hand, motioning for me to come back to bed. I twist my lips in fake contemplation and then cross the room to fall into his arms.

"This is the best morning of my life," he whispers, running his fingers under my shirt to touch the skin of my stomach. "Next time wake me earlier."

I smirk. "You needed the rest."

"I think I need you more."

Grinning, he flips me onto the bed to roll on top of me. He kisses the giggle from my mouth, slowly working his way to my jaw and neck. Heat blossoms from my heart to travel down my stomach, sending tingles through the rest of me.

A knock sounds on the door, drawing my attention away from Ryan, and he lowers his weight on me to muffle his groan in the pillow. I laugh, kiss him once, and nudge him off me to answer the door.

"I think we need a few more minutes," I say, smiling at Giselle in the hallway.

Fake glaring, she shakes her head. "We've already picked up breakfast. Talia is ready and waiting." She slides past me and into the room. "You're going to be on a boring ass island with nothing to do but each—"

I reach out and cover Giselle's mouth with my hand, cutting off her words. "We'll meet you downstairs."

She tips her head back and laughs before turning around to leave. I start to close the door, the both of us smiling at each other, and she points at me. "Two minutes."

"Make it thirty," Ryan calls out.

I close the door completely, cutting off Giselle's laughter, and pad my way back to the bed. As much as I want to fall back into Ryan's arms, I also want to get out of here for the day planned with Talia. I pull Ryan to his feet, making him groan again, and I laugh when he lifts me off my feet to carry me with him toward the bathroom.

The phone rings from the nightstand, and I wiggle and kiss him until he sets me back down. "It could be Talia."

He fakes a deep sigh. "It's not even seven."

"And I've been up since six," I say, laughing.

"I'm never sleeping in again."

I blow a kiss to him from over my shoulder and spin out of his way before he grabs me again. Ryan narrows his eyes while smirking, watching me long enough to answer the phone. I wave him toward the bathroom and hear him turn the sink faucet on.

"Is this Luna?" a masculine voice says, erupting in the line.

I'm too surprised by the voice that I don't respond.

"Luna, I can hear you on the line. I don't know what Ry has told you about me, but you don't have to be afraid." I knew Ryan's dad found out we were staying here, and I knew he wanted to meet me, but I hadn't expected him to call me.

I clear my throat, trying to suppress the fear raging through me. "I—I'm sorry. You surprised me is all. I was expecting a call from someone else."

"Is Ryan around?" he asks. He sounds different this time, not as condescending or angry. It's the only reason I haven't hung up yet.

I peer at the closed bathroom door. "I can get him."

He hums a breath in the line. "Oh, don't worry about it. I was hoping to talk to you anyway." A car horn blares, and other street traffic muffles through the line. He's outside somewhere.

From my position, I can't get a good look at the street below, so I pick up the whole phone and pull it as far as it'll go to the balcony. I can't see anyone loitering. Mostly people heading toward the beach and pier.

"Me?" I ask a little late.

"I'd like to get to know the young woman who caught my son's attention so much so that he doesn't wanna come home."

I suppress the urge to yell, swallowing so I don't speak right away. It takes everything in me not to tell him that of course his son doesn't want to go home to someone who thought it was a good idea to threaten him. To return to a man who arranged someone to break into my condo. Instead, I say, "I'm sorry. I have to go. Maybe we can talk some other time, but I'm busy."

"Wait," Ryan's dad says, his voice growing in desperation, making me hesitate. "Please, don't hang up. He's my son. You have to talk some sense into him. I'm his dad. We can make this work out for everyone."

I sulk for a second, drooping my shoulders. I have to remind myself he's trying to use his bond to Ryan against me. Pressing the phone to my ear, I say, "That might be so, but you're asking an awful lot considering you stole from me. I even gave you what you wanted so that you would leave Ryan alone."

"I had to know if you were worth my son's time. I can't have you breaking his heart. I've seen your type, Luna. Pretty girl from a rich family, probably mad at her daddy and wants to do something to spite him. You find a thrill in the bad boys only to run scared."

My mouth falls open at his accusation. "You don't know me, and Ryan isn't bad. He's sweet and smart and—"

"Quick to take whatever you offer him. I know my son, and if you don't break his heart, then he'll break yours. If you think he'll ever settle down, he won't. It's in his blood."

"You clearly don't know your son."

He releases a laugh, but not a light-hearted one. It's condescending. "I know where he comes from, and you won't like it. I bet he hasn't even told you much. I bet the second you find out, you'll run."

"I won't. I love Ryan."

"Yeah, sure. Come on, you've known him for what? A week? Why don't you tell me that after you really get to know him," he remarks. "Wait until he's no longer trying to impress you."

Tears burn my eyes. "I want you to leave us alone. I mean it. If Ryan doesn't want anything to do with you, then I'll do what it takes to make sure of it. Just tell me what you want."

"I want to meet you," he says. "That's it."

"I—"

"You and Ryan can meet me for dinner tonight. Families go through rough patches, but we're still family. You get that, right? My kid is all I have left since his mom died."

Ryan opens the door to the bathroom, and I meet his bright eyes. I must wear my unease and worry on my face, because his smirk melts into a frown, and he rushes across the room to me.

"Luna, what's wrong? Is it Talia?" he asks.

I shake my head.

He snatches the phone from me before I can get the words from my mouth and holds it against his ear. Ryan glances from me to the balcony door, and then slams the phone back in the cradle. Looking over me, Ryan closes the distance and slides his arms around my waist.

"Was that my dad?" he asks, resting his chin on my shoulder.

I nod.

Ryan stretches back to look into my face. "What did he say? Did he threaten you?"

I rub my lips together, trying to find my words. "No, he wanted me to reason with you and for us to meet him for dinner."

Sighing, he brushes strands of hair off his forehead. "We'll switch hotels this afternoon. We can handle a few more days, right?"

"Maybe we should meet him," I whisper.

Ryan scowls at the balcony. "No way."

I touch his hand. "He's your family."

Ryan reaches up and rubs his thumb along my jaw to push my hair behind my ear. His eyes shine in the sunlight streaming in from outside, reminding me of the dozens of pieces of green sea glass I have in the same color. "Not if I have anything to say about it."

"Ryan..."

He leans in and kisses me. "Let's enjoy today, okay? I don't want you to worry about him. He'll get the hint when we disappear."

"Are you sure?" I ask. Because I'm not. His dad reminds me of my own, and the only reason my dad ever gave up was that he had no choice otherwise. Ryan's dad is human. He doesn't follow the same laws as the seas, and he doesn't even follow the laws of the land. Someone like him doesn't give up.

Ryan bobs his head. "Positive. He's not going to risk you bringing in the police. He's trying to see how far he can push me, but I'm not afraid of him anymore. He doesn't deserve my time and definitely not yours."

I stifle the dread threatening to steal away my happiness with a deep breath. Ryan's right. His dad isn't worth our time or even a second thought after what he's done. I have too many other things to look forward to. Finding Talia, discovering the map and letters from my mom, being with people who love me—it makes living on land now more real than ever.

"Okay, let's enjoy the day then. You, me, and our friends hanging out on a boat, the sea—"

"Kissing my mermaid princess future mate and tasting the salt on your lips, tangling my hands in your beautiful hair, seeing you in a bikini."

I grin. "Only half."

He chuckles. "Do all mermaids buy tops from land or—"

"It's a fashion choice."

"Hmm, well I don't care about fashion."

I laugh, pressing my hands to his chest to nudge him to the door. Giselle and Sun meet us on the sidewalk outside the hotel, and Ryan hooks his fingers to my side, walking in step with me as we make our way to the private marina. Talia waves from the deck of her boat, and the security guard opens the gate for us to allow us in.

"I can't get over how identical you two look," Giselle says, hugging Talia. "Like sisters."

"The Torres gene is strong," Talia says.

"Luna Torres," Giselle says smiling. "That's a way better name than Luna Stevens. Don't tell Carter I said that."

"Carter?" Talia asks.

"Queen Ava's mate," Sun says, speaking up.

Confusion crosses Talia's face, and I smile and sling my arm over her shoulders. "When you're comfortable, I'd love to introduce you to my friends. They're like my pod."

"I think I can handle that," she says. "It'll give me a chance to get the boat out more. Maybe you can join me."

"Of course I'd love to," I say, excitement coursing through me as she willingly makes plans to hang out together. It's something I hadn't expected, but I'm so thankful for. I was right about Talia, and the ocean made sure I'd be able to grow the bond between us, even if it wasn't exactly the best approach. "And Ryan loves adventure, so I'm sure he's in."

Talia half hugs me. "Then today will be perfect. I thought we could spend the afternoon treasure hunting outside the bay. I never did find what I was looking for last night."

Giselle claps her hands. "Ugh, yes! I'm in. Snorkeling with merpeople is the best."

Ryan grins. "Wait, what? I'll get to see the ocean instead of being pulled through the dark abyss?"

"So true. Last night was the worst. It made me anxious to be a mermaid," Giselle tells him, glancing at Sun. "In a few years."

"Years?" Ryan asks.

"I kind of like my legs."

"And I love your legs," Sun says, wagging his brows at Giselle.

Talia smiles at us, getting to work to prepare to launch from the dock. Ryan helps her inspect the boat and unties it to set us off through the bay. The bright sunshine warms my skin, and I stand at the bow of the boat, staring into the rippling water as we head to the open sea to where I saw the underwater caves last night.

It's almost surreal, being out here, feeling the wind through my hair instead of the waves. I never dreamed coming to land would fill in the part of me I never realized I was missing. I thought I was just curious about the land, yearning for adventure, wanting to only emerge for the fun of it. But the ocean knew all along I wasn't meant for a life of my dad's making. I wasn't meant only to experience the world mirroring back to me from below the surface. I was destined to breach up instead of dive under. I was fated to turn Ryan's dangerous waters to ones of magic and mermaids, of love. Of completion.

A wondrous life that starts today with those I care about.

Talia makes her way to my side, allowing Ryan to take over in the cockpit. The wind picks up her black hair from her neck, and she closes her eyes, inhaling a breath of the sea air. Everything about this moment feels so perfect. I'm glad to have these few extra days with Talia—with Ryan, Giselle, and Sun, too. I can't wait to plan more.

"I've been meaning to ask you this since last night," Talia says. "Everything that happened in the water is kind of fuzzy, but I do remember something."

I keep my eyes trained on the bluish-green stretch of vast ocean, listening without responding. I didn't think she'd remember anything apart from Ryan saving her. I'm almost afraid of what she'll say.

She touches my hand, so I finally look at her. "I heard your voice in my mind, and I saw something strange. Like fire underwater."

"Oh." I swallow, gripping the railing at her words. She

does remember I tried to save her, and as much as I wanted to do so, I was hoping I could forget I had. Not because she didn't deserve my efforts—I don't regret trying—but because I don't know what it means about me.

"It was the prettiest thing I've ever seen, and it reminded me of something from Charles's journal," she continues. "He mentioned something about Marina's spark."

"He was referring to a mermaid's essence," I whisper, the words struggling to come out. "And what you saw was mine."

She pushes her hair from her face to look at me. "You tried to give it to me." It's not a question. If she knows anything about mermaids, it's something she knows.

"I did." My heart races at the memory—how I was willing to give up my one chance to transform a human into a mermaid to save Talia. When I saw her take her last breath before Ryan saved her, it was all I could think about, how I wasn't willing to let her go. "But it didn't work."

She bobs her head. "It didn't feel right. It didn't feel like it belonged to me, so I didn't take it."

"Oh." My mind whirls at the thought and how Talia unintentionally saved my future with Ryan even if it meant she'd lose her life. Tears blur my eyes, and I sniffle, trying to control the sudden wave of emotions I can't hide from her.

"Whoa, don't cry. It's fine. I'm fine. Maybe it was fate that I wasn't supposed to be changed, like with Charles," she says. "Your essence is meant for someone who can bring something to the sea that I can't."

I blink away my tears. "What do you mean fate? I thought he chose the land and decided not to go through with the transformation ceremony."

She shakes her head. "He loved the ocean and Marina more than anything. He dreamed of the merpeople life."

"I don't understand. Why didn't my great-grandmer change him?" I ask.

"She couldn't. She gave up her spark to save someone else—a woman named Evelyn. They were best friends and neighbors on land. Marina divided her time between the land and sea until Evelyn coupled with a merman and had a daughter named Coral. Marina returned back to Charles and then had your grandma, which made her split her time again."

I blink a few times in surprise. "Coral? I know her. She's—oh, Ocean." I can't believe it. My great-grandmer is responsible for transforming Carter's great-grandmer. Marina chose a different kind of bond to share, one that's unheard of, because if a mermaid is going to change a human, it's always her mate—but I guess not.

"There's more in Charles's journal. I want you to have it. It belongs to you," she says.

I hug her. "Thank you. It means so much to me."

"It's the least I can do. You don't know how good it feels to look at the water and not expect to be dragged away at any second. I can enjoy the place I love again because of you."

I leave Talia at the bow of the ship and head back to Ryan to watch him navigate the yacht to the location where my mom hid something for us to find. He shows me how to steer, standing behind me with his head on my shoulder.

Ryan kisses the nape of my neck. "You know, as much as I like the idea of being a merman, I'd be okay remaining a human if I had to."

I purse my lips and crane my head to look at him. "You heard my conversation?"

"It's a small boat," he says. "I didn't mean to listen."

"I'm sorry, Ryan. Last night was—"

He brings his hand up and touches his finger to my lips. "You don't have to explain or apologize. I just wanted you to know that I love you. I'm lucky you show me even a second of attention."

"Why does it sound like you doubt yourself and us?" I ask.

He hums under his breath. "It's not that I doubt us, but I still feel like you deserve more than me sometimes, even if I'm who you want."

"Is this about your dad?" I ask.

"Partly. I—"

I spin around and kiss him, interrupting whatever it is on his mind before he puts it out into the world. "Coupling isn't about what we have to offer each other. It's about what we are together as a whole. I don't even know what to do with myself half the time. All I need is the sea...and now you."

"I swear I'll be the best mate I can be for you," he says. "On land and in the sea. It's all I can promise."

I smile. "I know, and I promise the same."

Ryan kisses me once more and spins me back around to peer at the sea ahead of us. The rippling water sparkles white under the shining sun. The coastline blends into the cerulean sky, and he cuts off the engine after a few more minutes of gliding over the water.

"I think this is it," Ryan says. He steps from the cockpit, pulling me with him, and heads to where Talia's already releasing the anchor.

Sun peers over the edge of the boat into the clear water. "There are a lot of caves to cover, Princess Luna."

"It's a good thing there are five of us." I tug my dress over my head, smiling at Ryan when he trails his gaze over me in my bikini, reminding me of what he said this morning.

"Technically four," Giselle says. "I'm only here for the merman watching."

Sun scoops up Giselle and throws himself backward with her in his arms from the small bathing platform. She pops to the surface, laughing, and swims to the boat where Sun lifts her up to get her snorkeling gear on.

Ryan adjusts his mask and fins from beside Talia, and she peers into the water, watching Sun swim a lap around Giselle, spinning her in his current. I jump in and take off my bikini bottoms, tossing them at Ryan. He dives in, swimming up to me underwater, his eyes widening when I complete my transformation in front of him without the dark of night obscuring his view.

I swim closer and kiss him, jetting us both to the surface.

Talia dips under, hovering in place to glance around the vibrant sea. Oxygen clings to her face, and her lips puff slightly from holding her breath. She studies me for a long moment, taking in my shimmering gold tail.

As much as I want to swim closer to her, I remain in my spot, gripping Ryan's hand, though he treads to keep his head above water. Talia releases a few bubbles and kicks her legs, finally closing the distance between us to look into my eyes before launching upward to the surface.

I spit out water over Giselle's head, making her laugh and splash me in the face. "You sure you want to stay here? I think Sun can handle both you and Talia to dive."

"She's right, my love," Sun says, smiling.

"I'm good. I prefer shopping for my treasure. I'll keep an eye on the surface for other boats," Giselle says.

Sun kisses Giselle once and then turns to Talia to explain to her how to hold on and the signal to let him know if she needs to surface. Adjusting Ryan's arms around me, I dive us under, winding through the kelp forest teeming with life. Ryan reaches out his hand over my shoulder and points to a group of sea stars crowding the rocky bottom, and I dive him closer for a better look.

Sun and Talia dart past us, stirring up sand in their current, and I gaze around the glittering kelp forest in front of some natural underwater caves covered in algae and other plant and animal life.

"There are two here big enough to fit us, but all the other

openings are much too small," Sun thinks to me, projecting his thoughts through the sea. "Let's surface to let the others know."

I follow him up and expel water from my lungs. Talia and Ryan both gasp for breath, and I turn my gaze to check on Giselle, now sitting on the bathing platform with her wetsuit pulled down to show off the new bikini she bought yesterday. She flips her sunglasses up on her head and smiles, and I turn back to the others.

"There are two caves we can swim in, but I don't know how deep they are, and I don't want to risk your safeties," I say.

"That's fine," Talia says. "I don't mind watching from here."

"I'll follow you down but won't go in," Ryan says, sliding his arms around me. "I'll swim up if I need air."

"If they're diveable, I'll take you," I say, smiling.

Sun nods and dives before us, and I pull Ryan with me to save his oxygen for the wait. He holds onto the rocks to keep him in place outside the tunnel, and I peer at Sun's tail disappearing inside.

I touch Ryan's cheek and then swim into the cave, my vision adjusting to the dimming light. Glittering stones not unlike the ones from my home colony of Pearlestria decorate the walls, creating a soft glow of their own, enhanced by ocean magic. It reminds me of my mom already.

"Princess Luna?" Sun calls to me. "This cave dead-ends into nothing."

I swim another few feet forward and run my fingers over

the glittering stones of the wall. "This one does—" The rock wall shifts under my pressure, rolling forward into a cavernous space big enough to fit all five of us if the others wanted to look. "Whoa. Come here, Sun."

I spin around, staring at what looks like many of the merpeople's homes throughout the colonies. Among the glittering walls rests what looks like a rusted metal trunk. Rocks have been arranged into a seating area, and one of the walls has been carved out into shelves with dozens of shells, stones, sea glass, and braided fishing line not unlike my workroom in Pearlestria.

Settling into the sand, I lie back and stare at the ceiling. The roof glows with sunlight from above coming in through small holes that look like stars. I can almost imagine the mermaids who stayed here before me. Maybe Marina. Maybe my mom, even. I roll on my side and catch sight of my reflection in the mirror, my blue eyes glowing in the dim light. I feel closer to my mom than ever, laying in a spot she had visited, being near a shore she loved so much because of who was on it.

It's like everything that happened in my life was to bring me to this moment where everything seems so clear. I've spent all my life thinking my existence was about finding my mate, about living a life for my perfect half, in a simple world where all I needed was love and the sea.

But I need the land, too. I need all the bonds I've created.

Ryan swims into the room, surprising me, and Sun follows behind him. I push from the floor and wrap my arms around Ryan, smiling as his eyes widen when he looks around.

"This is a house," I say out loud, sending bubbles shooting to the surface.

Ryan peers around, running his fingers over the rocks. I know he only has another minute or two of air, so I swim toward the metal trunk in the corner and flick it open. I'm sure it contains whatever my mom wanted us to find.

Sun swims up behind me. "Queen Celestiana used ocean magic everywhere in here."

He's right. And it's more than treasure. There are documents in plastic within the air bubble protecting the contents in the trunk, but I have to surface to see what they are. The moment I disturb the water, the magic will disperse and return to the sea.

"Allow me to swim Ryan back to the surf—"

The cave dims, and I glance at Sun and Ryan who both tilt their heads back to glance at the porous ceiling. Something blocks the sun from above, and I blink when the sunlight returns a moment later.

"A boat," Sun says.

Without waiting for me to say anything, Sun darts from the cave, and Ryan points his thumb up, motioning he needs to return to the surface for air.

I scoop up the contents of the trunk in my arms, holding everything against my chest, and swim Ryan out of the cave on my back. I freeze outside the cave, staring at Sun hovering in his merman form below the surface.

He glances at me. "The boat's approaching ours."

Ryan lets go of my shoulders, and I swim up in front of him, searching his reddening face. "Don't surface," he says into the water, releasing his air in the process.

"I'm going with you," I say back.

He shakes his head and motions for me to stay while handing me his waterproof bag. Sun swims up next to me at the same time Ryan kicks toward the surface. We look at each other and then toward the boat closing the space to Talia's.

My mind screams to surface, but I stay in place, clutching the treasures my mom left me. Ryan bobs back under once more, his eyes narrow, a strange look crossing his face, and he motions for me to stay under again.

Something feels utterly wrong. All the happiness I had moments ago washes away with the cool current playing with my hair. Flicking my tail, I swim after Ryan, reaching to grab onto him to pull him deeper. But I'm too slow. Hands reach into the water and yank him out.

And then he disappears.

23

THE OCEAN'S KING

THE SPARK IN MY chest blinks in quick successions as I count the passing seconds, waiting for the other boat to leave. But it doesn't. It remains floating on the surface so close to Talia's that I'm certain whoever is on the strange vessel isn't someone passing by or asking for the best dive spots in the area. This is different. And the vessel is much bigger.

"We have to transform," I say.

Sun nods, taking the stuff I pulled from the cave from my arms so I can open the waterproof bag. He helps me put everything inside, and I untie my bottoms from the strap Ryan had secured them to.

If we don't hurry, we won't be able to explain how we surfaced from being underwater for an amount of time humanly impossible. Cramps seize my muscles, and I arch my back, transforming next to Sun. He takes my hand and kicks us to the surface together. We soundlessly emerge without splashing, close enough to Talia's boat that no one sees us, but I can't see on the boat either.

"This is an interesting collection of stuff you have here," a familiar, masculine voice says.

"Dad, leave them alone. I'll come with you, okay?" Ryan says, sending my heart into my stomach. I knew the voice belonged to his dad, but I didn't want to believe it. "You didn't have to come all the way out here."

"But I wanted to meet your girlfriend," Ryan's dad says. Annoyance rushes through me, and I bob up and down, trying to get a better look. I never dreamed Ryan's dad would follow us out here. He was upset Ryan didn't want to give him the time of day, but this? He had to have followed us from the hotel and to the marina.

"And you have, so you can leave now," Talia says. "You're ruining our dive."

I frown at Sun. Ryan's dad thinks Talia's me. We look similar enough that I can see how we can be mistaken since Ryan's dad has only seen me in photos. But I wish he didn't assume. Bringing Talia, and Giselle too, into this mess was the last thing I wanted. I underestimated Ryan's dad. I thought maybe he'd try to approach me on land. But Ryan did mention he lived on the sea, and what better place to corner us than somewhere he thinks we can't get away.

"Hey, Wren. Look at this." Another masculine voice sounds through the air. "I found these in the galley. Looks like maps. Old letters. Seems we're not the only treasure hunters. No wonder Ry likes the girl. One of the bags is loaded."

"Anything like the pearl?" Ryan's dad, Wren, asks.

I inhale a small breath. Ryan's dad is a thief. He stole from my condo and threatened me for the pearl I gave to Ryan. Now, if he sees all the treasure my mom left for me and Talia to find, things will go beyond making Ryan leave with him. Both possibilities ignite a fear in me that makes me want to pray to the ocean to rise up and help me. But if it does, the others can get caught in the same rough waters. I can't risk it.

"Better." Footsteps tap across the deck, and I press my lips together to stifle my gasping breath to hear things more clearly over the humming sea. "I think this is the Siren's Soul diamond."

I cringe, turning to glance at Sun quietly waiting for my command. As an ocean warrior, he'll wait by my side and follow my orders as princess. But I don't know what to do. I don't want to reveal myself. I need the advantage of surprise.

A low whistle sounds through the air, and a shadow crosses the water over me as someone moves along the perimeter of the boat. "Now how did someone like you get your hands on something like this?"

"I—"

"Who'd you steal it from?" Wren asks, cutting Talia off.

"No one. I'm not a thief," she snaps. "I found it."

"You found it? Sure, sweetheart. You saying that because of her?" he asks. Without having to see, I know he's referring to Giselle. And the tone of his voice makes me nervous. I know he knows Giselle has a wealthy family. He knows she's a relative of Ruby and Carlton King. "Because I found something interesting looking into you. Six months ago, you didn't exist, Luna. And then you started showing up around the Kings. Other wealthy families. I think me and you are a lot alike."

"We're not," Talia says.

The strange man laughs. "If you don't want to talk in front of the heiress, I can take care of—"

"No!" I scream, covering my mouth a little too late. Just the thought of anyone hurting Giselle sends a wave of fury through me, igniting my spark in my chest to heat up the rest of me in the cold water.

Sun ducks under, transforming back into a merman a second before a figure blocks out the sun above me. Strong hands lock under my arms, dragging me from the ocean, and I slide across the rough deck, scraping my hip. Pain burns my skin, and I touch the blood trickling down my leg.

I scramble to my feet, using my waterproof bag to shield myself like somehow having my mom's belongings in front of me will protect me. But the ocean magic is gone from them, and the sea might protect me in a way the others couldn't survive.

The boat rocks, sending me forward a few feet. Ryan grabs me and pulls me into his arms to spin me away from a man who is as handsome as Ryan but older, his dark hair streaked with strands of silver. The other man, much taller and stockier than any of us, stands with Giselle, holding her against his chest with a knife drawn.

"If you hurt her, you will regret it," I say. "If you want to know where I found the Siren's Soul diamond, then you have to let my friends go. Only I have that information."

Wren releases a low whistle, looking me over in Ryan's arms. "And who are you?"

I clear my throat, swallowing to keep my voice from shaking. "You know exactly who I am, and I meant what I said. They have nothing to do with any of this. Those are my maps. My treasure. You hurt them, and you won't get your hands on more than what is on this boat. And even then, I doubt you'll get anything." I grip Ryan's hand, praying to the ocean this works. Because I don't know what else to do. Ryan's dad is a thief. The idea of getting his hands on things no one else can should appeal to him enough to get him to let us go.

Wren glances at the man holding Giselle and nods. The man lets go of her and shoves her toward Talia. The boat rocks again, the water rising with Sun's movements. He's acting as the ocean's warrior, and I wouldn't put it past him to sink the vessel to get to Giselle. If he does, he'll reveal what we are. I do not doubt that the ocean will claim these men.

And I can't let that happen. It's not our way. It's something my dad would do. I'm afraid the only person who could talk Sun down is Giselle, because it takes the words of a mate to help a merman see reason when his sole purpose is protecting and caring for the one he plans to couple with.

If Sun sinks the boat, even Talia or Ryan could get caught up in the ocean's wrath. I can't allow it. I won't allow it.

Ryan's dad grabs the side of the boat, bracing through the next swell created by Sun's powerful fin. The other man peers over the side of the boat, looking into the water. The vessel shudders, knocking into the yacht tethered to Talia's boat, and the man swears under his breath.

"What in the hell is—"

A swell rises next to the yacht, crashing over the side to wash over the man. The sudden force knocks him away, and he falls over the side, his scream cutting off as he plunges into the water. Wren rushes to where his friend fell overboard, and I pull myself from Ryan and gaze into the water as Sun drags him deeper.

Without thinking, I dive over the side of the boat, breaking the surface. Millions of tiny bubbles sprinkle through the sea, and I peer through the haze, swimming deeper in my human form. Sun lets the man go, allowing him to float a dozen feet toward the surface and then yanks him back down.

"Sun, stop!" I yell out loud, releasing my breath. "Stop!"

His eyes meet mine, and I dive forward, refusing to change into my true form. Sun releases the man, letting him drift up toward the surface. Darting my way, Sun gets close enough for me to see him clearly. He leans forward and brushes his lips to mine, sending me a dozen images of Giselle.

"I will get her off the boat. I promise," I say with my last breath of air.

Sun pushes me toward the surface to the man, and I grab onto the back of his shirt and yank him the rest of the way up. He gasps, yelling and thrashing, and I dip back under to avoid the swing of his arm.

"Stop fighting. It's me," I say, pulling him closer. "I'm trying to help you."

Wren stands on the bathing platform, holding out some sort of metal rod for me to grab, but I don't take it. I keep my distance from the boat, and Sun swims around us, creating a strong enough current to make the man yell again.

"Untie the boats," I say. "If you don't, I'll shove him under, and he won't ever come back up."

Wren glares from me to Giselle and Talia. "No. He's expendable. I have a bigger crew."

"Dad," Ryan says. "Are you kidding me? Giselle is related to the Kings. You will never get to stop at another port in this region again. You don't think they'll hunt you down? Just let my friends go, and I'll stay with you."

"Ryan, no," I say. "You can't."

"I promised to protect you. I don't know how else to," he says.

Wren rubs the back of his neck. "You think I'm stupid, kid? The girls know who I am. I should take what I can and sink this damn boat with all of them on it."

Swimming forward, I push the man toward the bathing platform. "Please, don't. No one will say anything. You can have the maps and whatever you want. Just please, I don't want anything bad to happen. I'll do anything."

Wren narrows his eyes on me, touching something on his belt under his long shirt. My breathing quickens, knowing it's some sort of weapon, but he doesn't show it. And I'm not as afraid as I should be, because the ocean would swallow this whole boat if he intended to harm me. I just know it. But the ocean is giving me a chance.

"Okay," Wren finally says. "Everyone's free to go. Except for you."

"No!" Giselle yells.

Talia holds her back, covering her mouth before she unleashes a flurry of threats I doubt Wren will take kindly to. Wren strides up to the two of them, making me tense. The man I rescued extends his arm in front of me, not restraining me, but warning me to remain where I am.

"If I even suspect you tell anyone about me, you will not like what happens to your friend," he says. "And it'll be easy enough to explain how Ryan set you all up."

"You're not—"

"Giselle," I say, stopping her from threatening Ryan's dad. "I'll be fine, okay? You have to trust me, and please, don't get anyone involved. You know what happens. This is Ryan's dad."

"I don't give a sh—"

Wren reaches for his belt, and I rush forward, grabbing his arm in one hand while pushing Giselle with the other. She crashes into Talia, and they both fall overboard and splash into the water.

I grip the front of Wren's shirt, keeping him from glancing over the side. He locks his fingers around my wrist, a scowl morphing his face, sending a blip of panic through me. Ryan yanks me away from his dad, pulling me to him, and wraps me in a hug.

"Jump off the boat," he whispers into my ear. "Jump off the boat and leave."

I swallow, my eyes burning with tears. "No."

"Luna."

I shake my head. "I can't leave you with him."

"He's dangerous. What if—"

I cut him off with a quick kiss. "I'm dangerous, too. We will figure this out. I just need him to leave Giselle and Talia."

Strong fingers lock onto my arm, dragging me away from Ryan. Wren pushes me toward a rung ladder on the side of his yacht. "Go."

Inhaling a deep breath of the sea air, I board the yacht with Ryan behind me. An old woman with long, silver hair appears from a door, surprising me, and she motions me forward, her forehead crinkling in a frown.

"It's best you come inside," she says, holding her hand to me.

I shake my head. "I need to make sure my friends are

okay."

"You're brave. I always knew my Ry would fall for someone brave and strong. Loyal. You'll make a lovely addition to our family," she says. "I'm happy Ryan's come home with you."

I sneer, nearly baring my teeth. She makes it sound like we had a choice, like I'm some guest.

Ryan pulls me from the woman and points at Giselle and Talia treading water with Sun circling below without revealing himself. "That's Luna's family."

She shrugs. "From what I hear, she'll fit in here fine. She might even like it. I don't know why you're always rebelling, Ry. Breaks my heart."

I stare in silence as Wren and the man I rescued clear Talia's boat of everything they deem valuable. It takes Ryan covering my mouth with his hand to stop me from screaming out when they reel in the anchor and start the engine, driving the boat a good mile away from Talia and Giselle, leaving them in the choppy water.

"They're going to be fine," Ryan whispers into my ear. "This vessel isn't documented here, so my dad is giving himself a head start if Talia radios for help."

"You've done this before." It's not a question. Everything these people do is calculated, well thought out, perfected even. Ryan's dad isn't an ordinary thief. He's a thief of the sea. He's the type of man my dad would leave alone because he kept the surface empty.

"I come from a long line of pirates," Ryan says, confirming

my suspicions. "But I'm not one. This isn't me."

I release a breath, a dozen thoughts crossing my mind. "Oh, Ocean. I know why the sea didn't rise to protect us."

He frowns. "I don't understand."

"I'm supposed to be here, Ryan."

He shakes his head. "These are dangerous waters, Luna. This isn't like the land you're used to. My family—these people—they control the surface."

The yacht glides forward, and I sway with the sudden movement as it sails away from those who tie me to land. Sun pops up next to Giselle and Talia, hooking an arm around the both of them.

I raise my hand to them, wishing I could've gotten to say goodbye, but I know this isn't the end. The sea has laid out a path for me on the surface, and I must learn the way.

"I'm not afraid, Ryan," I finally say, turning away from the ocean when Sun dives Giselle and Talia under. "The ocean protects me, and I need to protect it from the surface. Can't you see?"

Because the tides are changing. Merpeople are evolving. I'm exactly where the ocean wants me. Things haven't been so clear in the shallows of the shore, blurred by the sand and the cresting waves, but the deeper I swim, the clearer I see. The quieter the world becomes. The easier it is to hear the call of the ocean. It speaks to my very essence. And I have to listen.

"There are other ways. You deserve so much more than this. The things I've seen—I want to protect you, too."

"You will protect me, and I'll protect you. I promise."

Someone clears their throat, and I turn and meet Ryan's dad. His brown eyes shine with flecks of green, trailing from me to Ryan and the ocean beyond us. Something indecipherable crosses his face, and he presses his thin lips into a line.

He offers me the towel from his shoulder. "Welcome aboard the *Ocean's King*. Like I told you over the phone, you don't have to be scared of me."

I meet his gaze. "I'm not scared."

His lips tilt upward. "Good. As long as you don't try anything stupid, we'll treat you like a real princess here."

I turn toward Ryan. "Does that make you my pirate prince?"

For the first time since we've boarded, he gives me a smile he can't control. "I guess so."

Wren chuckles and smacks Ryan on the back, pushing him forward. "Why don't you show Luna your room? Make her feel at home."

Ryan only nods.

"It's going to be okay," I whisper to Ryan as he pulls me away. "It's you, me, and the sea."

He slides his arm around my waist. "You, me, and the sea."

EPILOGUE

PIRATE PRINCE

THE WAXING MOON SHINES above the midnight waters, setting a path aglow into the horizon. The glittering stars twinkle like millions of pearls haphazardly scattered through the deepest part of the ocean.

The door creaks open behind me, and I turn and spot Ryan entering our stateroom. I rush the few feet to him, sliding my hands around his neck to kiss him. He breathes a sigh into my mouth, his sweet lips tasting of chocolate instead of the salt I dearly miss. It has been two days since I've been in the sea, and I'm getting restless the fuller the moon gets in the sky.

"You're back later than I thought. Are you okay? Did you do it?" I ask, tugging him toward the bed.

He scoots on the bed to rest his back on the headboard and pulls me closer, shifting my legs across his lap so that I can snuggle with him. He plays with strands of my dark hair, just watching his fingers wind the tresses over and over again.

"Yeah, but it wasn't easy. If my dad finds out what I di—"

I frown, turning to cup his face in my hands. "He won't. And if he does, he'll have bigger problems if he tries anything." Because my friends need to know I'm okay. I can't continue this new journey if they search for me. I have to make sure they don't intervene. The clues of where I'm at should be enough to ease their worries. I'll make sure they always know. "I'm in a terrible mood, so—"

"What else can I do for you?" he asks, shifting to look at me.

I shrug. "I'm antsy is all. The full moon is coming, and I'm a little nervous. I have to be in the sea when it arrives or I'll die."

He stiffens, sucking in a breath and nods. "We'll figure it out."

"I wish I could swim now. Even for a few minutes."

Ryan glances toward the small balcony overlooking the sea. "How about you jump, and I'll keep watch until everyone's asleep?"

"Then you'll join me?"

He nods. "Maybe I'll convince you to swim away with me."

If only it were so simple. But Wren knows where Giselle lives. He knows the people I love on land, and even if he doesn't threaten them, I know what he's capable of. I'll do any-thing to protect them, even if it means I must remain where I am.

I bite my lip between my teeth, smiling at Ryan. Tugging my tank top over my head, I change from my pajamas and into a bathing suit. Ryan's warm fingers slide around my sides, and he runs his fingers up my back and into my hair while hugging me against him.

"Maybe I'll jump, too," he whispers. "Who cares if anyone notices."

I grin, locking my fingers to the hem of his shirt. "I don't. Plus, the water's warm here."

Ryan releases a moan, brushing his lips to mine as I trail my fingers up his stomach, taking his shirt off for him. I tug him with me toward the balcony, kissing him harder, our breaths mingling, his skin touching mine, his heart beating against mine.

My back presses into the cool metal rungs of the railing, and I kiss him once more, sending him a dozen images of us swimming in the sea. Leaning back, he grins at me and nods, only letting go of me to climb over the railing. He helps me over, locking his fingers through mine, and a rush of adrenaline sends my heart racing.

"You ready?" he asks.

Cramps roll through me, the anticipation of jumping into the sea triggering my transformation before I even hit the water. He loosens the ties on my bikini bottoms for me and hooks his arm around my waist.

"Take a deep breath," I say, touching his cheek with my

now shimmering hand.

He inhales the sea air, and I hug him, launching us both from the balcony to dive head first into the sea. The glowing waters wrap me in comforting warmth, sending my spark blinking through the quiet ocean. Ryan hovers in front of me, his dark hair floating on top of his head, his green eyes peering at me in the light of the moon lightening the ocean from above.

Reaching out, he brushes his fingers over my chest, my mermaid essence lighting his hand aglow. He kisses me while I finish transforming, and I flick my tail to send us both to the surface.

He gasps a breath against my lips. "You're glowing like the first time I saw you."

I smile. "It's my essence, remember?"

He nods. "What does it mean that I can see it?"

"That you're my perfect mate."

"I can see everything so clearly. The water isn't so scary now."

I smile and kiss him. "With me you'll always know your way."

Water splashes between us, and he hugs me tighter. "And I'll follow you anywhere."

Voices echo through the quiet night, drawing our attention away from each other. Ryan sighs, watching the yacht, and a beam of light cuts over the water. I dip back under, forcing myself to transform into a human, even though I don't want to.

"What the hell are you two doing?" Wren calls out, shining

the light on us.

"Swimming," I say, tugging Ryan with me.

Wren descends down the stairs to meet us on the swimming platform. "You're going to get swept away or drown."

"Hasn't Ryan told you I'm a mermaid? I can swim in the roughest water," I say, letting Wren pull me back onto the yacht. "Shark infested and blindfolded even."

He chuckles, thinking I'm joking. "Want to prove it? We're going to hit the first destination on the map soon."

I turn to Ryan, but his face remains expressionless through the saltwater dripping down his face. We stare at each other for a long moment, and I wish I could hear his thoughts. I wish the ocean would guide me again.

Licking the saltwater from my lips, I say, "I agreed to be here, not help you. Plus, people don't work for free."

"Of course you'll be rewarded," Wren says. "That's how this works here."

"I don't want money or jewels or whatever."

He raises his eyebrows. "I have something that might be more meaningful."

"Doubt it."

"I'll return to you the belongings I took from you," he says. "The documents you were carrying."

My lips quiver. I can't help it. I've been dying to read over what my mom protected with ocean magic in the long forgotten mermaid cave.

"You should give it back to her anyway," Ryan says. "It belongs to her."

"I know it does. Her name's all over it." He looks at me. "That was one helluva spot to hide your birth certificate, but what I want to know is why?"

I blink my surprise away. I had no idea I had one of those. I was born in the sea. My mom had chosen the sea. But she chose the land for me.

"I didn't even know I had one," I admit. "But I'll do it. I'll dive if you give it to me."

Wren slings his arm around my shoulders, guiding me away from the water. "See, this isn't so bad, is it?"

I shrug away and take Ryan's hand. "Could be worse."

Wren wags his eyebrows, looking between us. "You're right about that. It could be much, much worse."

To be continued...

If you loved *Mermaid Waters*, make sure to sign up for Ginna Moran's newsletter to stay up-to-date on new releases, including *Pirate Waters*, book two in the *Call of the Ocean* series. By signing up for her newsletter, you'll also gain VIP access to exclusive www.GinnaMoran.com stories and content.

OTHER YOUNG ADULT SERIES BY GINNA MORAN

PARANORMAL

Destined for Dreams Series
Demon Within Series
Finding Nate Series
Going Ghostly Series
Spark of Life Series
When Souls Collide Series
Demon Watcher Series
Call of the Ocean Series

CONTEMPORARY

Falling into Fame Series

STANDALONES

Life After Lila

 ACKNOWLEDGMENTS

I OWE A HUGE thanks to my mer-mazing team, who I dearly appreciate for all their hard work to make these books possible. Sarah, Katie, and Jan—you are incredible, and I'm so lucky to have the chance to work with you.

Also, I wanted to give a shout out to AAYAA and 20Books—I've learned and have grown so much from these wonderful groups of authors.

Lastly, thank you to all the readers who showed so much enthusiasm for my Spark of Life series and for loving my mermaid world. I'd have never written Luna and Ryan's story if it weren't for you all. Here's to more mermaid adventures! XOXO

ABOUT GINNA MORAN

GINNA MORAN IS A writer from sunny Southern California. She started writing poetry as a teenager in a spiral notebook that she still has tucked away on her desk today. Her love of writing grew after she graduated high school, and she completed her first unpublished manuscript at age eighteen.

When she realized her love of writing was her life's passion, she studied literature at Mira Costa College in Northern San Diego. Besides writing novels, she was senior editor, content manager, and image coordinator for Crescent House Publishing Inc. for four years.

Aside from Ginna's professional life, she enjoys binge watching television shows, playing pretend with her daughter, and cuddling with her dogs. Some of her favorite things include chocolate, anything that glitters, cheesy jokes, and organizing her bookshelf.

Ginna Moran loves to hear from her readers so visit her online at www.GinnaMoran.com. You can also find her on Facebook, Twitter, Instagram, and Snapchat. To stay up-to-date on new releases, sign up to her newsletter. You'll not only get exclusive access to extra stories, but you'll be able to participate in monthly giveaways!

Ginna Moran is currently hard at work on her next novel.

www.ingramcontent.com/pod-product-compliance
Lightning Source LLC
Chambersburg PA
CBHW051647180726
48284CB00006B/1904